A Sour Chord

M. Jandreau

To find out more about M. Jandreau, please visit
http://www.twitter.com/jandreauwrites
http://www.facebook.com/jandreauwrites

This is dedicated to you, reader, for having the courage to read
something from an unknown author.
Thank you.

Chapter One

It was raining pretty heavily as Sal made his way from the parking lot into his band's rehearsal space, a large, old building that'd been converted into dozens of separate sound-proof rooms, for bands, artists, and musicians to practice their craft. So Say The King, Sal's band, practiced every Monday, Wednesday, and Thursday, from around five until midnight, sometimes later. Almost like a second job, each member of the band showed up after their day job ended, often carrying a drink or two along with a meal for the evening. Sal knew it was going to be a long night when he entered the room. Greg raised his beer to say hello and Sal could tell from the look on Paul's face that this wasn't Greg's first of the night.

Sal had been friends with Greg for most of their lives and no two guys in the band knew each other as well as Sal and Greg. They'd been working on music together since their early teen years and as their band, So Say The King, since their early 20s. While Sal, Derek and Paul took the band seriously, none of them took it quite as seriously as Greg did. Greg often went off on what Sal referred to as a "mood" where he'd push the rest of the band members harder and longer than usual, insisting that if they didn't make it, they had nothing to fall back on.

Sal stood at five feet ten inches and was in good shape. His dark brown hair was long enough that he often slicked it back, where it would stay by itself. He was full-blooded Italian and proudly so. His skin was tan, his eyes dark, his eyebrows full. He usually had a 5 o'clock shadow. He'd just turned 31 not long ago, but you'd never have guessed his age from looking at him.

"I think we need to work some more on the chorus for 'Night Before Dawn'," Greg said. "I don't think it's quite there yet."

"We spent most of Monday night working on that," Paul groaned. "Can we work on something else? I'm getting sick of that chorus."

"Well perhaps you can come up with a better bass line so it's not so boring for you," Greg snapped back.

"Guys, let's take a breather, huh? We literally just got here. Let's step back a minute and try to work out a game plan for the night. You know it's going to get hectic when other bands start showing up," Sal said.

Sal was usually the peacekeeper when tempers got a little hot under the collar. Sometimes he wondered how therapists managed to try to solve problems all day every day. After most rehearsals where the guys would argue, he would feel like shit when he left.

He was right this time, as usual. They had the distinct advantage of usually arriving at the rehearsal space before the majority of other bands did. While mostly soundproof, music would often bleed from one room to another, making it more difficult to have a conversation.

Sal sat atop his guitar amplifier, sipping on the Coke he'd bought himself from the vending machine.

Greg, Derek and Paul all opened one of the beers that Greg picked up for the night. Sal, being the one member of the band who didn't drink, knew that if it was going to be anything like last time, he was going to end up driving at least one of the other guys home, or most likely, all three. He didn't mind though; he sometimes enjoyed taking care of the guys.

Despite Paul's protest, Greg insisted starting on "Night Before Dawn". They looped through the chorus into the bridge for what seemed like an eternity. Sal, as he often did, sang the lyrics he'd been writing in his head, while listening for the changes that Greg proposed to the music they'd been working on for the past few weeks, trying to spot the time changes that Derek was adding in, and listening for any licks that Greg tossed into the mix. Sal may have had the least experience in the band, but the others recognized that he had the vision. He heard the songs before they were complete and gave a lot of input into the orchestration of the song. Derek often joked that Sal was a musical prodigy, that he could see the song on the paper without even realizing it. Sal didn't always agree. Unlike many people with his talents, Sal was humble, almost to the point of embarrassment because of how shy he was.

By the time other bands started showing up, it was around 7:30pm. At one point there was a break in the music coming from all directions around them and in between takes of "Night Before Dawn". It was so quiet that you could hear the rain bouncing off the tin roof. Paul suggested they take a break to have some dinner. Greg, usually liked to work through dinner, but decided that Paul was right and put down his guitar, a beautiful Paul Reed Smith Artist IV that his parents had bought for him when he graduated college. Greg babied his guitar like it was his child. Sal was a bit jealous. Working at Starbucks didn't exactly afford one a lavish lifestyle, but it paid the bills and gave him the flexibility to rehearse three nights a week, which he liked.

The guys all sat around the room. Derek on his drum stool, the others on their amplifiers. As usual, they didn't say much. They had the tendency to only talk about music when they were at the studio.

After dinner, the guys progressed more on the chorus from "Night Before Dawn" working until close to midnight, at which point Greg pointed out the time and the fact that he was a bit tipsy.

"Okay, let's call it for the night. We'll pick up on the chorus to bridge on Friday," Derek said, as he turned to the whiteboard on the wall behind his drums, making a note of what they'd work on next.

"You guys want a lift?" Sal asked Paul and Derek.

"I'm all set, I've got the van," Derek responded.

"If you're going by my place, it'd be nice to not have to run down to the T," Paul said.

"No problem. You're on the way to Greg's anyway," Sal said. "Let's go."

Greg waited for the others to leave the room, shut off the lights and fans and made sure the door was locked behind them as they left. Two by two they walked down the long hallway towards the stairs, listening to other bands through the walls and doors.

Chapter Two

Sal's apartment was just a short ten minute drive from Greg's. After dropping Paul and Greg off at home, Sal got back to his place just shy of 1:00 a.m. He loved this time of night, the world was quiet and serene, his mind usually clear, the neighbors in houses and apartments around him long since asleep. When he didn't have to wake up for an early shift, Sal spent his late nights in near darkness writing, overanalyzing, and dreaming of a better time he knew was coming.

He entered his one-bedroom apartment as he always did: flipping on the overhead light by the door, illuminating the majority of the 400 square feet. He tossed his keys, wallet, and iPhone onto the small table that sat to the right of the front door. Sal maintained the same routine when he gets home every night. Keys, wallet, and iPhone go on their table next to the day's mail. His jacket gets hung on the same hook, his shoes go in the tiny closet by the front door. He often defends himself saying that he's not obsessive, he just likes things to have their place.

His apartment was by no means fancy, but a typical one-bedroom apartment in downtown Somerville, Massachusetts, where many struggling musicians opted to live. It was close enough to the city, but far enough away from city rents.

His living room was sparse with a television on an IKEA stand, a small couch big enough for Sal and one other person, and a desk where his iMac sat along with numerous stacks of paper. By the foot of the desk sat a plastic legal-sized container with hanging folders. In the folders resided every lyric that Sal had ever written. From the very first song he wrote when he was eleven years old to the most recent from just last night. He kept every song meticulously, saving a handwritten copy and a typed copy which were each held together by a single staple, then paper clipped to one another, and sorted alphabetically in each folder.

After stopping in his kitchen to grab a drink, Sal made his way to his desk. Sliding the keyboard back out of the way, he grabbed the pad he'd jotted ideas down on for "Night Before Dawn" last night. He grabbed his favorite pen — a blue Pilot Dr. Grip that he'd had specifically for writing and had filled its ink cartridge a dozen times — and turned on his desk lamp. Before beginning his writing process, he made his way back over to the front door to shut off the overhead light. He liked to write in near darkness.

He always started off the same; all electronic devices are off; left leg folded up onto the chair with the foot tucked against the right leg; all extraneous items moved off the desk. Once he was settled into his desk, lights dim, Coke at the ready, he began reviewing his lyrics for "Night Before Dawn" from the night before. Almost feverishly, he began crossing out lines, rewriting parts of the chorus again and again.

"This has to be perfect. This is the song," he muttered aloud.

Sal was a perfectionist when it came to his lyrics. He loved to write songs that let the song's listener try to figure out what the song is truly about. It was his method of connecting with the audience and something that he'd prided himself on after so many years writing.

He got up from his desk and walked laps around his couch while trying to think of the perfect chorus. Sal swore that So Say The King would be the only band that he'd ever be in, and that he'd give everything he had to make it. He told himself that he'd worked too hard, come too far, and invested everything he had to start over.

He began questioning everything he'd written thus far, the longer he spent working on the lyrics, the less satisfied he was. Lyrics that he wrote in a matter of minutes, plowing straight through to the end, always seemed to be better. "The less you think, the better the end result," he'd tell himself from time to time. For some reason "Night Before Dawn" had him stumped. Perhaps it was all the pressure that Greg had put on this particular song. Perhaps it was that the band wanted to perform it at a gig they had booked in a few weeks — just a quick half hour set at a less-than-famous spot where bands from Boston often played. He knew that he had to finish the lyrics before Friday and was beginning to beat himself up over it.

Before he knew it, his alarm was going off. It was ten in the morning. Sal woke up in a very common place for him — the couch, still fully clothed, television on, and his pad of paper on the small IKEA coffee table in front of him. He glanced down at the legal pad and found that he'd scribbled out most of what he'd written last night, before he passed out.

He groaned at the sight of the scribbles and got up, shaking his head.

Chapter Three

Friday was Sal's favorite day because Jess would make the entire band dinner at she and Greg's place. Sal saw so many great qualities in Jess and in her relationship with Greg that he was sometimes jealous. They were lucky to have found each other and fallen so deeply in love, so quickly. He hoped that someday he'd have that same feeling. Greg and Jess had met the first day of sophomore year in high school, but didn't start dating until after college. They were getting married a week from tomorrow.

Derek and Sal showed up to Jess and Greg's apartment around quarter to five, as they usually did. Living not far from one another, Sal usually picked Derek up. Paul snuck in with just a few minutes to spare, barely making it before the five o'clock cutoff time. Jess was a stickler for showing up on time. If you were five minutes late, she wouldn't open the door for you. She said being prompt taught you lessons in how to manage yourself later in life. As usual, Jess had crackers and cheese waiting and handed everyone a drink as they arrived. By day she was a successful blogger for a number of websites; by night she was the typical housewife despite not yet being married. She worked more than any of the guys did, she just happened to be able to do it from home in her pajamas. Sal was especially jealous of that fact. Jess rushed around in her 1950s-era apron that had little pockets on the front of it, bouncing from here to there, topping people's drinks off while the timer gleefully ticked away in the kitchen.

"What's on the menu for tonight?" Paul asked.

"It's the third Friday of the month. We always have Mexican on the third Friday of the month," Jess replied.

"You're like a calendar," Greg laughed as he grabbed her around the waist and pulled her into him.

"Honey! The meat!" she exclaimed as she pulled herself out of Greg's arms and ran back to the kitchen.

"Oh! I almost forgot. My friend Samantha is joining us tonight. One of the sites I write for just hired her and it turns out she lives in Medford, too. We've been chatting over IM and e-mail for weeks, so I figured I'd invite her. She's probably lost, I'm going to call her," Jess yelled from the kitchen.

"Oh sure, her friends can show up late, but you guys are two seconds late, and you're out in the cold," Greg joked.

"Her friends are probably cuter than we are," Sal said, laughing.

"She'll be here in a sec, she's coming up the stairs now," Jess reported as she rushed back into the kitchen.

As if on cue, a knock came from the door.

"Greg, honey, let Sam in, will you?"

"Yes, dear," Greg responded. "I'm on it."

Greg made his way across the apartment which was substantially larger than Sal's and opened the door. Samantha came in, shaking Greg's hand as she did. There were some pleasantries exchanged, but Sal couldn't hear them from where they were seated in the living room.

"Samantha! You made it!" Jess called from the kitchen in an excited girl voice.

"It's so nice to meet you in person," Samantha responded as she made her way farther into the apartment to greet Jess.

"Wow, she's hot," Derek said, nudging Sal's shoulder.

Sal was following Samantha across the room with his eyes. His mind raced and he immediately wanted to be closer to her. Even to just sit next to her at dinner. He felt that if he wasn't close to her, something bad would happen. It was an instant attraction. A school-boy crush.

Sal guessed she was around five foot five, very trim and it was obvious that she exercised. Her long brown hair flowed down to the middle of her back. She had the most electric blue eyes that he'd ever seen. They seemed to brighten the room. She was wearing a button down blouse that accentuated how slim she was. Her dark pants combined with the lowly-lit room made it hard to make out her full figure, but Sal liked what he could see. Her lips were small and thin, but fit perfectly on her symmetrical face. Sal found himself staring harder than he knew he should.

Samantha had offered to help Jess finish the preparations for the meal and the two walked into the kitchen. Checking the clock on his phone, Sal knew that dinner would be ready in a few minutes. Jess was like a well-oiled machine. Guests arrive at five, dinner is served at quarter to six.

With minutes to spare, Sal knew he had to somehow signal to both Paul and Derek that they must sit next to each other across from he and Samantha. At a table designed for six, when Greg and Jess sat at either end, there were only four seats left available, two on either side.

"Oh, how rude of me," Jess said from the kitchen. "These are Greg's bandmates."

As she called out each of their names, Derek gave a nod and Paul a smile. Sal actually waved and immediately wished he could delete the movement like a line from his lyrics. *What is wrong with me?*

he thought to himself. He took a moment to compose himself —
shook his head briefly, closed his eyes for a second — and stood up.

"It's nice to meet you, Samantha," he said as he crossed from the
living room to the dining room table.

"You too. I've heard so much about all of you guys from Jessica,"
Samantha responded.

"Jess, do you need a hand with bringing anything to the table?"
Sal asked.

"Um, sure. I guess we could use some help," she responded,
looking at him quizzically as Sal made his way to the kitchen.

Jess proceeded to hand him sour cream, mixed cheese, and gua-
camole and shot Greg a look. Greg had been with Jess long enough
that he knew what the look meant and immediately jumped up from
his recliner to make his way over to the kitchen.

After he dropped off the round of items Jess had given him, Sal
looked around for an excuse to reenter the kitchen and made his
way to the fridge.

"You guys need another beer?" he Paul and Derek.

They both nodded and Sal turned to Samantha.

"Anything special you'd like to drink?"

"I'll just grab some water," she said.

Sal made his way from the fridge back to the table and placed a
beer for Paul and one for Derek on the opposite side of the table
from where he planned to sit next to Samantha. Surely this would
work.

Jess proclaimed that dinner was ready and everyone that wasn't
already in the dining room made their way over. As Sal had hoped,
everyone took their places. Paul and Derek sat across from him. Jess
and Greg took their seats at each end of the table.

Samantha made her way to the empty chair. As she approached, he stepped back and pulled out her chair for her. A smile crossed her face and Sal even noted a hint of a blush.

"Well thank you," she said.

"My pleasure," Sal replied as he sat down.

"Dig in," Greg said from the head of the table and everyone complied.

"Sam, did you see that piece that Mark published today?" Jess asked.

"I did!" Sam said. "I figured you saw it and were going to say something."

Sal caught himself looking to his right to see Samantha as she looked to her left to talk to Jess.

"Mark has terrible grammar and the editors never correct him," Jess informed the guys who were a bit lost.

"It's so terrible because these stories go out without any real editing, like they're afraid of Mark!" Sam laughed.

At one point during the conversation, Sal and Sam caught each other's eye and looked away quickly like children on the playground during recess.

Sal's plan of seating her on his right lead to a comedy of errors as they bumped elbows throughout the evening. She being left handed and he being right handed lead to them bumping elbows each time one of them tried to pick up their taco. Each time it happened, Sal turned red and Samantha giggled a little bit to herself.

"Don't forget what you're in charge of for next weekend," Jess said out loud. "All of you."

"Don't worry honey, everything's going to be perfect," Greg assured her.

"How long have you worked with Jess?" Sal asked Sam semi-privately.

"A few months now," she said as they bumped elbows again.

"I'm so sorry," Sal said. "I guess we didn't think this seating arrangement through that well."

"It's okay," she blushed.

The conversation around them seemed to fade away to a dull roar as Sal got engulfed in his chat with Sam.

"What do you do?" Sam asked.

"I work at a Starbucks. It's not the best job, but I survive."

"Jess says you're the singer and that you guys are really good."

"Yea, I play guitar, too." Sal said.

"That's pretty cool."

At the same moment, they both reached for the sour cream resulting in another awkward but adorable moment of clumsiness. Rather than dwelling on the moment, Sal scooped some onto her plate for her without missing a beat.

"Have you been playing long?" Sam asked.

"Most of my life and most of the time that I've known Greg we've been a 'band'."

"You do the writing too?"

"I do, I write all of the lyrics and the band works on the music collectively."

Sal got lost in her eyes for a moment and seemed to stop hearing the words she was saying. He was so focused on how blue and beautiful they were that he realized he'd not heard Jess at the end of the table calling his name.

"Sal? Sal?" Jess called out, louder and louder.

"Huh? What?" he replied, his friends laughing.

"I was just saying how I thought you and Sam would get along well, but it seems like you've taken matters into your own hands."

"Sorry, we were just chatting. I didn't mean to ignore the rest of you." Sal apologized.

As dinner wound down, Sal found himself wishing he'd spent more time talking to Sam. The smaller conversations that they'd had as a group sufficed to help him get to know her, the way she spoke, the movements she made when she talked. In some small way, he knew that Jess had brought her there to try to set them up together.

Before everyone left, Jess reminded them of their responsibilities for the wedding next weekend again. Everyone got little laminated cards with their tasks, due dates, and phone numbers.

"Oh, and I invited Sam. She'll be coming by herself," Jess said, staring directly at Sal.

His eyes lit up a bit at that news.

Chapter Four

"Thanks for dinner, Jess! It was nice to meet you guys," Samantha said as she made her way to the door.

As she put on her coat, Jess came over, glanced in Sal's direction and whispered something in Samantha's ear. Samantha turned a bit red and turned her back to the rest of the group.

She thanked Greg and Jess again as she left. As she made her way down the stairs out onto the street, the spring air hit her, so she took off her coat. For an April night in New England it was surprisingly warm.

She daydreamed while walking the few blocks back to her own apartment, a tiny one-bedroom apartment above a 24-hour convenient store. She couldn't help but smile after having a great night with some new friends.

She tried to force herself not to dwell on it. She hardly knew anything about him, after all. All she knew was the few pieces of conversation they'd had over dinner and the few things that Jess had told her over the last few weeks of working together — and yet she felt more comfortable with him than she did with anybody else she'd met so far.

It was a short ten minute walk from Jess' apartment to her own, and being that it was still early, she stopped into the store below her apartment to grab a few items that she needed for the weekend. She said hello to Mr. Juang, her landlord who also owned the convenient store. It seemed like he was always there.

The small bag of groceries was placed on her cafe table when she got into her apartment upstairs and put her shoes, coat and purse in their places, neat and organized.

On her way by the cafe table, she grabbed the pint of Ben & Jerry's she bought and dropped it in the freezer on her way to her desk. Samantha's desk was at the far end, with a small desk lamp and not much else. Her iPad sat on its stand to the left of the computer.

As she sat down she pressed the spacebar on her laptop to wake from its slumber. She opened her browser and went right to Facebook. First, like any good guest would do, she updated her status to say what a great time she'd had at dinner, purposefully tagging Greg and Jess in her status so that they'd see it.

From there, she went to Jess' profile page, and looked through her list of friends to see if she could find Sal. Facebook profile stalking was something everyone did and despite being called stalking, Samantha didn't feel creepy about it. To her surprise, she didn't see Sal listed in Jess' friends, which was odd given how long they'd known each other.

She saw Jess' relationship status and clicked on Greg's name to get to his profile. Again, no luck. Sal didn't come up as one of Greg's friends. Confused, she thought there must be a mistake.

"I can't believe I'm doing this," she said out loud.

Then she saw an icon light up in the top left corner of her screen, indicating that she had a new friend request, followed almost immediately by a Messages icon. A friend request and a new message all at once?

This wasn't a too uncommon thing, Sam spent most of her free time online building a large following on Twitter and a large group of friends on Facebook. She found it easier to interact with people online, especially ones she didn't know. Not being a drinker, she didn't go to bars, so she opted to meet her friends electronically.

Sam had her share of attention over the years but had never been able to break out of her shell enough to be as bold as she wanted to be. She'd always been fairly reserved, never going out of her way to stand up for herself and point out the things she wanted in life.

She clicked on the message first. It was from Sal Maggione. She let out a small squeal and felt herself turn bright red.

I know this is rather forward, and I apologize for stalking you through Jess' page. But I figured if you're going to be around Jess and Greg a lot in the future, then you and I should get to know each other. Hope that's okay, Sal.

She read it three times before clicking over to accept the friendship request, making Sal her 516th friend on Facebook.

Her phone, iPad, and Messages on her laptop all popped up at once. A text from Jess: *Friends already?!?*

Chapter Five

SAL HAD EVERYTHING PLANNED for Jess and Greg's big day. His tux was in the trunk of his car, his trusty iPad in his bag with a copy of his best man's speech, and he was on his way to pick up Derek.

As he drove from his apartment to Derek's, he ran through some of the lines of his speech that he was having trouble remembering, hoping that he could get through the whole thing without having to rely on the iPad as his backup. It got him thinking of how complete Jess and Greg had made each other, almost instantly and completely. From the moment they met, they were inseparable. He often referred to them, at least in his own mind, as his Marshall and Lilly. No other tv couple had personified his best friend's relationship so perfectly over the years.

Though a bit jealous of their relationship, Sal knew that seeing them as happy as they were meant that there was hope for this type of happiness for him. That, someday, he'd meet someone who complimented him as well as Jess complimented Greg. Someone that loved every ounce of him and his imperfections. Someday, she'd arrive.

"Got your speech?" Derek asked when he jumped into the passenger seat of Sal's car, after dropping his tux in the trunk.

"It's on my iPad in my bag. Is that tacky?"

"Nah, you're keeping up with the times. Plus, you've got that thing glued to your hands anyway. If you didn't have it on you today, I'd think you weren't feeling well," laughed Derek.

"I've rehearsed it enough that I almost know it by heart. I brought it just in case," Sal said.

The drive from Derek's place in Somerville to Paul's place in Arlington was pretty quick one this morning. They drove in silence, listening to music on the radio, changing stations to find a song that they both liked the entire ride. Sal daydreamed of a day when his songs would be on the radio and knew that Derek had the same ambition.

He let the idea of hearing one of his songs on the radio float around in his head, wondering if any of their ballads would ever be played at a wedding, wondering if anyone would fall in love to one of those songs. The band had been working so hard for so long, Sal knew that their hard work would have to pay off eventually.

For some reason, he had the thought that he wouldn't be the first one to hear the song on the radio. He'd just be at work or home, doing whatever he was doing, and one of the other guys would call him and tell him to put the radio on. He imagined he'd sit in silence and listen, wondering what the rest of the world was thinking, hearing his lyrical emotion for the first time. He wondered how his parents would react and could already hear Cassie squealing in excitement.

When they arrived at Paul's complex, Derek sent him a text and Paul came out, adding his tux to the pile in the trunk.

"Are we picking Greg up, or is he driving himself in?" Paul asked.

"He's already at the church," Sal replied. "He's been there for about an hour now."

"Aside from seating people, what do we have to do? They didn't cover much last night at the rehearsal dinner."

"The wedding planner and the church people will walk us through it as we go. You guys seat the guests, I wait up front with Greg," Sal told the guys. As best man, his duties were to hold the rings and make sure the groom didn't run off.

"Seems easy enough," the others agreed.

When they arrived at the church, Greg was waiting in the back, already in his tux even though the wedding wasn't scheduled to start for another two hours. He wore a lobster bib to protect his tux while he ate a chicken parm sub.

Sal was the first to notice and couldn't control his laughter.

"Jess will literally kill me, in a church, if I have sauce on my tux when we get married," Greg said while Derek and the others continued laughing.

"Don't worry, they can work wonders with Photoshop these days," Sal said.

Each of the guys took turns getting dressed in the men's room, a room barely bigger than a closet.

"Thank God for clip-on bow-ties," said Derek as he emerged in his tux.

"Dude! You're in a church, don't say that!" Greg yelled, motioning at their surroundings.

Derek shrugged, attributed Greg's irrationality to the events of the day, and left the small back room followed by the rest of his bandmates.

The church was old, beautiful and warm. The sun flooded through the stained glass windows, casting blues, reds, yellows, and oranges on the walls in a beautiful scattered pattern, and causing bits of light to shine on parts of the altar, creating multi-colored layers of light. Sal watched as Greg made his way over to the altar and up the few steps, counting aloud to make sure that when he and Jess left as husband and wife, he knew how many steps to take down.

The priest came over and introduced himself to Sal and Derek.

Father Williams repeated the same instructions he'd given hundreds of times about how great God is and how beautiful their love is to the group. You could tell it was rehearsed, but not in a bad way. He was on his game, was good with words, and was going to make today special for Jess and Greg.

Sal and Greg stood on the altar watching as Paul and Derek sat all of the guests. As Samantha sat down near the front behind Jess' parents, she gave a small smile to Sal. He couldn't help but smile back. He wanted to skip the wedding and go right to the reception so he could talk to her and spend more time with her.

He knew at that moment that he'd make sure he got to dance with her as soon as his obligation to the maid of honor out of the way. The ceremony itself went by in the blink of an eye and before Sal knew it he was passing Sam's smiling face as he followed Greg and Sam out of the church.

The reception was just down the street at one of Greg and Jess' favorite restaurants. Everything was set up earlier that morning by the wedding planner and her staff, so that the newly married couple could walk in, and go right into their first dance to Jason Mraz's "I'm Yours".

The guests had all arrived and were standing when Jess and Greg came into the DJ's announcement.

"Ladies and Gentlemen, it's my great pleasure to introduce to you for the first time Gregory and Jessica Wincomb."

The crowd of nearly two hundred erupted into applause as Greg and Jess, red-faced and a bit shy, entered the room and started their first dance.

"I'm surprised Jess' tiny frame can hold up that dress," Derek commented to Paul, "it probably weighs half as much as she does, she's so tiny."

Jess' whole life she'd been barely five feet tall and never had broken a hundred pounds. Her blonde hair was pulled up and twisted this way and that, accentuating her blue eyes.

Greg's curly hair had been tamed for the first time in as long as Sal could remember. Standing over 6 foot 3 inches and slightly more than two hundred pounds, you'd think that they would make an awkward couple, but they always just worked. Their whole lives Sal had always joked that Greg looked like someone took Corey Matthews and made him bigger, a throwback to one of their favorite childhood shows, *Boy Meets World*.

As practiced, at the sixty-second mark Sal, Derek and Paul took the hands of the maid of honor and bridesmaids and took the floor alongside Greg and Jess. Jess had jumped at the opportunity to not be the only couple out on the dance floor.

As Sal danced with Victoria, Jess's younger sister by a few years, he looked around at the restaurant. Large enough to comfortably seat every guest plus a couple of hundred more, the place was decked out beautifully.

"The wedding planner did an amazing job with this place!" Sal said, as he noticed that Victoria was crying on his shoulder.

He couldn't help but try to find Samantha in the sea of onlookers while they spun and twirled on the dance floor. The song felt like it went on forever and when it finally ended everyone took their seats. From the head table, which was elevated a foot or so off the floor, Sal could clearly see over to the table where Samantha was seated.

Sitting alongside some other bloggers and writers that Jess had worked with over the last few years, Samantha was conveniently facing the head table. He caught Jess' eye, who then glanced at Samantha and back at Sal, smiling.

As the crowd began to settle down, doors all around the restaurant started to pop open, spilling endless lines of waiters and waitresses carrying armfuls of plates. Without a word, each waiter and waitress knew which of the two choices of entree the guest in a given seat had and placed a meal down in front of them.

Sal could hear people talking about how delicious the food was.

Jennifer, the wedding planner, made her way over to Sal, tapped him on the shoulder and indicated that it was almost time for him to make his best man's speech. He turned to acknowledge her and quickly finished his meal. Before grabbing the wireless microphone from the DJ he made his way to the men's room to make sure he didn't have any food in his teeth and that his pant zipper hadn't become unzipped. Making a speech in front of 200 people, most of whom were strangers, made him a bit nervous and he was overthinking everything.

With clean teeth, a fully zipped zipper, and his iPad laid gently on the head table in front of him, he took the microphone from the DJ and took the stage, standing just behind Greg and Jess.

"Good afternoon, everyone. My name is Sal Maggione. I've been Greg's best friend for the better part of our lives, and it's my honor to be up here in front of you today on the greatest day of Jessica and Greg's lives. They've asked me to say a few words and anyone that knows me knows that I'm anything but brief, so I apologize in advance."

The crowd collectively chuckled and Greg grinned.

"I've known Greg since I was a teenager and met Jess the same day that he did. It was clear from the moment that they met that they were destined for this day. Their love for one another was instant, obvious, and heartwarming.

"You hope, throughout your entire life, that not only do those you love find someone who suits them so completely, but that you can find that same love for yourself."

Jess had started crying as soon as Sal started talking, but now began weeping louder. Sal reached out and put his hand on her shoulder.

"Jess has changed Greg in ways that she doesn't even know. But I'm about to open that can of worms right now. I'm sorry Greg." Sal took his hand from Jess' shoulder and gave Greg a gentle punch.

"Here are the top five things that Jess doesn't know she's done for Greg. Number one: Greg never wore his seatbelt until the first time he drove a car with Jess in it. He later told me that he would never be able to live with himself if something were to take either one of them away from one another. Number two: Greg wouldn't have gone to college if it weren't for Jess. She'd so often told him that she wanted to marry an educated man and he so wanted to be that man. Number three: Greg always said he never wanted to have kids. He wanted to be a career man and find a job to support himself and his future wife. That changed the day Jess told him that she loved him. Number four, and this one's a good one: Greg turned down a date with the head cheerleader at our high school to stay in on a Friday night and help Jess put together her new TV stand. You remember that, Greg?" The crowd laughed.

"And finally, number five: First period, September 7th, 1997. Our first class together of sophomore year. Greg leaned over to me in our seats, just three rows behind and two seats over to the left of Jess and said 'I'll bet you $20 I'm going to marry that girl someday.' Twenty dollars I'm glad to lose." Sal handed over a crisp twenty dollar bill to his buddy, who was laughing through his tears.

"I've never known a love even a tenth of what you guys share. I hope, and I pray, and I ask all the things that I believe in that I find someone who'll love me as much as you guys love each other. I've watched you grow into an amazing couple over the years. You've had many more ups than downs, and you've learned to let the other take care of you when you can't take care of yourself. Everyone always says that their friends' marriage will last. I know I can say that and never have to worry about it not being true. You are my family and I love you both. I needn't wish you the best of luck, because when you're as in love as you two are, there's no need for luck."

A tear started to form in his right eye, so he wrapped up quickly.

"Please join me in raising a glass to the greatest couple on the face of the planet. My friends and yours, Mr. and Mrs. Greg Wincomb."

Through tears, the crowd sipped their champagne, placed their glasses down, and erupted into applause. Jess and Greg took turns standing and hugging Sal.

"Great speech," Jess said through her tears.

After dinner ended, the DJ put on some typical weddings songs — "The Electric Slide", "YMCA", "We Are Family". Sal finally gave up waiting for a slow song so that he could ask Samantha to dance and approached the DJ.

"Hey, I'm trying to get something a little more mellow to dance to for couples. Got anything in mind?"

"I'll see what I can do after this one. How 'bout a little Clapton?" The DJ said.

"Clapton it is," Sal agreed.

He stepped down from the platform and approached Samantha. As he got closer, her smile grew wider, her cheeks became flush, and her eyes focused on him. Sal could tell that she was expecting him to come over.

"Your speech was beautiful. You have a way with words."

As she finished her sentence, the end of "We Are Family" faded out and "Wonderful Tonight" started playing.

"I think that's for us," Sal said as he extended his hand.

Samantha blushed and looked away but eventually took Sal's hand and stood, following him to the dance floor a few feet from her seat.

He pulled her into his arms and began twirling and spinning to the tune of the music.

"This is such a fantastic song," Sal said.

"I know. I've always loved that the lyrics are so beautiful, yet so sad." She was still blushing but a smile started to break through.

"I wish I could write something that touches people the way this song has touched so many."

"Jessica told me that you're kind of a wordsmith. I have to believe her now that I've heard your speech."

"I've been writing for years. I never really saw myself as a great writer. I just write what I feel or what I think."

"I know what you mean. I basically get paid to write, but I always feel like it's not good enough. Maybe I could hear some of your songs someday?"

"Really?" He was taken aback for a moment, not sure how to respond. "Well, we don't have anything recorded just yet, but we've got a show lined up in a few weeks. When Greg gets back from their honeymoon. Maybe you'd want to come to that?"

"That'd be great. I'm guessing you have hard copies of the stuff you've written? Or digital?"

He laughed. "Yeah, I have three copies of everything, actually. Greg gives me a hard time about it. I have the original handwritten version, a typed version, and then a copy I keep on my iMac."

"Do you think I could maybe read them sometime? "

"I suppose we could make arrangements for that," he said as the song wound down.

Sal glanced over at the DJ and nodded. The DJ went from "Wonderful Tonight" right into John Mayer's "Your Body Is a Wonderland". Sal and Samantha didn't miss a beat and kept right on dancing.

"I have to travel to San Francisco this week to meet with a client. I'll be back on Friday."

"Ohh, Friday is no good. That's when we have our weekly dinner at Jess and Greg's," he said with a look of disappointment washing over his otherwise happy face.

"You're right. But there's two things you're forgetting."

"What's that?"

"For starters, they'll be gone this week. Honeymoon, remember?" She gestured around the room as if to remind Sal that they were at a wedding, "and secondly, I'll be at those Friday night dinners for a while, so you're kind of stuck with me either way. Maybe one day I'll follow you home and sneak into your apartment like a ninja." She made a ninja-like chopping action on his left shoulder.

"I see. So now that I Facebook stalked you, you think it's okay to real life stalk me?" he joked.

"Well, truth be told, I was trying to stalk you on Facebook too. You just have some hard-to-get through privacy settings. I couldn't even find you to send a friend request, but I was literally doing it when I got your friend request. I guess we're even."

"I guess we are. So I'll talk to you when you get back from San Francisco?"

"You will. And hopefully we'll talk while I'm out there, too," she said as the song ended. "Thanks for the dance." She kissed him on the cheek and then ran off to talk to Jess at the head table.

Sal watched her walk towards Jess, smiling so widely that he wondered if people were noticing. He felt the warmth from her lips on his cheek, and looked forward to the next time he'd get to see her.

Chapter Six

The Monday after Greg and Jess' wedding, Sal visited his little sister at college. Cassie was in her last year at Boston University about to graduate with a degree in Journalism. Sal, being so many years older than her, was often a bit too protective and sometimes over the top. It was raining, so their usual routine of taking a walk along the river was swapped for having some lunch at Rhett's in George Sherman Union, right on campus. They agreed to meet at noon.

"Cassie May!" Sal yelled out to his baby sister from across the crowded and long hallway as she stood at the ATM withdrawing money.

"Sal!"

She made a gesture to the ATM to hurry up, as if it would have an effect on how quickly her receipt would print, ran the few yards to Sal and leapt into his arms. It had been a few weeks since he'd visited and Cassie was stressed out about all of her finals, so it was nice to see family.

"I'm so happy you're here! I've missed you so much and Mom and Dad never visit me. It's nice to have a family member here! How are you?" The questions and statements seemed to all come out of her mouth in one big mess.

"Calm down, Cassie May. We have as much time as you need," he reassured her while leading her to the line at Rhett's.

Were there not such an age difference between the two of them, they could have been twins. Cassie was a few inches shorter than Sal and much thinner, but they shared the same facial features, both a spitting image of their mother. Cassie looked almost identical to photos of their mom from when she was a teenager — the long brown hair, dark eyes and tanned skin tone.

They ordered, making small talk about Cassie's classes and finals while they waited for their orders. Once they had their food she led him to the back of the dining room to a quieter area. They sat down across from each other and she dove into her burger.

"I saw some pictures from Greg and Jess' wedding on Facebook. Who's this girl you're dancing with?" she asked.

"What girl?"

"There're a few photos of you dancing with some girl. Didn't you see them?"

"No. I must not have been tagged," he said.

"Let me show you. Hang on." She took a bite of her burger and reached for her iPhone, which was adorned with a pink glittery case.

"Here, look," she said pushing her phone towards him.

There they were in color on Cassie's screen: Sal and Samantha dancing, arm in arm. He scrolled to the next photo. The same moment, but from a different angle. This time, Samantha had her head on his shoulder.

He immediately missed her. A woman he barely knew and had only been apart from for a day and a half, but he missed her.

"Oh, that's Samantha. She works with Jess. We were introduced at their apartment a few weeks back."

"She's making lovey eyes at you in some of them, you know."

"She is? No way." he said, defensively, trying to make it seem as if that wasn't what he wanted.

"She is."

Cassie showed him another photo. This time Sal was nodding to the DJ to play the second song and Samantha was staring at him affectionately.

"I had no idea."

"Do you like her?"

"I don't know, I just met her."

"That doesn't mean that you don't like her, Sal."

"Let's talk about something else," he suggested.

"Let's talk about this girl that my big brother has a crush on," she said a little louder than Sal would have liked.

"Ok, fine. You win. Yes, I like her. I barely know anything about her, but I like her so far."

"She better be good to you or I'll beat her up," Cassie joked.

Sal laughed at her joke, knowing full well that she was joking.

"What's going on with you? Another few weeks until finals, right?"

"Yep, I've studied all I can study. I don't think there's anymore that I can learn at this point."

"Good. I'm sure you'll do great. You were always the brains of this operation," he said with a smile.

They finished lunch and made their way to the trash and recycling bins to discard their waste.

"While I'm here, do you need anything?" Sal asked.

"You're such a big brother."

"Well, yea, I am. That's the whole point. What do you need? I know when you don't say no it's because you want something, but won't ask. So what is it?"

"My laptop's been acting up lately," she said, avoiding eye contact.

This was both good news and bad news. The good was that Sal and their parents were planning on buying her a new MacBook Pro for a graduation gift. The bad news was that he worried that she'd be unable to finish her finals without a working laptop.

"Okay, let's go take a look and see," he said, following her out the door towards her dorm.

The made their way from George Sherman Union through as many connecting buildings as they could before they had to go out in the rain to get back to Cassie's dorm.

They dried themselves off and Sal sat down at Cassie's desk.

"What's it doing this time?" he asked.

"It's just really slow, which makes it hard to get anything done. Can you fix that, Mr. Wizard?"

"I can try, sure," he said, thankful that he'd already pre-ordered the new MacBook Pro for her with his parents help.

After a few minutes of clicking and dragging and dropping, he was confident that the laptop would continue to function for just a little bit longer and handed control back over to Cassie.

"Here you go, kiddo. That should do the trick."

"You really are the best!" she said as Sal grabbed his coat and made his way to the door.

"I'm glad you think so. Give me a hug before I go."

Cassie ran over to him and wrapped her arms around him.

"I mean it. Anyone would be so lucky. I love you the most," she said.

"I love you the mostest."

That's how all of their conversations ended. In a family as close as theirs, they always believed that you should never say goodbye without telling the other person that you loved them.

As he left her dorm, he felt good about helping his little sister and for coming clean about liking Samantha. Even though Cassie was his little sister, he felt good telling someone about how he felt.

Chapter Seven

By the time everyone arrived at the rehearsal space on Wednesday night, it was evident that Sal was in a rotten mood. He hated his day job and from time to time someone would come in and just ruin his day, whether it was a complaining customer, a rude homeless person or someone who was just being spiteful for any reason. Today was one of those days and Sal had been stewing over a rude customer earlier in the day ever since leaving work.

"What's up with you?" Derek asked as he arrived and sat down at his drums.

"Just had a shitty day. Some asshole at work threw coffee all over the counter because it wasn't hot enough."

"What a dick. Did you throw him out?" Paul asked.

"Nah. I'd rather not talk about it. Let's just see what we can jam out tonight. Since Greg's not here, we can just kind of relax a bit. Everyone cool with that?"

Paul and Derek nodded.

"How about some Zeppelin?" Derek suggested as he began playing "Communication Breakdown."

As Paul and Sal joined in, Sal let his mind wander. He knew the song well enough; they'd played it countless times on Greg-less nights before. He couldn't help but think of Samantha. Of the photos that Cassie showed him of the two of them. Of how happy it made him. Of how he couldn't wait for her to get back from San Francisco.

From "Communication Breakdown," the guys went into a jam session, free-styling riffs and bass lines along with Derek's drumming, making sure to note anything that they liked along the way. Derek was pretty quick to jump up and turn around to the whiteboard to jot down notes, usually a time signature and some name that he'd come up with that would describe what the song sounded like.

"We should find some way to just record when we jam. It'd make it easier to remember what we played that we liked, wouldn't it?" he suggested.

"Yea, but with all the other noise that happens in this building? It might be hard to do," Sal pointed out.

"Sure, it won't be perfect, but it's not like we're going to sell it. It's just so we can refer back to it and remember."

"We could even just drop an iPhone on the floor in the middle of the room," Paul said.

"I doubt we'd be able to even decipher what sounds were being played doing that. The iPhone's microphone isn't really made for such extreme volumes," Sal said to Paul's disappointment.

"What if we buy one of those handheld multi-directional recorders?" Derek asked.

"You mean like one of those little Zoom devices, or something?"

"Yeah, exactly. Those can't be too expensive, can they?" Derek said.

"I don't think so, but I don't really have any extra money right now. Do you guys?" Sal said.

"I think we could scrounge something up. But let's wait for Greg to get back. You know how he is when he's not involved in decisions to spend band money," Paul suggested.

He was right. Greg was Sal's best friend, but there was no doubt that he had a tendency to try to control everything. It was a fault of Greg's that Sal had learned to live with back in junior high.

In fairness to him, Greg did have the best job and would likely be responsible for the biggest portion of anything that they bought for the band. The band had always said that they would split purchases equally, but Greg knew that the other guys didn't have the salary that he did and he didn't mind helping out a little bit extra here and there. While controlling, everyone still thought Greg was a great guy and they were lucky to know him and have him as a bandmate.

After a few hours of jamming, they decided to take a break for dinner. Derek and Paul ate their dinners in silence, while Sal continued to daydream about his dances with Samantha. He could still smell her hair, still feel her body pressed against his. And what a body it was, he kept thinking to himself. He'd never admit it if you asked him, but Sal thought he was a pretty good looking guy. He'd had his share of women, but never any that made him feel the way that Samantha had and he barely knew her. He kept coming back to the fact that he barely knew her and wondered what that meant for his future.

"What's up with the girl?" Paul asked in Sal's direction.

"What? Me?" Sal replied.

"Yeah, you. The girl from Greg's wedding." Derek added in.

"Samantha? I don't know. She's just a girl," he said, feeling exposed.

"You sleep with her?" Derek asked.

"Dude, come on." Sal said, defensively. "Greg's not here and you guys turn from picking on him to picking on me?"

"Well, you're the interim leader," Paul said.

"So you have to bust my balls?"

"Busting someone's balls is part of our routine," Derek said, leaning over his drums to high five Paul.

"You guys are assholes."

"Come on, spill. You dig her?" Derek pressed.

"She's pretty cool. Yeah, I like her."

"Sal and Sam, sitting in a tree," Paul mocked.

He tried his best to ignore them, but decided that quickly finishing their dinners and getting back to work would be the easiest way to get them off his back.

It worked. Once they started jamming again, they let up on nagging him about his feelings towards Samantha. He'd known both Paul and Derek for a while now and he knew that they wanted to keep razzing him, but knew that focusing on the music was more important.

Sal stayed a few hours after Paul and Derek had left. He spent some time sitting in the silence of their room and trying to ignore the music coming from other rooms, working on lyrics in his head. He wanted to keep working, as it helped get his mind off Samantha.

Chapter Eight

It was just shy of eight o'clock Friday morning when Sal was awoken on his couch, as usual, by the sound of his phone vibrating on the coffee table. He sprung to his feet, wiped his eyes, and grabbed his phone. Still a bit groggy, he tried to make out the caller ID, but it was a number he didn't recognize.

"Hello?" He answered.

"My stalking level is greater than yours," the voice on the other end said.

"Who is this?"

"Guess."

"I have no idea. I'm barely awake. Give me a hint."

"I missed you," she said.

"Samantha?"

"I got your number from Jess before they left for the honeymoon. I've wanted to call you all week, but was nervous."

"You should have called. I'll be honest, I've been missing you too. Is it weird that we feel that way? We just met."

"It's a bit weird, yes. But I feel it, too. The good news is, I bumped my flight up. I was on the red eye last night and just landed at Logan."

"I thought you weren't coming home until tomorrow!" he said, almost a bit too excited.

"I wasn't supposed to, but I wanted to make sure I was rested up. I've got some reading to do tonight and if I flew in later today, I'd be asleep by dinner time. I slept the whole flight home, so I'm ready for tonight!"

"You didn't have to, but I'm glad you came back early. How are you getting home from the airport?"

"I'm waiting in line for a taxi right now."

"Oh, okay. If I knew, I would have come and picked you up. "

"That's sweet, but I can manage. You have to work this morning anyway, don't you?"

"Nope, I have Fridays off every week. Despite working a crappy job, they're pretty accommodating with my schedule."

"So then we're on for tonight?"

"Are you hitting on me, ma'am?" he said, jokingly.

"Yes, I am. I hope that's okay," she sounded a bit reserved.

"You bet it's okay. In fact, it's perfect," he said, smiling.

"Well, in that case, I think you should take me to dinner first. It seems only customary before bringing a girl back to your apartment, doesn't it?"

He could hear the adorable look on her face. That look of surprise that she was just so forward, but also smiling because she knew he'd say yes. He'd never had a woman be so forward with him before and he kind of enjoyed her taking the reigns.

"Text me your address, and I'll pick you up later tonight. Let's say five?"

"I think that sounds good. Anywhere you'd like to take me is fine, but I don't eat seafood."

"That makes two of us," he said jokingly, "anything that swam while it was alive isn't for me."

"Let's not go too formal, though. After all, it is a first date."

"Okay, I'll think of a place that we can go that isn't too far. You still want to come back here and read some of my stuff afterwards?"

"That's the whole point of us getting together, isn't it?"

"It is. Just don't be too hard on me."

"I'll never be as hard on you as you are on yourself, Sal."

That was the first time he'd heard her say his name. It was music to his ears. He suddenly felt flush, his skin warming, his eyes glimmering, and a smile across his entire face that he felt that she could hear through the phone. He'd felt happy before, but this was a new level of happy. The type you only read about or see in cheesy movies. This was happiness above all other happiness. And he loved it.

"I guess I have my work cut out for me today. I have to wow you," he said.

"Why?"

"So that you'll want to go out with me again."

"I already do, silly."

"You already want a second date? What if tonight goes horribly wrong?"

"It won't."

"How can you be so sure?"

"I won't let it. I know it's going to be great. There's something about you. There's something that I just feel is destined for greatness."

"You're putting a lot of pressure on me," he laughed.

"No more than you've already put on yourself. I know how you are."

"You're right. I'll try to not overdo it," he assured her.

"Okay, so I'll see you at five?"

"You bet. Just don't forget to text me your address. I'll see you then."

Sal, knowing he had plenty of time, decided to go back to sleep for a bit so he was rested up for what would likely be the best date of his life. Or so he hoped.

He woke up an hour or so later, to find a text message on his phone from Samantha, as she promised. Before he forgot, he saved her number into his Contacts list so he'd have it in case he got lost later tonight.

Chapter Nine

DESPITE BEING TOLD TO not be too formal, Sal still put on a pair of nice pants and a button down shirt.

In typical Sal fashion, he arrived to her apartment half an hour early. Just after 4:30. He usually left early to get to places he'd never been before to make sure that he'd be able to find where he was going. He didn't want to drive around lost and end up being late. This particular time it worked in his favor since it took a while to find some parking on the busy Medford street where Samantha lived.

He sat in his car, waiting, watching the time pass on the radio's clock.

"Don't blow this," he said to himself as he got out of the car to approach the front of Samantha's building.

A few hours left of daylight this time of year meant that they could take a walk after dinner if they wanted to. The air was warm and the sun flooded between the closely nestled houses as he made his way down the sidewalk.

He stopped at the convenience store below her apartment and got some flowers. Not roses, just an assorted bouquet to let her know he was sweet.

When he made his way to the back entrance, he checked the name above the doorbell.

"St. Allen" it read. He was in the right place.

He pushed open the door and made his ascent up the creaky stairs that Samantha had known so well. At the top, he knocked gently and heard Samantha call out from inside.

"Be right there! Hang on!"

He could hear her rushing around inside. A moment later the door opened.

A rush of wind flew over his face. His hands got sweaty. His eyes glimmered. He felt like a schoolboy again.

"You found it, good! People often get confused because of the convenience store. They think I gave them a fake address."

"That thought had never crossed my mind," he said as he handed her the flowers, "these are for you."

"Aww, you shouldn't have. That's so sweet," she said ushering him inside.

He watched her walk to the kitchen and open a cabinet for a vase. She filled it with water, grabbed some scissors to cut the stems, and within moments the flowers were in the vase on her small kitchen table.

"Your place looks a lot like mine," he said, "but cleaner and bigger. And it's obvious that a girl lives here."

"Well I'd sure hope so," she said, poking fun at him.

"How long have you been here?" he said, looking around at how similar their apartments were.

"Let's see, I moved to the area two years ago from upstate New York. And stayed at my first apartment for a year and a half. So I've been here around six months or so. It's not perfect, but it's home. I don't go out all that much, but I do spend a lot of time shopping online for home decor," she replied.

"You don't have to explain that to me. I get it. My apartment is tiny, but it does the job for now. And I can afford it, so that's all the better."

"I guess I'll see that eventually, won't I? Or did you change your mind on letting me read your work?"

"You will, yes. I didn't change my mind. I even made sure to clean up today!"

She smiled and made her way towards the door.

"Shall we?"

"We shall," he said, "after you."

Samantha grabbed a cardigan from her closet and Sal opened the door for her. It was a bit awkward to both stand at the top of the stairs while he took her keys to lock her various locks for her. He noted that she smiled when he offered to lock up for her.

When they got to the bottom of the stairs, Sal reached around Samantha and opened the door for her, to which she smiled again and thanked him.

"I don't mean to be too forwarded," Sal said as they walked the short distance from the back entrance to his car, "but you look beautiful."

She blushed and managed to get out, "Thank you."

As they approached the car, Sal opened the door to let her in. He waited for her to be seated, closed the door, and walked around to the back. In today's modern age, you don't have to perform the test from A Bronx Tale. The girl never has to reach over to unlock the driver's side door anymore. Ever since the invention of keyless entry cars, that test had been null and void. Sal was confident that she'd have unlocked his door, though.

He got in, buckled his seatbelt, and started the car. The GPS in his dash was already set to their destination. An Italian Restaurant called Polcari's, just north of the city in a town named Woburn.

He'd already called in a reservation for 5:45 and set the GPS to take back roads, going north on Route 93 on a Friday at this time would be a nightmare due to all of the traffic. They had plenty of time and it'd give them an opportunity to talk.

"I guess we should start at the beginning. Do you want the story of Sal first, or do you want to tell the story of Samantha?" Sal started the conversation.

"Tell me about you. I know little bits and pieces here and there from Jess, but I'd love to hear it from the horse's mouth. So to speak."

"Okay, let's see," he began, "I suppose it all started when I was a little kid. I don't remember being a baby much, but who does? I'm the oldest of two very Italian children, in case you couldn't tell. My grandparents came over on a boat in the '40s, when they were just teenagers. They were together for almost 70 years when they both died. Within weeks of each other, my grandfather first, then my grandmother. I'm pretty sure she died of a broken heart."

"That's so sad. Were you close with them?"

"Yea, I mean what Italian family isn't close, right? We went there every Sunday for dinner as a kid. We were lucky that they lived close enough that we could visit them often. So we went every week, and made sure to spend a lot of time with them. It was really tough for my little sister when they died. She was barely a teenager and she cried for days. Our grandmother was a big influence on her. I took it pretty hard, too, but not as hard as Cassie."

"How old is she now?"

"Cassie?" he asked, "She's 22. She's a senior at BU and is taking her finals over the next few weeks so she can graduate with a Bachelor's in Journalism."

"Did you go to college?" She asked.

"I thought I was telling you my story, I didn't know you were interviewing me," he said jokingly with a wink, so she'd know he was kidding.

"I'm sorry, I guess it's the interview gene in me."

"No, it's fine. I'm just teasing. To answer your question, I never went to college. It's one of those things that I kind of regret now, and wish I'd done. I know I could go back now, but it'd probably be weird being a freshmen in college in my thirties, don't you think?"

"Probably, yes. But you could do online courses or night classes to get a degree, if you really wanted to."

"True. I never thought of it that way," he said, "anyway, back to my story. So Cassie is 22, I was just about 9 when she was born, and growing up it was both a chore being that much older than her, but also awesome. I got to look out for her as she started dating, help her with her homework throughout junior high and high school, and just be that cool older brother. It was kind of hilarious when she was 16, and all her friends would come over and flirt with me. I was 25 at that point and I loved the attention, I'm not gonna lie. I'd go out and wash my car in the summer and let them watch from her bedroom. I was such a punk."

Samantha laughed, but tried to choke it back, "I'm sorry," she said, "I just can't picture you doing that."

"I know, it was so out of character for me. It wasn't something that I would normally do. I was a different person then."

"I know what you mean. It's crazy how much people change from their teens to their twenties to their thirties."

"Some for the better, some for the worse."

They were approaching Polcari's and had made good time. Their reservation was at 5:45, and it was just about that time. Before Sal could make it around to the passenger side, Samantha had already gotten out of the car. Sal saw that as a missed opportunity, but vowed to himself that he'd make up for it.

They walked up the few steps to the restaurant's front door, and Sal was pleased to see that it wasn't that busy for a Friday night. The earlier reservation worked out, he thought. It's usually not a great first date if you're in a crowded and loud restaurant trying to yell to your date over the dozens of other people talking.

They were seated rather quickly and began looking over the menu. Sal, being a picky eater, immediately settled on having chicken parmesan.

"Are you a vegetarian?" He asked.

"No, why?"

"I was going to get chicken parm, but didn't want to order something that wasn't vegetarian in case it offended you."

"That's thoughtful. It won't bother me, I'm actually considering getting veal parm, myself."

The waiter came over to take their drink order and ask if they needed more time reading the menu. Sal said they didn't and ordered for both of them, letting Samantha order the drink she wanted. A Diet Coke. Sal asked for water and dove back into his story.

"So, let's sum up what we talked about in the car: grandparents passed away, together a long time; little sister; no college. Let's see what else can I tell you?"

"What else do you want to tell me?" She asked, playfully.

"Everything," he seemed to surprise himself. "Wow, I can't believe I said that. I'm sorry, that sounded so tacky."

"No, it's sweet. You're sweet," she replied, "tell me about your parents."

"Mom and Dad. Okay. They've been together since they were 22. My dad's three days older than my mom, so they take a vacation somewhere together every year to celebrate their birthdays. They usually go for a week and we got to go with them when we were kids. It was our annual family vacation in August. Mom and Dad would go off on a date one night and I was in charge of Cassie when I was old enough. Otherwise they'd find someone local to watch us for a few hours. It was always great to be a kid and see how in love my parents were with each other. I never really saw that with a lot of my friend's parents. Ask Greg, he'll tell you how his parents only stayed together because of him."

"I know so many people in that boat. It's kind of terrible, but that's the way life goes for some people."

"At this point they've been together now for almost 35 years. It'll be 35 years in a few months actually and Cassie and I are planning a surprise party for them. It's so easy now with Facebook. You just go look at their friends list and invite everyone all at once. I remember as a kid trying to figure out who your parents actual friends were was a nightmare. You had to find their address book and call people. It was a pain. The internet's made that whole process so much easier."

"I agree! I thought the same thing when I planned a 50th birthday for my mom a few years back."

"Wow, your mom's only in her 50s? She had you pretty young, then?"

"Like your parents, mine were in love to the point where others wondered how they did it. They were sweethearts their whole lives. My mom had just turned 18 when she had me. They split up when I was just about four. It was really hard for me, growing up with such a loving family, and then one day my dad just decided he didn't want to try anymore. He just upped and left. I came home from the park with my babysitter one day and there was a note on my pillow. All of his stuff was gone. My mom cried off and on for weeks."

Sal could tell that tears were starting to form, so he reached across the table to take her hand in a comforting way. She smiled and apologized that she was getting teary eyed,

"Even 25 years later, it's hard to think about."

"Do you still see your dad, or did he disappear all together?" Sal asked.

"Up until college, I still saw him from time to time. We were never close, but larger life events would bring him out of the woodwork," she said, sipping the last of her Diet Coke.

"That's terrible. I can't imagine a life without my dad."

"Well sure, because you had him around and were close to him. But having one that barely wants anything to do with you makes it tough to miss that person, ya know?"

"I guess you're right, I didn't really think of it that way."

The waiter brought over their food and asked if they needed anything else. Sal motioned to her empty glass and the waiter immediately went to retrieve another. Sal had barely had any of his water, so his throat had gotten dry. He was quite familiar with this, being a singer, so he gulped half his glass to hydrate himself and get rid of the scratchiness in his voice.

"It's not a big deal," she continued, "my mom and I grew much closer because of it. It was just the two of us for years, and we never let it slow us down."

"And you're still close today?"

"Yea, it's tougher now with the distance between us, but we FaceTime twice a week, and I call her a few times, too. I think she's sad now that she's all alone in that big house, so I try to call her whenever I can."

"That's admirable. Cassie and I try to go see our parents for a Sunday dinner at least once a month. We don't always make it, but we try to. Family is important."

"It is, I agree. So we might as well get that question out of the way."

"What question is that?" he asked.

"The 'do you want children?' question."

"Ah. That one. Yes, I'd love children. Not too many of them, though. I think 2 or 3 is more than enough. Life is expensive, right?"

"I think I want the typical one boy, one girl routine that most people want."

"What else should I know about you?" he asked.

"Well," she began, "I guess you could say I'm a typical shy girl. I've been through some tough times in my life; dad leaving, a far-too-long and terrible relationship, and moving hundreds of miles away from my mom to a place I knew nobody. I try to keep myself guarded."

"That's not a bad thing, though."

"No, I don't see it that way," she continued, "it just tends to put people off. It's not that I'm not interested in getting to know someone, I'm just protecting myself and trying to stay at bay until I'm comfortable. To be honest, I'm surprised I've been so forward with you chasing you down like I did. That's so not like me. Do you think I'm a crazy person?"

"If you are, then so am I," he said, still touching her hand across the table.

Sal wondered to himself if she'd noticed he turned the topic of conversation from him to her, without really meaning to. He didn't mind though, he just loved hearing her talk. She had this non-descript accent that had he not known it was upstate New York, he'd have never guessed. It was just smooth and calming. He felt like he could listen to her talk forever and it felt like he had.

"I have a question," she said, "may I?"

"Go ahead," he replied.

"Why don't you drink?"

"I get that a lot, actually."

"So what's the answer?"

"I don't really have one. I just never have. When I was growing up, probably in my late teens, one of our friends got really heavy into drinking. I remember being at Greg's house one night when his parents were out of town, we were probably 17, and our buddy was so drunk that he just kept throwing up on the front walkway. I stood there with a hose, washing away his puke for hours, well into the night."

"So in seeing how much your friend suffered and how miserable that made him made you not want to do it?"

"I guess on some level, yea. I just never wanted to be that way. Never wanted to not have control over myself like we saw him do all those times."

"Whatever happened to that friend?"

"To be honest," he said, "I have no idea. Greg and I haven't spoken to him since were just out of high school."

They opted to skip dessert and head back to Sal's apartment to continue the evening. Though she insisted on paying for dinner, Sal refused.

A playful tug of war broke out over the table, each with their hands on the bill, tugging it back and forth over the small candle in the center of their small table. She knew that she was going to let him pay the bill in the end but decided to be polite and at least try to pay.

Sal finally won the battle, paid the bill, and escorted Samantha back to his car.

By 7:30 the roadways were clear, and they jumped on Route 93 South to get back to Sal's apartment in Somerville. A quick ten minute ride and they were making their way up the stairs to his apartment.

"Oh," Sal said, "I don't have any Diet Coke. Did you want me to run to the store and get some?"

"Thanks, but I'm fine. I had two at dinner, and I think that's enough caffeine for one night," she said.

Sal unlocked the door and let her into the apartment. He followed her in and performed his usual routine. He then took her coat and said she could feel free to take her heels off if she'd like. She did and they made their way over to his couch and sat.

"Can I get you anything to drink?" He asked.

"Some water would be great, thank you."

Sal left her in the living room to get some water for the two of them while keeping an eye on her from the kitchen. Even though he was just seeing the back of her head, he could tell how beautiful she was. She had a glow about her, this warmth that radiated from her.

When he came back, he placed the glasses of water down, and made his way over to his desk, picking up the plastic file folder that stored his life's writings. Mostly songs, but also a few poems here and there. He had a bit of a struggle to get it off the floor — years and years of writing weighs quite a bit.

He made his way back to Samantha and put the box down by her feet, sliding the coffee table slightly out of the way to make room.

"Any specific time frame or material matter that you'd like to start with?" he asked.

"That's a great question. I was figuring you'd likely just give me one of your favorites to read. Don't you want to give me the best one to impress me right off the bat?" she joked.

"I hadn't even given it a thought," he said, "I assumed you'd pick one. How about we grab one at random?"

"Ok, that sounds fine."

Sal reached into the file folder and grabbed one filed under the letter S, a song called "Subtracted: 49", and handed it to Samantha a bit reluctantly.

"What's wrong? Why the hesitation?" she asked.

"It's been a long while since I let anyone read some of this stuff. To be honest, a lot of this is really personal. And it's not that I don't want to share it with you, I'm just nervous."

She leaned over and kissed him on his cheek.

"Don't be nervous," she said, "it's just me. You have nothing to be nervous about."

She took the handful of pages — two printed and two handwritten, and opted to read the handwritten version.

"There's something more personal about the handwritten version," she said, "and I want it to be as personal as possible. I assume that's okay?"

As she began reading, she reached out and took Sal's left hand from his lap, while he was innocently watching her read. He knew this song well, despite having selected it at random and knew when she read certain parts. Based on the severity of the verse she'd just read, she'd clinch his hand tighter and tighter.

"Subtracted: 49" was a tale of a young man visiting his father's grave, trying to convince him that he's grown up in a way that his father should be proud of.

Let me stand up here on my ownLet me show you, how much I've grownLet me make you proud, of who I amNot a little boy anymore, I'm a man

Take a look at me, I'm so wiseYou knew I'd be great, no big surpriseI became what you, told me to beNot a little boy anymore, look at me

Take a better look at who I becameYou'll see I'm no longer the sameI've grown a little older, a little wiser, a bigger manI'll be the same in your eyes, until you see what I am

Let me grow more today, like I have doneNo longer do I tolerate, no longer do I runI faced my fears, to let you know I still careSitting in the darkness, I still can't leave you here

I can't just walk away, like I do all the timeI can't slip away, you'll always be mineLook at me now, not what I used to beI've grown, I've changed, but I'm still me

Please realize, that I never blamed youYou did what was right, you did what you knewAnd I never meant to leave youI never once said I didn't care

Take a better look, at who I becameYou'll see, I'm no longer the sameI've grown a little older, a little wiser, a bigger manI'll be the same in your eyes, until you see what I am

I never once said, you meant nothing to meI've just changed so much, I just want you to seeI grew up so much, in these last few yearsBut one things remains, I still cry your tears

Just look at me please, see me nowHere in the darkness, shine down on my somehowFill me with love, like you used to doPlease tell me I'm okay, cause I never knew

I can say the words, till I'm blue in the faceI can beg for another, but you can't be replacedI can hold you so high, I can tell you I'm fineBut all of your memories, still infect my mind

So I leave you tonight, with a teary good-byeI ask you again, I cry out why?It may fade away, but I still feel it insideI still feel it hurt, like the day you died.

"Has Greg read this?" she asked.

"No, he's never read it. In fact, I've never even really told him about it. It's never fit with any of the music we've written as a band."

"It's so moving. It's like I'm there. This is wonderful, Sal. Really. Wonderful."

"Wow, that… that's so… kind of you," he was taken aback by her positive reaction.

"It tells such a story and it's so clear what's happening. It's like you wrote this as a short story rather than song lyrics."

"That's how I usually write. I like to tell the stories. I think it makes for better songs. Greg and I have known each other since we were kids, and as his best friend it was tough for me to watch him grow up in a household where it was clear that his parents stayed together for his benefit. They were always fighting constantly. There was an entire summer where he stayed at my house every night — all summer long — just to get away from everything. I think we were ten that year. It was never easy for him, but he never let it show. He's one of the strongest people I know. Or will ever know."

"You don't often hear grown men talk about their friends that way," she said, "it's very endearing."

"To be honest, I don't have many people in my life, aside from family, who've been there through thick and thin like Greg has. He isn't just my best friend, he's like a brother to me. And now, Jess inherits me as a brother-in-law, of sorts. At first she was sort of just stuck with me, but I think she's grown to accept and love me, over the years."

"Don't tell her I told you," she said, "but you're right. She thinks of you like a brother, and is glad you're around to keep Greg in check. She knows he can be bossy at times, and she says you balance him out quite nicely."

Samantha handed "Subtracted:49" back to Sal and he placed it back in its spot, searching for another.

"Oh, this one's good. This is one that I like to refer to as 'open to interpretation'. There's a clear story in the way I wrote it, but it could be read in any number of ways. Let me know what you think," he said, handing her the handwritten version of "Lost Without You".

She took it and immediately took his hand again. He looked down at it and up at her, smiling as she read the lyrics. He loved that she was taking the initiative to take his hand and enjoyed the closeness. He decided that he was going to move over to his left some to close the gap between them.

As he moved slightly closer, she paused from reading and looked up at him smiling.

"I was hoping you'd do that," she said, "you were a bit too far away, but I wanted to hold your hand anyway."

She went back to her reading, flipping to the second page after a moment. When she finished, she handed the lyrics back to Sal, and he could tell she was contemplating what the song she'd just read was about.

"Well," she began, "there's a number of possible things that come to mind. I think what you wanted people to interpret it as was a simple story of boy meets girl, girl leaves boy, boy is lost without girl. A typical Hollywood love story. But I don't think that's it."

"Go on," he urged, "what else do you have?"

"Well, part of me wants to think it might be about something less serious, like a puppy. There's some lyrics in the second verse that support that, but I don't buy that you'd write an entire song about losing a puppy. Would you?"

"As much as I love dogs, no."

"So then it must be something less obvious."

"It's whatever you want it to be," he said, "within reason, of course."

"I don't know," she pouted, "tell me!"

"You really want to know?"

"I do!"

"Well, if you re-read it knowing what it's written about, it'll be obvious. Kind of like when you re-watch *The Sixth Sense*. It's the story of a man who's recovering from being a drug addict. Although he knows he'll never do drugs again, he still feels lost without the drugs as part of his routine."

"Wow. I would have never pegged that. Though I suppose if I had lived through it, I might have. Were you a drug addict in the past?"

"No, not at all. Sometimes I just like to pretend I know how people think and how they feel and I write about those experiences as if they're first hand. This particular one is something we've written music to and will be playing at the show next month."

"That's pretty deep. I'd have never guessed that's what it was. It's really well written and I get it now that you've explained it."

"It still makes sense if you don't know the story, though, right?" he asked, making sure that it wasn't gibberish without the key.

"Yes, it definitely does. Another, please!"

This repeated for another couple of hours. Before they knew it, it was after eleven and Samantha was yawning in the middle of almost every sentence.

"I'm so rude!" she said, "I keep yawning, you're not boring me, I promise!"

"It's okay, it's getting late anyway. And I have to work at 6 tomorrow morning. Perhaps we call it a night?"

"I didn't know you had to work so early. I feel terrible now."

"Don't. You're worth a night of not enough sleep."

Sal left the file folder of lyrics where it was and began the process of gathering his wallet, car keys, and a jacket. Though it was late April, the weather still got a bit chilly this late in the evening.

"Will you be okay in just the cardigan?" he asked.

"I should be fine. We're not going far. Thank you, though," she replied.

They walked down the few steps and along the side of the driveway. Sal opened the door for her and she kissed him on the cheek again.

The ride from Sal's apartment to Samantha's was quick. They held hands the whole way there, but didn't say much. Parking was easier this late at night on a Friday and they got a spot right in front of her apartment.

"I'll walk you up," Sal insisted, "those back stairs are kind of sketchy."

She smiled and nodded, knowing full well that the reason she had the extra deadbolt put on her door was precisely because of the sketchiness of those back stairs.

At the top of the stairs, the light above her door was faint, but bright enough to allow her to find the right key for each lock. The door swung open and she turned on the light inside. He helped her take off her cardigan and hung it on the hook near the door.

"Tonight went as well as I promised you it would," she said, "exactly like I knew it would."

"I'm glad you had a good time. I did too."

He made the last step up into her apartment from the stairwell, and pulled her into his arms embracing her tightly. It was warm and romantic, but not overly pressuring. He felt the urge to kiss her, but decided against it. Kissing her on the first date, while perfectly acceptable in today's society, may have left a bad impression on her. He decided to wait for the second date to kiss her.

"Make sure to lock the door behind me. I wouldn't want anything to happen to you."

"Of course. Will you do me a favor?"

"Anything," he said.

"Text me when you get home, so I know you're safe?"

"As you wish, dear."

She liked that he referred to her as dear. It was the first sign of an affectionate nickname and one that was both old fashioned and current at the same time. It gave her butterflies.

"Good night, Ms. St. Allen," he said making his way down the stairs.

"Good night, Sal," she said as she closed the door behind him.

He took a few steps down the stairs and waited until he heard the distinctive clicks of the locks latching behind him.

He drove home with the windows down and the night air rushing through the car. The radio was tuned to Magic 106.7, the sounds of David Allen Boucher filling his car with soft rock almost putting him to sleep.

He was home by midnight. Wallet, keys, and shoes went to their respective places and he sat on the couch where Samantha sat just an hour ago. She had a smell about her that he just couldn't place and he could still smell it now.

He toyed with the right words to send via text message were. To the point that if he waited any longer, she'd worry that something happened to him. He opted simply for:

Home safe. You're amazing. Thank you for brightening my life.

Samantha read the message, laying in bed while nearly asleep and she smiled. A single tear fell from her right eye onto her pillow. Tonight she would sleep happily, soundly and have dreams of her new crush.

Chapter Ten

"I'm going to spa with Sam," Jess called out to Greg early Sunday morning.

"Okay," he mumbled back from their bed, "all day?"

"At least for a few hours," she responded, "love you."

Jess stopped by Sam's apartment and sent her a text from the car, letting her know she was downstairs.

The sun had just started to peak over the tall houses on Sam's street, the grass still fresh with morning dew. The air had a slight chill in it and Jess was thankful for the seat warmers in the car.

The engine had just started to warm up when Sam came down and got in.

"Good morning," she said as she buckled herself in.

"Hey, how was San Francisco?"

"You know how they are out there," Jess replied, "everything's more laid back. Deadlines aren't really deadlines, they're more of suggestions."

"I know!" Jess said, "I love going out to meet with them. They're so relaxed, it's hard to feel stressed out working on their stuff!"

Jess wove in and out of back roads and side streets as they journeyed a few miles to the spa. Jess had made appointments for both of them to get manicures, pedicures, and a massage before Sam left for her business trip. Jess thought it would be a good idea for them to get to know each other better.

She was doing her best to not blurt out and ask Sam all about how her date with Sal had gone. She was overly eager, but didn't want to come across like someone desperate to set up her husband's best friend.

It wasn't until they arrived at the spa and checked in that Jess brought it up.

"So," she said, "I guess elephant in the room… How'd it go Friday night?"

"You mean on the date?"

"Of course on the date!" Jess yelled a bit too loudly garnering some looks from others in the waiting area.

"I think my favorite part was back at his apartment," Sam said turning red, "we went there after dinner."

"You slut!" Jess joked.

"Not like that, Jess," Sam was turning more red, "I wanted to spend some time getting to know him. He suggested that reading the lyrics he's written would do that."

"So you sat around reading all night?"

"I know," Sam defended, "it sounds lame, but it was actually amazing. Have you read any of his stuff?"

"Not in a long time, not since we were in high school, I think. Back when they had dreams of being famous rockstars."

"It's amazing, Jess, it really is. He's got this way with words."

"Did you swoon?"

"I think I did. At least a little. That's so unusual for me. "

"I know!" Jess said, "I'm surprised you even agreed to go out with him. That's so not you."

"It took me a few weeks to start talking to people at work. I'm usually so shy when it comes to meeting new people."

"Why is that?" Jess asked, "You're smart, fun, funny, beautiful. You'd think you would have an easy time meeting guys and making friends."

"It's not that," she said, "it's how I've always been. I think it got worse after my last break up. I guess I just have a hard time trusting people now."

"You want to talk about it?" Jess asked.

The receptionist called both of their names and escorted them from the waiting room to the back, where the manicurists were waiting.

"No, not really," Sam said as they both sat down in their chairs, next to each other, "it's not really important."

"Okay, I understand," Jess replied.

After each instructing their manicurist on what color they'd like their nails, they continued their conversation about Sal.

"So, you think he's pretty great?" Jess prodded.

"I do. We're going out again on Tuesday."

"My plan to set you up with him worked then?"

"I guess it did. I still can't get over that first dinner. Did you see me giggling like a little girl every time we bumped elbows?"

"I thought that was adorable though!"

"I guess he did, too."

Their nails and toes were polished, primed, painted, and complete before they knew it. Balancing on the balls of their feet, as to not let their toes touch the floor, they made their way to the waiting area for their massages.

Sam was called in first.

"I'll meet you back here when we're done," she said, carefully following the masseuse, "enjoy your massage!"

An hour later, Sam was done with her massage, showered, and back in the waiting area. Jess must have gotten called in shortly after Sam did, as she came out just a few minutes later.

They paid their bill on the way out and decided to have brunch together.

Chapter Eleven

THE SOUNDS OF MULTIPLE hi-fives could be heard echoing through the halls of the complex that Monday night.

"Welcome back, buddy. Did you guys have a good time in Italy?" Derek asked as Greg got settled down in front of his amp.

"Man, you have no idea. To say that it was an incredible week would be an understatement. I wish we had the money to stay longer or see more of Europe."

"Someday," Sal interjected, "someday they'll pay us to visit their countries."

"It's good to have you back," Paul offered up, "we were like kids in a candy store while you were gone."

Greg looked up at the whiteboard behind Derek and nodded.

"Anything noteworthy?" he asked.

"A few parts here and there. We worked out a nice 5/8 jam, and a couple of chord progressions in some unique keys that I think could work," Sal said, "we can play some of it to show you later tonight. Let's finish getting all set up and we'll run through a few of them."

The guys each went through their usual process of getting things in place. Sal took his guitar out of its case and plugged into his amp, adjusting his various levels. Greg had a similar process, but his included some effects pedals needing to be turned on, as well as adjusting his guitar's strap, which he seemed to do endlessly. Paul was pretty simple, toss the bass on his shoulder, plug it in and turn it on. He had a sound that he liked and he hardly ever touched any of the settings on his amp. Derek was easy too, turn on his fan, sit down, and find a pair of drumsticks that weren't broken.

"'Night Before Dawn'?" Greg asked.

Sal sighed under his breath. The chorus from that song was starting to turn into his nemesis. He was losing his passion for it all together. He wasn't sure if it was because they'd played the music so many times or if it was because he just couldn't figure out the best chorus for the song. In either case, he was frustrated by it and was starting to let it show to the rest of the guys.

He understood and appreciated what Greg was trying to do. The more they played the music, the more Greg hoped the lyrics would just come to him. He was just frustrated with himself for not being able to finish the song, especially given that the rest of the guys wanted to debut it at the show next month.

He'd been writing "Night Before Dawn" with the premise that he wanted it to be about someone struggling to make it through their first night after coming down off of some sort of drug. Until he realized that Samantha had picked "Lost Without You" to read Friday night, which is essentially the same story but told slightly differently.

Over the years he'd written many songs about the same subjects – love, growing up, death – but "Night Before Dawn" was supposed to be the big song, the one that people would listen to and come to their own conclusions about. It was supposed to be the song that people would email them about and post to their Facebook page to start discussions on. It was supposed to be huge. And now Sal questioned what the whole thing was about. Should he really try to write a better song than "Lost Without You"? That was a great song and was something that was filed away under "someday" in his mind.

While the band started off on the music, Sal left his guitar part out, so he could think to himself. He nodded and bobbed his head to the music as the rest of the band played, all the while not writing lyrics in his head, but talking to himself. Questioning himself.

While he'd been focusing on the chorus as the primary part of the song that just didn't click for him, he started to realize that perhaps the chorus didn't work because the rest of the song didn't work. Just maybe the song that was almost complete was just getting started.

He grabbed his pad of paper and pen and sat down on his amp, staring at the incomplete lyrics that he'd written what seemed like months ago. Listening to the music and reading along to the lyrics on the sheet in front of him. They worked as lyrics to the music that was playing, but they didn't make him feel anything. They didn't make him want to force himself to finish writing this song. He hated that feeling.

Flipping to a new page on the pad, Sal wrote the date in the top right corner, as he always did. He then wrote "Night Before Dawn" in the top left corner of the page. He'd made the decision that he was going to start over with new material. "Night Before Dawn" was taking a turn to new subject matter and he felt good about the song for the first time in weeks. Normally he'd talk to the rest of the guys about a decision like this but it didn't matter much. The guys usually only wanted to be involved when the decision came to the music of a song. They left the lyrics to Sal and knew that it was his specialty. If someone had an objection about a particular set of lyrics once they were done, they'd sit down and talk about it.

"Night Before Dawn" was now the story of a man struggling to survive the night after being hit by a drunk driver. He planned to in-corporate the unconscious sounds of the ICU, doctors checking on the patient, and write the whole thing from the patient's comatose point of view. He felt good about the new direction.

After a few hours of rehearsing, Sal had a good portion of the new lyrics to the song done. He'd gotten through the first four verses, a pre-chorus and the chorus itself. A few scratched out marks here and there on the pad, but nothing nearly as bad as the original lyrics.

Greg looked at his watch around 11:30 and the rest of the guys knew what that meant. Paul instinctively turned his amp off and Sal followed suit. Derek got up, added the notes about tonight to the whiteboard and asked, "What were you working on, Sal?"

"New lyrics to 'Night Before Dawn'. I'm changing the story."

"What? Why?" Greg chimed in.

"It just wasn't working with the original story. I couldn't get the chorus right and I think it was because of how I felt about the song. So I'm changing it. You guys will like this new version, I promise."

And that was that. They agreed to let him do his thing because he was the singer. Being able to put your heart and soul into singing a song was important to Sal. He needed to be able to feel what he was singing and by the rest of the band letting him write the lyrics, he was able to accomplish that.

As they left their rehearsal space, Greg and Sal lagged behind to lock up. When Derek and Paul were out of earshot, Greg said,

"I heard you and Samantha went out last week. You know Jess had that planned the whole time, right?"

"I had a feeling, but I honestly don't care. That girl. Wow. She's just amazing."

"So it went well? Jess talked to her this morning online, but Jess wouldn't give me the details. She just kept saying 'ask your friend tonight' when I asked her how it went."

As they left for the night, Sal filled him in on the details. Not all of them, as he wanted to maintain his "I'm a macho guy!" mentality, but enough so that Greg knew he was serious about her.

"I'm seeing her tomorrow night, after work," he said as they got to his car.

"I'd say to call me after, but let's face it, that's not something dudes do," Greg said with a laugh, as he got into his car.

Sal waved, and made his way across the parking lot to his own car.

Driving home, he smiled. Not only about his revelation for "Night Before Dawn", but because of Samantha. In less than 24 hours he'd get to see her again, and he liked that idea.

Chapter Twelve

SAL ROUNDED THE CORNER and bound his way up the creaky stairs to Samantha's. He knocked twice when he got to the top.

"Just a sec," he heard her voice from inside, "be right there."

He heard that warm tone of her's right through the door. The clacking of her heels making their way across the room to let him in. Both deadbolts unlocked and she emerged from behind the closed door.

She invited him in and asked if he'd mind waiting a few more minutes while she finished getting ready.

"You look beautiful, what more could you need to do?" he asked.

"You're sweet. Two minutes, I promise," she replied, as she went back towards her bedroom.

Sal made himself at home on the couch, flipping through an issue of Entertainment Weekly that was on the coffee table. She said two minutes and she meant it. He had barely gotten to the table of contents when she came back to the living room and announced that she was ready.

She was remarkable. Her long brown hair was straightened and reached down to the center of her back. Her dress was sleeveless and her shoulders bare. He liked seeing this new portion of her skin. She was wearing a new perfume, he could tell, but didn't want to point it out. When one is on a second date, you don't want to come across too creepy, he told himself. She was wearing heels, which brought her closer to his height. There was only a five inch difference when barefoot, so her three inch heels brought their eyes almost level with one another.

"Again, you look beautiful," he said, "as always."

"Thank you. You're always so sweet," she said and kissed him softly on the cheek.

"I made us reservations at California Pizza Kitchen over by Emerson in the city, and then we've got tickets to a movie right after. Work for you?"

"Sounds great," she said, "I trust you picked something we'll enjoy."

She smiled and stood up from the couch. Sal followed suit and made his way to the door, opening it and reaching for her keys.

Samantha waited on the third step down while Sal locked up her apartment and checked to make sure everything was secure before they left.

Down the creaky stairs, along the driveway and to Sal's car they trekked. Both excited for the evening.

As she'd find it was customary, Sal opened the door for her when they got to his car, making sure she was seated completely before shutting the door behind her. As he walked around to his side of the car, he glanced in through the windshield at her and saw that she was smiling. That made him smile. He didn't know why.

He took his place behind the wheel, waiting for Samantha's seatbelt to click firmly before starting the car. Once sure that she was buckled and safe, he pulled away from the curb and headed toward the city. On a Tuesday night the roadways going into the city are almost empty. The other side of the highway was a different story. Car upon car upon car of people who'd left their offices in the city and were heading home on Route 93 North. Sal tried to think of a job he'd love so much that he'd voluntarily sit in traffic for hours in each direction to and from it, but he couldn't come up with a single one.

They pulled off 93 South at the Fanuel Hall exit, weaving through tourists and pedestrians towards Government Center. The sun was still high overhead and the roads were clear of snow. Samantha marveled at the tall buildings as they drove through the busy streets of Boston. As they approached the Commons, she let out a short gasp. A sight she clearly hadn't seen before.

"Have you never been in the city before?"

"To be honest, no. Well, just one time when I had to come in for an interview at the staffing firm that failed to find me a job as a writer anywhere in the city limits."

"Oh, wow. I had no idea. If I had known, I would have planned a whole day to show you around."

"That's okay, I think this will be a good first experience. I don't want to overdose on the city all at once. I live here now, so I should get familiar with things, right?"

"Definitely. But you have to let me bring you back in for a weekend day, where we can see all of the touristy things. Deal?"

"Deal," she said, as they rounded the corner of the Commons heading toward the underground parking garage.

Sal reached out the window to take the parking ticket and headed to the third level down, tires screeching as they rounded every corner.

"I swear that's not me doing that," he said, "it's the garage."

Samantha chuckled a bit, and responded, "I know. It's like they coat every garage on earth with some magic surface that forces your car to sound like you're peeling out."

A few minutes later they discovered an empty spot and parked. As they headed towards the elevator to the surface, the sounds of other cars peeling out could be heard throughout the echoing garage.

She followed him through the endless maze of cars to an elevator at the far corner of the structure. He pressed the call button.

"I did the math once. If this garage is full every day, it brings the city over a million dollars. For parking. Isn't that crazy?" Sal said nervously trying to fill the silence.

"What's crazier is that you did that math!" she responded.

"I've always liked figuring out that sort of thing. I feel like it keeps my mind sharp, which I like."

The elevator arrived, chiming and the doors slowly opened to the smell of urine.

"Ugh," Sal said, "sometimes the homeless people come in and sleep in the elevators when it's cold. I think that's what we're smelling."

"Is there another way?"

"Of course," he said as he took her hand, "come with me, my dear."

They headed back across the garage towards a staircase, leading them from the third basement all the way up to the surface. The "Common Garage", as it's named, is literally below Boston Common, a giant park in the heart of the city. When you emerge from the structure, you're in the heart of the Common.

As they exited from the parking garage, Samantha commented on how much she loved the surrounding area.

"Wow," she said, "this is beautiful."

"Wait until Spring when everything in the Public Garden is in full bloom. We'll go for a walk in a few weeks when we come back. You made a deal."

She smiled while still holding his hand as they walked towards the far corner of the Commons.

Crossing the street, Samantha couldn't help but look up at the tops of the tall buildings. To her right she could almost see the top of the John Hancock building, Boston's largest, and The Prudential Center, arguably Boston's most famous building. Sal had to tug her hand to remind her to not stop in the middle of the crosswalk. Typical Boston drivers gave a honk to get them to move out of the way, which they did.

They took their time walking up the slight incline of Boylston Street. Mainly so Samantha could look at the expansive Boston Common.

"I can't believe I've never been here before," she said, "it's so spectacular."

"It's one of my favorite parts of the city. It's just so amazing that it's been here so long and they've never paved over it, or put buildings there. It's survived the test of time," he said.

They reached the back entrance to California Pizza Kitchen, and entered City Plaza just as their reservation time struck. He approached the "Wait to be Seated" sign and let the hostess know that he'd called ahead.

They were whisked away to a quiet table in the corner by the back entrance. It was away from the crying babies, large families, and other couples on dates.

"Did you pay them to give us our own corner?" Samantha asked.

"I plead the fifth," he responded smiling.

"Sal!"

"I'm just joking. A friend from high school is a manager here and he said he'd do what he could to keep the tables around us empty. Which, by the looks of things, shouldn't be a big deal."

Most of the restaurant was empty, which was expected for a Tuesday night. The waiter made his way over to them, weaving around the empty tables and dodging his colleagues making their way around delivering food. He introduced himself as Giovanni which by looking at him very well could have been his real name. He took their drink orders and gave them a minute to look over the menu.

"I think I'm going to try something new tonight," Samantha proclaimed, "something I've never tried before."

"Daring, are we?"

"You do the same. It'll be fun!"

"I don't know about fun, but okay. I'll try something I've never tried before."

Giovanni came back with their drinks in hand and asked if they were ready to order.

"I'll have the chicken picatta," Samantha ordered, "but with no capers, please."

"And I'll have a buffalo chicken pizza."

Giovanni thanked them for their order and made his way off to the terminal to input it. Once done, he came back bearing a basket of bread and butter packets.

"I always wonder why they give you these little packets of un-spreadable butter with bread," Samantha pondered aloud.

"I wonder the same thing," Sal said, a bit too excitedly, "it's like, 'here, have this nice soft bread and a brick to smash against it while you try to spread it'."

But Sal had a secret weapon, his iPhone. He took the iPhone out of his pocket and opened one of the games that he had on it. This particular game had a tendency to make the phone run hotter than usual, a defect that the developer was working on fixing.

"I'm not ignoring you," he explained, "this particular game makes my phone get really hot. So," he continued as he placed the butter packets down on his phone, "if we let them sit for a minute they should soften up."

"You're a mini-MacGuyver!" Samantha proclaimed.

"Sometimes the solutions to life's little problems present themselves to you when you're least expecting it. I discovered the phone melting trick by accident and have used it ever since."

He handed her a softened butter packet and took the other for himself.

"I started working on a new story for 'Night Before Dawn'," he said, "I scrapped the old lyrics I'd been working on."

"Oh no! Why?"

"Well, the other night when you were reading my work, I realized I'd already written a similar song. I didn't want to revisit the same material, so I opted to write something else."

"Is it done? Can I read it?"

"Not yet, I just started it last night. I should be able to finish it tomorrow night while we're rehearsing."

"That's amazing. Do you feel better now? I could tell that it was bothering you the other day while we were chatting about it."

"I do. I feel a lot better. It's tough to sing lyrics that you don't feel or even don't agree with. I think that's why it's easier for me to write the lyrics myself. It lets me connect on a level that makes it easier to convey the song's message."

"Even if the song's message is unclear?" she asked while taking a bit of bread with warm butter spread evenly on it.

"Even if, yes. When it's something I've written, even if the message is unclear, I know what I think the song is about and that helps me perform it better than if it were something that say Greg wrote."

Giovanni brought their food over. Sal's friend from high school, Phil, followed behind to say a quick hello.

"Go ahead and eat, I don't want your food to get cold. I just wanted to say hey," Phil said.

Sal introduced him to Samantha quickly and Phil made his way back to where he was watching over the dining room.

As they began eating, they kept talking about Sal's writing, specifically about "Night Before Dawn". She was curious and loved trying to get inside his mind. Having known him only a week and a half, it was a fun game for her to try to read his facial expressions. When posed with something he didn't want to talk about, he had a tendency to answer the question with a question of his own. Samantha picked up on this pretty quickly and called him on it.

"You know you often answer a question with a question, right?" she asked.

"Do I?" he said smiling.

"You do! Do you really not notice you do that?"

"I guess I notice it. I just feel like by asking questions in return I'll keep the conversation moving."

"That's true. But you can also answer the question first, and then ask your question."

Throughout the rest of their meal, they discussed various topics. From Samantha's blogging and how she got involved with that, to the more technical aspects of what tools she used. While still technically an amateur, Sal dabbled with building websites and picked Samantha's brain from time to time about certain tools she used to do it. He liked learning and was trying to teach himself more of that type of technology.

"Can I interest you in a dessert?" Giovanni asked as he cleared their empty dinner plates.

"I hear the Belgian Chocolate Soufflé Cake is to die for," Sal responded, "let's share one of those."

"Excellent choice!" Giovanni said leaving to enter their order into the computer.

Samantha smiled at the idea of sharing a dessert.

"Compliments of Phil," Giovanni said as he returned a few minutes later to drop the dessert off.

Sal gave a wave in the direction of Phil, who nodded in return.

Samantha picked up her fork first and dove right in.

"You snooze, you lose," she said playfully.

"Never get between a man and his cake," he said starting a faux fork-sword fight over the plate, "to the death!"

She laughed out loud and immediately threw her hand up over her mouth to cover the laugh so no one would stare. A few onlookers gave her a glance, but neither Sal nor Samantha cared.

They enjoyed their dessert down to the last bite, which Sal let Samantha have. She swirled it around in the leftover chocolate sauce on the plate before devouring it.

Giovanni brought their bill, which Sal immediately grabbed.

"Don't even think about it," he said, "my treat."

Samantha smiled, "Fine! But next time is my treat."

They left California Pizza Kitchen, thanking Phil for the dessert. Samantha was again amazed at the buildings, notably the W. Hotel. Sal guided her through the streets to the corner of Tremont, where they took a left. They walked between many buildings owned by Emerson College, passing students and tourists alike.

It was just starting to get dark now and they made good time in the short walk up to the Loew's Theater, right next to the Common.

Inside, Sal approached the counter, got their tickets, and lead Samantha up to the ticket taker and eventually into the theater.

"Where do you want to sit?" She asked.

"Next to you," he joked.

She gave him a playful jab in the ribs.

The plan to see a movie on a Tuesday night worked out well, the theater was mostly empty. A few couples sat scattered throughout, but Sal still had his pick of seats. They settled on some seats that were in the center of the theater a few rows up. Samantha sat on his left to avoid bumping elbows, placing the soda they were going to share in the armrest on her left. Sal noticed and subconsciously figured out that by placing the soda on her left, she was leaving her right side open for him to sit closer to her, which he gladly would.

During the trailers, they whispered back and forth about how good or bad each movie was and made mental notes of which they wanted to make sure they saw.

As the movie started, she scooted right in her chair, closer to Sal — and rested her head on his left shoulder. He may have been mistaken, but he felt like she took a deep breath in, not in a sigh, but of happiness. Being close to her made him feel the same way.

She didn't notice exactly when it happened, but at some point during the movie Sal had taken her hand. She didn't mind and was hoping he'd do so.

After the movie ended they left the theater and made their way outside. Another short few steps up Tremont Street was a crosswalk to get across to the Commons, which they could cut through to get back to the parking garage. Sal reached for her hand again pulling her up next to him as the Walk signal turned to Don't Walk. They rushed across the street to the other side making their way into the Common.

It was after ten now and the night sky had set in. Hundreds of glowing stars, mostly eclipsed by the bright lights of the city, but some still visible. The streetlights throughout the Common had been on for hours, illuminating the pathways for them as they walked back to the parking garage. The air was warm and the sky clear. They walked together hand in hand in silence until Samantha spoke.

"This park is gorgeous. I really can't believe I've never been here before."

"It really is beautiful. It's even more beautiful tonight because I'm here with you."

At the junction of some of the paths thad lead through the Common, Sal noticed that her hand had gotten cold.

"Are you cold?" he asked.

Before she could answer, Sal had taken off his light coat and wrapped it around her shoulders. To help warm her up, he pressed himself up against her, wrapping his arm around her shoulder.

"I feel so dumb," she said, "who goes out without a jacket?"

"You're not dumb. It was warm earlier, you just didn't plan well."

They continued walking toward the center of the Common where the various paths lead off to the different entrances to the garage. To their right was Parkman Bandstand, a small gazebo like structure where the city sometimes put on concerts.

"Can we go sit for a minute?" she asked.

"Of course. Are you warmer now?" he asked. He was getting cold himself but had no intention on asking for his jacket back.

They walked across the grass which was slightly wet with night moisture, to the bandstand area and climbed the few steps. The structure had wrought-iron fences around it, so they couldn't sit as she wanted to. But they leaned up against it, looking around in 360 degree views of the city and the Common. From this location they could see the top of the Prudential building illuminating the night sky like a beacon of Bostonian hope; the State Building's golden dome reflecting the moonlight; the tennis court nearby had some college-aged kids playing on it. Despite being one of the more heavily trafficked areas of the city, it was quiet at this moment. The other people around them seemed to fade away and it was just them, the city and the night sky.

"It's magnificent here," she said.

"It is. This is one of my favorite places in the city," he said, "there's only a few places that I like more. I'll show you those when we come back in a few weeks when it's warmer."

"Is the Prudential building taller than everything else?" she asked, pointing in that direction.

"No, it's actually an optical illusion from this angle. See the building next to it, with the blue light flashing on top? That's the Hancock building. That's the tallest in the city. It just looks shorter from over here. Weird, right?"

They spent another few minutes talking about various parts of the city. She'd ask a question and marvel that he knew the answer to what she'd just asked. She loved that about him, he seemed to know everything about the things she asked. A feature that she found reminded her of the few memories she had of her father.

Just after midnight, Sal made note of the time and suggested they get a move on. Not because it was too late but because being in the Common that late was sometimes not the best thing to do.

Sal lead her to the edge of the stairs taking the first step down himself and stopping, turning to face her. He caught her by surprise and she startled a bit having expected to make her way down the stairs.

"I just think…," he said, "this is the perfect time."

"For what?" she asked.

"For our first kiss," he said.

Chapter Thirteen

He put his hands on her waist and leaned in, waiting a moment to make sure she didn't pull away. She was the perfect height now, maybe a tiny bit too tall for the perfect kiss, but he went for it anyway.

Their perfect moment of bliss was cut short by a drunk homeless man yelling "Get a room!" at the top of his lungs from just a few yards away.

In that perfect moment, it was like every star in the sky lit up twice as bright as it was. The world seemed to have stopped spinning, and the noise of the city was gone. In that moment it was just the two of them. Just Sal and Samantha and their city. The rest of the people weren't there, there was no noise, there were no lights except for the stars. Sal heard music and Samantha pushed herself into him, pulling him in closer than he'd put himself.

He leaned in, stretching up the stairs to reach her and kissed her again.

"I wouldn't be able to sleep tonight if I didn't do that one more time," he said.

"You're wonderful," she responded, kissing him back.

"Thanks for making tonight as amazing as I knew it would be."

Chapter Fourteen

ON THE WAY TO their practice room the next morning, Sal ran into Derek at the vending machines at the top of the stairs. There was an elevator, but Sal liked to get the extra exercise by climbing the three flights of stairs.

"Hey," he said, "you just get here?"

"Yeah, a minute ago. Figured I'd grab some snacks on the way down the hall."

The two walked side by side down the hall, listening to the myriad sounds coming from each door as they passed. So many sounds in a single building still amazed them after a year of renting this space.

Greg and Paul were already in the room. Greg was pacing back and forth waiting for them. He high-fived Sal as he walked to his corner of the studio space.

"What's that for?" Sal asked.

"Jess is a gossip. She told me all about last night."

"What was last night?" Paul asked.

"Sal went out with Samantha again," Greg answered.

"Yea, we went to dinner and a movie and then I took her home. It's no big deal," Sal played it modest. He didn't want to spill his feelings to his bandmates. Despite sharing his thoughts and feelings through his lyrics, Sal had always had an issue with expressing himself in the moment. Even to Greg.

"That's not all of it. Jess told me the whole story. You dawg!" Greg joked.

"Hey, come on now. Let's get to work. We don't need to talk about my love life, okay?"

Sal sat atop his guitar amp while the band started playing an older song that they'd written two years ago, called "Since You." He had written it about Jess from Greg's point of view. Greg had asked Sal to write it for one of their anniversaries, since Greg wasn't much of a writer.

As the music began, Sal's thoughts turned to Samantha. How she woke up and immediately thought to send him a text message. He liked that he was the first thing she thought about when she woke up.

Greg came over and kicked the bottom of his foot when he missed his queue for the first verse. He shot up straight up to the microphone and gave himself a moment to count in so he'd know where he was and picked up on the third line of the first verse:

"Since you came along, I found it all.

Living through today.

Since you brought your love, I need it all.

I'd never give it away."

They ran through that song twice before Greg put down the guitar.

"Our show is in two weeks," he said, "we should start working on the playlist."

"Good idea," Paul said.

Derek, somehow the designated note-taker, grabbed his white-board marker, pretended to lick the tip and turned to the whiteboard behind his drums.

"Clearly we have to play 'Since You'," he said to agreeing nods, "What about if we do 'Where Are You Now?'"

"I like that one. We haven't played it much, so we'd have to revisit it," Derek said while writing it down.

"'Polaroid' definitely," Paul chimed in.

It was one of Sal's favorite songs, so he agreed instantly.

It was a simple song, but Sal loved it.

They hemmed and hawed for half an hour and finally came up with a dozen songs that they'd like to play ranging in runtime from three minutes to five minutes, meaning they had enough material for, at most, an hour.

"They're only giving us 45 minutes," Sal said, "so we may end up cutting songs at the end."

"That's fine," Derek added. "It's better to rehearse enough than to not have enough."

It was just after six o'clock by the time they settled on all of the songs they wanted to play. Derek double-checked the list on the whiteboard and took a picture on his phone so he could transcribe and print it for the guys later that night.

Sal found himself zoning out as the guys made small talk about the songs they'd picked. He phased in and out while he heard mentions of stage arrangements, lighting choices and transportation arrangements.

He didn't want to cut things short. In fact, Sal had been telling himself all day that he wasn't going to leave early. He knew that if he did, Greg would be furious.

Instead of focusing on what was going to happen after rehearsal, Sal poured his heart and soul into the rehearsal, concentrating on remembering lyrics to songs that they hadn't played in quite some time. Thankfully for his sake, he had a pretty good memory, and only had to reference his iPad once throughout the next few hours.

As things wound down Sal looked at his watch. The guys were done, packed up, and heading out just after 10:30. Sal was excited.

He'd be at Samantha's by 11. Perhaps Greg knew that Sal was on his way to Samantha's and cut him some slack.

"We got done early," Sal said as Samantha answered the phone, "I think Greg knew I was coming there."

"I may have mentioned it to Jess earlier," she replied, "how long until you get here?"

He could hear it in her voice that she'd missed him all day and had to remind himself not to grin and draw attention to himself as he packed up and nodded to his bandmates on the way out of the studio.

"Maybe 15 minutes. That okay?"

"See you in a bit."

As he shut the door behind himself, he could hear his friends laughing. Whether they were mocking or were genuinely happy for him, he couldn't say. At that moment, he didn't care. He was on his way to see Samantha and that was all his mind would focus on.

Chapter Fifteen

In the alleyway to Samatha's apartment, Sal intercepted the pizza delivery guy and gave him $15 and a generous tip. Taking the pizza box, he bound up the creaky stairs and knocked loudly when he reached the top.

"Who is it?" Samantha called out from inside.

"Pizza," Sal said, trying his best to disguise his voice.

When she opened the door and saw that it was him, she was surprised, expecting the pizza delivery guy, but she played along.

"I didn't know you were moonlighting delivering pizzas," she said.

"There's a lot you don't know about me," he responded.

"Well come in and let's learn some new things," she said.

It was like the first time he'd met her all over again. His heart fluttered, his palms got sweaty, he had to catch his breath, and he couldn't help but smile. It was as though a missing piece of him was finally falling into place and all of his anxiety from the day and rehearsal had almost instantly melted away. Just from seeing her smile and hearing her voice.

As he entered her apartment, he took off his shoes, placed them neatly next to hers and followed her to the kitchen where she was already reaching for some paper plates and napkins.

"Soda?" she asked.

"Water is fine. Thanks."

They took their plates of food over to the couch and sat down next to each other.

Before they started eating, Samantha leaned over and kissed him. Not too forceful, but just decisively enough that he knew she had been waiting to do that all day.

"Is this okay?" Samantha asked while picking up the remote control and gesturing towards the television, where a rerun of *The Big Bang Theory* was playing.

"I love this show. I've seen them all a bunch of times," he responded. "This is fine."

Sal grabbed the remote when Samantha put it down and lowered the volume a bit, so that they could talk.

"How was your day?"

"Pretty great. I bet you're exhausted, though. I still feel terrible that I kept you out so late, and now you're here again."

"Don't feel bad. It's not like you held a gun to my head. I want to be here."

"I know, but you have work again in the morning. If you don't sleep enough, you'll probably do something horrible at work tomorrow morning."

"I make overpriced coffee for a living, what could I possibly do that'd be so horrible?"

"I don't know," she joked, "anything could have happened! You could have given someone espresso instead of decaf!"

Sal finished his first two slices of pizza and got up to get some more.

As he came back from the kitchen, he asked "Working on anything interesting this week?"

"No, just some press releases for a tech company. How was rehearsal tonight?"

"Pretty good. We ran through some of the songs for the setlist for the show."

"Everything went okay?"

"Yea, it's fun to play songs you haven't played in a while. It's like a game of memory trying to remember the arrangement, the lyrics, the timing. Everything. It was a lot of fun to revisit those parts of my life."

"What do you mean? What parts of your life?"

"Well, the songs, really. I have a tendency to write about certain things at certain points of my life. Which means that I flash back to those times when I revisit the songs. It helps me remember the songs pretty easily. I've never done it consciously. I don't sit down and say 'I'm going to write about that one time where that thing happened.' I just sit and write and most of the time it happens that when I read back what I've written, it ends up being something that happened to me in the past."

"Sort of like a mnemonic device of some sort?"

"Yea, sort of. Even if the song is something completely fictitious, I still equate it to a real event in my life. For example, one of the songs that we worked on tonight is called 'Polaroid.' It's this song about a young guy whose parents die in a freak accident. I don't explain what, but it's kind of irrelevant. Anyway, the parents are gone, and all he has left is this Polaroid picture of him as a little boy with his parents. And he brings it everywhere with him, and talks to it like it's his tele-communicator to his parents. I wrote it based on a photograph that we found at my grandmother's house after my grandfather died. It was my dad with his parents, probably back in the late fifties, when he was just a little boy. "

"So inspired by true events but not fully based on real events?"

"Sort of, yea. Songs stem from the strangest places for me, but they always tie back to something real in my life. So I just focus on that event, and the rest comes back to me naturally when I'm either writing or signing."

"That's amazing," she said, as she leaned into his side, lifting his arm to place it around her.

"Do you often find yourself trying to find inspiration in your writing?"

"Me?" she asked. "No, hardly ever. I write about tech stuff for a variety of blogs. I don't even need to think about things in most cases. I more or less take the technical information about a given product and turn it into something that a human can read."

"That sounds kind of boring," he said and then immediate cringed.

"Oh, don't get me wrong," she said putting her hand on his thigh. "It totally is. But it pays the bills. Well, most of them, anyway."

Though he'd never admit it to anyone, including Sam, Sal was almost completely broke.

"This is a great episode," Samantha said gesturing toward the screen where *Friends* had replaced *The Big Bang Theory*. "I love when Monica and Chandler get together and everyone knows about it but Ross."

"So you like *Big Bang* and *Friends?* You may be too good to be true. They're two of my favorite shows."

"I think they're two of everyone's favorite shows," she said. "I imagine next you'll tell me that you love *Full House* and *Boy Meets World?*"

"Like there's any doubt about it, c'mon! *Full House* was the show for us growing up. I could probably recite every line from every episode!"

"Me too!"

"Okay, pick your all time favorite television show. Don't think about it, just go," he said.

"*Friends*, that's easy," she said. "You go."

"*Boy Meets World*. Easy," he responded immediately.

"Why that one? Why not *Full House* or *Friends*?"

"I love *Full House*, don't get me wrong. But *Boy Meets World* is basically about me. So why wouldn't I pick that one? I am Corey Matthews."

She laughed, looking him up and down.

"But you're cuter," she said. "Why do you think you're Corey Matthews?"

Sal blushed a bit as Sam nestled in closer to him.

"We share so many of the same traits. He's shy but witty, has a best friend that he most likely couldn't live without and looks up to his parents despite not always seeing eye to eye with them. It's the story of my life."

Friends ended at 11:30 and Samantha reached for the remote to put *Late Night with Jimmy Fallon* on.

"Leave it on *Friends* if you want," Sal said, "I'm fine with it."

"You sure? You said you wanted to watch *Fallon*."

"I'd have told you anything you wanted to hear to get you to let me see you tonight."

"Sal, you're not supposed to say things like that. It's only our third date!"

"When you know, you know. It's that simple. I want to be around you and I'm okay with saying it."

Before he knew it, Sal was jolting out of a deep sleep. He didn't know how, but when he looked at his phone it was 2:15 a.m. Samantha was still pressed up against him, sound asleep, her feet curled up next to her on the extra couch cushion.

He slid from next to her and picked her up in one swooping motion. He turned the TV off with his foot and immediately realized that he'd made a bad decision; the only light source in the apartment was now gone. Having never been in her bedroom, or even down that end of the hallway before, he was lost. He waited a couple of minutes for his eyes to adjust before attempting the journey.

Managing to make his way in the dark, he found her bed and placed her down gently. He turned on the small light on the nightstand and pulled the comforter up over her. She woke and looked up at him.

"What time is it?" she asked.

"Just about 2:30. Go back to sleep."

"Oh, no! You have to be at work in four hours! I'm terrible. I knew this would happen."

"Shh, it's okay. You go to sleep," he said kissing her on the forehead. "I'll be fine."

"No. Stay here. Set an alarm and climb in next to me."

There was nothing that he wanted to do more, but he feared it was the sleep talking.

"You're delirious, you're so tired," he said.

"I am tired, but I want you to stay. It'll save you all that extra driving. And besides, you're like an electric blanket you're so warm," she said, tugging at his sweatshirt.

"I suppose you're right."

"Climb in. But don't try any funny stuff," she said with a sleepy smile.

It may have been a combination of the hour and exhaustion but she was right. If he went home, he'd lose 20 minutes and probably be wide awake when he got there. He took her advice and climbed over her. He wrapped his arms around her and squeezed in close to share her single pillow. Before dozing back to sleep, he remembered to take his phone out of his pocket and put it on the nightstand. His alarm was already set and should wake him up with plenty of time to get to work.

Kissing her shoulder was the last thing that he remembered. He was asleep in a matter of minutes.

Chapter Sixteen

By Friday morning Sal was still reliving Wednesday night in his mind, but forced himself to focus on working yet another morning shift. He began questioning why he got up so early to go make coffees for hundreds of people who didn't appreciate it. While he didn't love his job, it was secure and he knew that if he kept showing up, they'd keep paying him.

He snuck a peek at his phone and re-read the email she'd sent him when she woke up Wednesday morning.

I thought it was a dream, I didn't think you were really here. And then I saw your note.

He was relieved to see that she'd found the note he left on her nightstand, thanking her for the great date they'd had.

Reading her text over and over again gave him a warm feeling, a feeling of safety and trust. A feeling that he enjoyed and couldn't wait to feel again the next time he'd see her. He couldn't wait to see her tonight at Greg and Jess'.

He drifted off into his mind, thinking about how much he enjoyed feeling comfortable around Sam. It was something that he'd always wanted, saw others around him having, but had never been able to find it before.

"Excuse me. My coffee." An angry customer demanded.

Sal looked up from his phone, "I'm sorry, one second."

He noticed the line of customers piling up as it began to get closer to nine.

Sal had never been completely in love with the idea that he was a grown man who made coffee for a living. He'd heard, so many times in the last couple of years, that he was better than that job. As he handed over the cup of coffee, the customer snatched it from his hand. Sal thought, for the first time in a while, that he could leave this job and never look back. He wouldn't miss any part of it, especially the early mornings and rude customers.

After Sal had gone on his second date with Samantha, Jess had told Greg that she planned on inviting Samantha to the weekly dinners.

As the day progressed, Sal had been texting with Samantha, confirming that she was coming to dinner at Greg and Jess'.

She had text him one last time, asking him to pick her up at 4:15.

He didn't ask why, but he was dying to know why she needed him there so early. His mind went back and forth about what it could be before giving up.

The good news was that him thinking about what she wanted him there early for resulted in the rest of his shift going by in the blink of an eye. Before he knew it, it was 2 o'clock and his day was over.

He clocked out and made his way to the parking lot, heading home to shower, shave, and get dressed for dinner. It was the first Friday of a new month, which means Jess would make Italian. She made the most amazing baked ziti.

He made it home just before 2:30, which gave him over an hour to get ready.

Sal turned the hot water on, gave it a minute to warm up and jumped in. He smiled as he scrubbed. He knew it was just another hour until he could see her. He was a big fan of Edwin McCain songs and decided to sing a few. He related to him as a songwriter and appreciated how intricate his lyrics were.

Sal had felt compelled to sing in the shower today, something he didn't usually do. He found himself caught in his thoughts, not realizing that he'd switched from singing lyrics to other people's songs to songs of his own. He was halfway through "Night Before Dawn" for the second time before he realized he was singing it. There's no better way to learn than repetition, he told himself.

Before he knew it, he'd run through the lyrics to "Night Before Dawn" a couple of times, finding flaws in what he'd written and reworking things trying to improve them.

His mind had quickly locked on two things: Samantha and his music. He felt invigorated and reenergized with a clear set of goals.

He pulled back the curtain and glanced at the clock on the counter. Just after 3 o'clock, plenty of time left to finish up here.

There was just a little bit of traffic on his way to Samantha's apartment and the parking spot right out front was open. Before he knew it he was up the creaky stairs and knocking on her door.

"It's open," she called from inside. "Come on in."

He went inside, baffled. Her door was normally triple locked, but not today.

Inside, he found her sitting on the couch smiling in his direction.

"Hey beautiful," he said. "What's up?"

She motioned for him to join her on the couch and he complied, sitting next to her. Close, but not too close.

She pulled him closer and whispered, "I missed you."

"Is that why you wanted me to come early?"

"It is. I'm sorry if I made you rush. I just wanted to spend some time with you before we headed over to Jess and Greg's. There's no surprise, there's no secret. I was just trying to be cute. Is that okay?"

"That's more than okay."

They sat in silence together for a few minutes. After a few minutes, she pulled back a bit, which startled him. He had felt himself dozing off, and her jolt brought him back.

"What is it?" he asked.

"It's, well…" She leaned into him and kissed him.

It happened again. The moment their lips met, Sal could hear the roar of a crowd swelling in his ears. He could feel himself up on stage and performing in front of thousands of screaming fans. He briefly imagined that this is what heaven could possibly feel like. Their lips met with soft, gentle pressure and warmth. He could feel her smiling while they kissed, something that no person can fake.

Samantha thought to herself that there weren't enough hours in a day to kiss Sal. She'd never wanted to kiss someone as much as she wanted to kiss him. His lips were a perfect match for hers, his emotions coming across with every moment. As they kissed, she felt herself flashing back to a memory of walking through an amusement park with her dad as a very young child. Sal made her feel as protected as her father had made her feel, before leaving.

Each better than the last, each moment felt longer than the previous. She wanted to live like this — in his arms, kissing him. There was nothing that she could imagine she wanted to do more with the rest of her life.

She opened her eyes to look at him while still locked at their lips. As she closed them again, not wanting to get caught staring, he opened his, and did the same.

The second time she opened her eyes, she caught him looking at her and they both giggled.

Sal's phone chimed from his pocket, reminding him that it was 4:30 and they needed to get on the road to be at Greg and Jess' before 5.

"It's not that I don't want to keep kissing you," he said. "I do. But if we're not there by 5, Jess will definitely lock us out and start without us."

"I'll get my shoes!" she responded as she jumped up from the couch.

They arrived at Jess and Greg's with five minutes to spare. Sal made himself at home on the couch and greeted the rest of his bandmates while Samantha made her way to the kitchen to offer a helping hand to Jess.

"Yes, please!" Jess said. "Can you stir the pasta for me?"

Sal looked over at the kitchen area and smiled at Samantha. She smiled back and quickly turned back to stirring the pasta at Jess' request. He wondered if they were gossiping about things.

Jess made her rounds to drop off appetizers and wine. Samantha trailed behind with a glass of water for Sal.

"Thank you," Sal said smiling.

"You're welcome." Samantha said, walking back towards the kitchen.

Derek and Paul made their way to the table, taking the same seats they did two weeks ago, leaving the seat next to Sal's open for Samantha. Though he hadn't discussed his new relationship much with them, he assumed that Greg had said something, or possibly Jess before he and Samantha arrived.

Sal pulled out Samantha's chair for her, waiting for her to sit before taking his seat and draping his napkin on his lap.

"I'd literally have walked here for this baked ziti, Jess," he said. "It's out of this world."

"He's been talking about it all week," Samantha said. "You should hear him."

Jess motioned for everyone to dig in and dig in they did. Sal scooped some baked ziti onto his plate, and grabbed a few pieces of garlic bread. He grabbed Samantha a piece as well, since it was slightly out of her reach. He gave her two pieces, which was fair to all since Jess always made enough food for twice as many people than were invited. Most nights everyone left with leftovers.

"We've got tons of pictures," Greg said. "We'll show you guys after dinner if you want to stick around to see 'em."

It took Sal a moment to remember what Greg was talking about. He'd been so enthralled with his own relationship in its new and exciting phase that he'd almost forgotten that Greg and Jess had been on their honeymoon last week.

"I can't wait," Samantha exclaimed, "Jess sent me a few this week and I can't wait to see the rest."

"Greg said it was beautiful," Paul added.

The gang ate and chatted over the next hour, catching up on all of the things that Greg and Jess had missed while they were gone. Sal swore that he heard Jess say she wished they stayed in Italy longer a dozen times or more. Who can blame her, really? He imagined he wouldn't want to come back at all.

After dinner, Paul and Derek took care of the dishes. It was their week and they reluctantly made their way to the kitchen while the two couples made their way to the living room. Greg grabbed his iPad and turned on the TV, switching to the AppleTV so he could send the photos to the bigger screen for everyone to see.

Moments after Paul and Derek finished the dishes, they joined the group in the living room, taking their seats on the couch. The living room was feminine but you could still tell where Greg's corner was; the remotes were piled high by his end of the couch, a well worn coaster sat at that edge of the coffee table. The walls were painted subtle pastels to brighten up the space and enough seating was present for everyone to have their own space. Sal and Samantha shared an oversized arm chair on the far side of the room. Jess sat on one end of the couch with Greg sitting by her feet.

Their photos, in typical Jess fashion, started with them packing. She liked to document everything when they went on a trip.

It was just after nine o'clock by the time they finished looking at photos. Derek and Paul made their way to the door to silently say that they felt like third wheels.

"You guys leaving?" Jess asked.

"Yea, we're gonna go hit a movie," Paul replied.

"See you guys Monday night," Greg said, "we'll finalize the setlist for next week."

And like that, Derek and Paul were gone, and the pair of couples were left to hang out.

Sal and Samantha spent the night listening to more stories of Italy. Jess filled with laughter as Greg gave the details that were drowned out by Jess gasping for air, tears streaming from her eyes as she remembered how great their honeymoon had been.

"So I hear you two have been hitting it off quite well," Jess said, more to Sal than anyone else, "lots of dates."

He poked Samantha in the side.

"Gossip," he said. "But yeah, we've gone out a few times."

"It's all he can talk about," Greg joked.

"So far, so good," Samantha said, kissing Sal on the cheek.

Jess excused herself to the restroom and filled up her glass of wine on the way back. In her hands, she had a pile of board games.

"Do you guys want to stay for a bit, maybe play a game?"

They looked at each other for a moment and nodded almost in unison.

As the game ended it was close to ten thirty and the night was drawing to a close. Jess thanked them for coming and gave them both a hug before they left. Greg said his usual goodbye with a wave from the couch.

"That was weird," Sal said as they got in the car. "Very weird."

"What?"

"She's never hugged me when I was leaving before."

"Never?"

"Never."

"Maybe she's trying to make you feel like family? Maybe if she hugs both of us, she thinks it'll make us hug each other?"

"I dunno, but it was unusual. I think the only other time she ever hugged me was when my grandfather died. Oh, and at their wedding."

Sal drove the few blocks back to Samantha's apartment, finding a spot right out front, which started to feel like winning the lottery to him. It was a particularly bright night tonight - no clouds in the sky and the moon was large and full. He stopped in the alleyway, glancing up at the sky in between the houses nestled closely together, to look at the moon.

He pulled Samantha to in front of him, wrapped his arms around her waist from behind and pointed to the moon.

"Beautiful, isn't it?" he said.

"It is. I love when the sky's so clear."

They spent a few more minutes staring up at the sky before heading up the creaky stairs and inside.

"Do you want to stay for a bit? *Friends* is on soon," she said.

"I don't have to work until 11 tomorrow. I could stay a while."

By the time the first episode of *Friends* had ended, they were both sound asleep again on the couch, nestled together holding hands.

Sal woke up just after midnight, realizing that they'd done it again. Before shutting the TV off, he made his way down the hall to Samantha's bedroom. He turned on the small light on her nightstand

and looked around at her room. He spent a few minutes studying it, something he didn't have an opportunity to do last time. A queen bed, single nightstand with an alarm clock dock for her iPhone, a dresser and a closet. A small hamper sat in the corner by the closet. He appreciated that she kept her room neat.

He pulled the comforter down on her bed before making his way back to the living room to scoop her off the couch. As he did, he felt her face press into his neck and heard a small sigh. He pulled her in tighter and made sure to clear the doorway on the way down the hallway to avoid hitting her head, a mistake he was glad he didn't make last time.

He tucked her into bed, he kissed her forehead and made his way to the door of the bedroom.

"Stay," she called out from the bed. "You can stay if you want to."

"It's not that late, I can make it home."

"I know. I want you to stay though."

"Okay, I'll be right back," he said before making his way back to the living room to shut off the TV and double check that the door was locked.

He left his shoes next to hers, placed his wallet and phone down on the small table by the door and he made his way back to the bedroom. Samantha was barely still awake, so he took the opportunity to kiss her goodnight before she was completely asleep.

He shut the small lamp off and pulled himself in close behind her, wrapping his right arm around her stomach.

Samantha suddenly shot upright, almost immediately.

"I'm going to be too hot sleeping in this. Especially with you holding me," she said. "I have to change."

She jumped out of bed, grabbed her pajamas from the nightstand drawer, and walked to a dark corner of the room. Sal didn't look, but imagined he wouldn't have been able to see anything in the darkness anyway.

Before he knew it, she was back in bed, this time facing his direction.

"I'm glad you're staying," she said, "I like it when you're here."

"I do too" he said.

"I forgot to tell you, and I swear this isn't an attempt to blindside you, but my mom's in town later today for the night," she said, yawning in between words.

"You forgot, eh?" He gave her an evil eye despite her eyes being closed.

"I swear, I forgot."

"I believe you. I don't think you'd lie about something so silly. Can I meet her?"

He could tell she was tired, which made her effort of getting changed and then spending the next short while kissing him all the more meaningful. Sal ran his hands up and down her back, under her shirt, feeling her warm skin against his palm. The small of her back arching with his touch, her tongue darting in and out of his mouth. They held each other until they were both asleep.

It was perfect and they both knew it.

Chapter Seventeen

PARKING WAS A NIGHTMARE on a Saturday night, but Sal found one just a half block away from Samantha's and ran from the car to the creaky stairs.

Before knocking, he took a moment to regain his composure. He straightened his shirt, made sure his shoes didn't have any mud on them, and cleared his throat. He wanted to make a good first impression.

He knocked.

"It's open," Samantha called from inside, amidst laughter.

He entered and found Samantha and her mom milling about in the kitchen. They both seemed like they were ready to go.

"Hey," he said, joining them. "I'm Sal. It's nice to meet you."

Samantha's mom, Vanessa, reached out to shake Sal's hand. She looked much younger than Sal had anticipated. Without knowing that she had a daughter as old as Samantha, he'd have guessed she was only in her late 40s. Her hair still held its natural golden-brown color and was pulled behind her ears. She was slightly taller than Samantha but just as petite. It was easy to see the family resemblance. "What's your intention with my daughter?"

Sal froze. The first question her mother asked and he had no idea how to answer it.

"Uhh, well," he stammered, "I, um."

Samantha and her mom both burst into laughter.

"I'm sorry, I told her to do that. I thought it would break the ice," Samantha confessed.

"She put me up to it, I swear. I'm not a horrible monster," her mom added.

"That was probably the scariest thing that's happened to me all week," Sal said, putting his hand on his chest to mimic a heart attack. "Too funny!"

"It's so nice to meet you, Sal," Vanessa said. "Sam's told me so much about you. I thought you may not be a real person."

"It's so great to meet you, as well. Did you have a nice flight?"

"I did, thank you for asking. I'd have suffered through a terrible flight to see my baby."

"Mom!" Sam blushed.

"Where did you make the reservation?" Sal asked.

"There's an Italian place down the road called 'Pasta More-a' that's supposed to be pretty good. I thought we'd try that," Samantha said.

"We're ready if you're ready," Vanessa said, "and I'm starving."

"I'm ready, let's get a move on," Sal said.

He led the way down the stairs, waiting a few steps down for Samantha and her mom.

He made sure to offer to drive and open both doors for the women.

"This isn't an act, he always does that," he heard Samantha say as he rounded the front of the car to his door. Samantha waved to Mr. Juang as they pulled away and drove by the convenient store.

The restaurant was more upscale than Sal anticipated based on the name but not so busy that it would be too noisy to talk.

The host showed them to a table by the fireplace in the middle of the dining room and pulled out the chairs for Samantha and her mother. He waited for the women to sit before taking his seat, just as his mother had taught him.

The sommelier came by while making his rounds, asking if they would like any wine. Sal pointed to Vanessa.

"I'm planning to order the salmon. What would go well with that?"

"A nice red wine. We have a fine Pinot Noir that pairs nicely with our salmon dish," he offered.

"Great, I'll take a glass of that. Sam?" she motioned towards Samantha.

"No wine for me, thank you."

"Same here," Sal said. "Thanks."

"You don't drink?" Vanessa asked.

"Not a sip," he responded, "besides, even if I did, I'm driving."

Samantha said, "This place is a lot nicer than I thought it would be."

"I'm surprised too. Based on the name, I thought it would be a lower class place. Not a dump, but not as nice as it is," her mom added.

"We'll have to make note in case we're craving Italian some night. I bet Greg and Jess would love it here. It'd remind them of their honeymoon," Sal said.

"Greg is in your band and just got married, right?" Vanessa asked.

"Yes. We've been friends since we were kids, and I met Jessica the same day he did. They're an amazing couple."

"Their wedding was beautiful, Mom. You'd have loved it," Samantha said.

"What kind of band is it? Sam hasn't told me that part."

"That's a good point, I don't even really know what the music sounds like!" Samantha turned to Sal in surprise.

"It's hard to describe. We're kind of a mellow rock, something you'd hear on a mix station. Some of the songs are ballads and some are more edgy, but not too over the top."

"Kind of like… what's that band I liked as a kid?" Samantha asked her mom.

"I don't know, honey," her mom replied.

"Wasn't it Queen that I really liked?"

"You did cry a lot when Freddie Mercury died," Vanessa said.

They talked about Sal's band a bit more.

Just as he was reminding himself to relax, Sam reached over and gently touched his hand. Staring off into a void, Sal snapped back to it and looked over at Sam. She was smiling as if to tell him that this wasn't as big of a deal as he was building it up to in his head.

"You're coming to the show on Wednesday, right? You'll get to experience it first hand, and can report back to your mom."

"Of course I'll be there," she said. "Front row. With bells on."

"Bells on, huh? That's amazing, thank you. It'll be so nice to see a friendly face in crowd."

They opted to skip dessert, everyone was too full to eat any more. Sal had only eaten half his bowl of pasta, which Vanessa ribbed him about.

"There must have been three full pounds of pasta in that bowl," he fought back. "No human could have eaten the whole thing."

Their waiter brought take home boxes along with the check, which Sal insisted on paying.

"My treat," he said taking the folio directly from the waiter.

"A gentleman," Vanessa said and smiled in the general direction of Samantha.

"Where to from here?" Samantha asked.

"Spend some time with your mom. I know how important she is to you, and you don't get to see her enough," Sal said.

"It was a sincere pleasure to meet you, Sal. Thank you for taking care of my baby," she said, pinching Samantha's cheeks.

"I'm glad I got to meet you too. Next time you come back and visit, stay longer, and we can show you around the city."

"That would be splendid."

Chapter Eighteen

THE DAYS AFTER MEETING Samantha's mom flew by faster than any others Sal could remember, and before he knew it, it was Wednesday night, mere hours before So Say The King was set to play their first show in years. They were finally confident enough in the songs and their performances to play in front of a crowd.

And what better crowd could there be than at Cambridge's famed Middle East club.

The guys were lucky enough to have booked the upstairs venue for their gig, thanks to a friend of Derek's. They were one of two bands scheduled to play.

Sal met the rest of the guys out on the street and started helping unload the band's gear onto dollies and handcarts, wheeling everything inside load by load. They made sure to always have one member of the band stay with the van so no one walking by nicked anything. The natural finish of Derek's drums looked brighter than ever out in the sunlight as he grabbed them two at a time making his way inside. Guitar amps and Pauls' bass amp wheeled up the slight incline and over the door lip with ease.

The venue provided a PA system, so it was just drums and amps that needed setting up. Everyone knew better than to try to help Greg — he had his own process and needed to adjust his sound to the room. They'd learned this a few years back when they played their last show.

Sal finished first, then offered to help Derek get the drums setup, which took the most time due to the complexity of the drum kit. They managed to get everything done with some last minute help from Paul and started sound checking to make sure the sound was perfect.

The venue was small enough that the PA only needed to be used for vocals. The guitar amps were sufficient, and the drums would be loud enough to be heard in the room as well. Sal taped copies of the set list across various spots on the stage, and made sure everyone knew where their copy was.

By the time Greg finished getting himself ready to go, the rest of the guys were done. They all jammed for a short bit, to make sure their cohesive sound was there and everything sounded the way they expected. Working with the club's sound guy for the vocals, they had gotten everything to where they wanted it with a couple of hours to spare.

Greg was nervous. Sal could tell just by looking at him. As he glanced to the other members of the band, he could tell they were nervous as well.

"We got this," he said. "This is what we do."

His reassurance didn't seem to do much for the other guys' moral, but it helped him convince himself that he'd be fine. Based on best-guess estimates, there'd be close to two hundred people in attendance tonight. Paul had done some guessing based on their number of retweets on Twitter, as well as confirmed RSVPs to the Facebook event. Maximum capacity upstairs was just shy of 200 and Paul said they'd likely fill it to capacity.

They decided to head down the street to Veggie Galaxy, a completely vegan restaurant that Derek loved despite not being vegan.

They had two hours to kill, so they figured they might as well get something to eat. They didn't go on until nine o'clock and it was just after seven now. Samantha and Jess met them there.

"Hey, babe," Jess called out as they entered. "We found you."

"Let me grab a couple more chairs," Derek offered before scrambling around to find some spots for the women to sit. Though the largest of the guys, Derek was a big teddy bear. His tattoos often made people think he was more of a tough guy than he really was.

Sal greeted Samantha with a kiss. He was positive that the guys were all nervous now, normally they'd have done or said something childish in response.

After they all ate, they headed back to The Middle East, locating the night's promoter, and Derek's friend, Billy.

Billy looked like someone who promoted concerts for a living should — tattoos almost everywhere, neck included, long blonde hair that was pulled back and tied. He wore jeans and a Deicide T-shirt with his combat boots, his keys and wallet chain clanging as he walked around. The stench of smoke ensured a decent distance between him and the guys.

They talked for a bit at the back of the club while people filed in before the show was slated to start. They opted for the back of the venue since there really was no backstage at the Middle East upstairs. There was a door that lead to a hallway, which lead outside, but that was more or less it. There was nowhere to prepare, nowhere to get ready, nowhere to throw up because you're so nervous.

It was five minutes to nine when Billy ran down to jump up on the stage. At a mere 18" high, the stage was pretty tiny and sad, but it was a start. A place for them to re-invent and re-introduce themselves.

"We've got a great show for you tonight! Are you guys ready?" Billy yelled into the microphone, which the sound guy only turned on half way through.

The crowd cheered.

"For the first time in years, please welcome back to the Middle East upstairs: So Say The King!"

Each member took their place, Sal in the front, Greg to his left, Paul to his right, and Derek slightly askew behind him. Rather than launching into an introduction of any kind explaining who they were or where they were from, they went right into their first song, "Polaroid".

Sal felt alive. He felt like a rockstar, even if only playing for a couple hundred people. He felt proud of what they'd done and looked down to see Samantha in the front row, right where she said she'd be.

In the moment before the first chord of the first song struck, Sal felt at home. All the worries of his world drifted away and he felt at peace with who he was, what he'd done in his life, and where he was going. He didn't feel anything but excited, proud, and ready.

The first song seemed to fly by faster than he thought it should have, but he remembered all of the lyrics and the band played it perfectly. Greg's solo was received extremely well by the girl in the front row directly in front of him.

After the song ended and the applause died down some, Sal took a moment to introduce everyone.

"Thank you, it's great to be here doing what we love. We are So Say The King, and we hail from the greatest city on earth. This one," the hundreds in attendance went nuts at this announcement. My name is Sal, this is Greg, Paul is to my right, and the beautiful bastard behind me is Derek."

The applause continued and Sal couldn't help but take in the moment. He'd been smiling since he first got up on stage, but he took a good moment to look around and really absorb where he was. This is what he was meant to do and he knew it. He felt it in his bones. He, for the first time in years, had felt complete.

Their 45-minute set went by quickly and they were done and moving their gear off the stage before they knew it. They'd gotten through all of their setlist flawlessly. Every song sounded as good as they wanted it to and Greg was pumped.

"That was fucking awesome," he said. "I can't believe how well that went."

"They loved us, like, a lot." Paul added.

"I can't believe how awesome I feel!" Sal nearly shouted.

Jess and Sam made their way to the back of the venue, where the guys were waiting. Jess gave both Derek and Paul a high-five as she passed them, Sam followed Jess' lead and did the same.

"What'd you think?" Sal asked Sam and she wrapped her arms around him.

"That was amazing, Sal. All of you guys were great," she said, turning to address the other guys. "Really great."

She kissed Sal on the cheek, "Amazing. That's all I can say."

They decided to stick around and watch the other band of the night, a band from New Hampshire called Farewell Chat. They were okay, but Samantha kept telling the guys how much better they were.

While they hung out in the back of the club, a few new fans came up asking if they had anything in iTunes and what their website address was.

"I can't believe how great I feel. Thank you for being there," Sal said to Samantha.

"I wouldn't have missed it. Not for anything," she replied smiling.

One thing was clear, Sal wanted more. He wanted to play another show immediately. He tried to resist the urge to keep high-fiving the other guys, but he couldn't. Like some cheesy psyched surfer dude, he kept high-fiving everyone. He caught Samantha looking at him out of the corner of his eye. He could tell she was proud of him and that was all he cared about for the rest of the night.

Chapter Nineteen

Samantha didn't wait for them to fall asleep watching *Friends* on the couch.

"Will you stay tonight?" she asked him.

Their night together had started fallen into the same rhythm as the others. Samantha changed into her pajamas in front of him this time. The light on her nightstand was dim, but he could still see her body. Once she put on her T-shirt, she slipped her hand inside, unhooked her bra and slid it out from under her shirt. Magic.

As they climbed into bed, she took his phone and placed it on her alarm clock dock, making sure it was set for him to wake up in the morning. The light clicked off and he felt her head hit the pillow next to his.

"You were excellent tonight. You know that, don't you?" she asked from the darkness.

"I don't see it that way. I mean — don't get me wrong, it went great. I just don't think that I'm as great as you think I am."

"You don't see it. You didn't see the faces on some of the people in the crowd. I was looking around at other people while you played."

"What do you mean?"

"You connected with people, Sal. You touched some of those people with your lyrics."

"Really?"

"Really."

He laid in silence for moment. It was, in fact, precisely what he'd been looking for his whole career. Validation that what he was doing, what he was writing, was worth it.

"It meant so much to me that you were there tonight," he said.

"I wouldn't have missed it for anything. It was a big deal for you and I'm glad to be there to support you."

She leaned in and kissed him softly. Their lips melted together in passion, their bodies pressed together. He slid his hand up the back of her shirt, touching the small of her back. Her skin was so soft that he couldn't help himself.

He moved from kissing her lips, around the side of her face to her ear, and down to her neck, caressing her skin with his tongue, moving his hand up and down her back, feeling her press against him. She let out a soft gasp and grabbed his shoulders, pulling him on top of her.

The kissing turned feverish and she yanked his shirt up over his head. Grabbing the back of his arms, she pulled him in close to kiss him again, pressing her body against his, kissing and breathing heavily the whole time.

"I want to go on record and say that I don't think we should sleep together yet," he said. "It's too soon and I care about you too much to let you think, even for a minute, that all I want is sex from you."

She kissed him on the nose. "I understand," she said, "I'm glad you feel that way. My body wants nothing more than to be with you, but my brain keeps trying to tell my body to stop rushing."

Sal stayed perched on top of her, shirtless, for the next hour or so, kissing her neck and ears, as she caressed his back and arms. It was the perfect ending to the perfect night.

She kissed him one last time before he watched her fall asleep. It was close to one o'clock before Sal finally dozed off. Normally he'd have been awake at home and using this time to write, but he much preferred to sleep next to her.

Sal fell asleep on his back. When he woke up the next morning, she had curled up next to him with her face on his chest and her left arm draped across his stomach.

He was close enough to the nightstand so he managed to reach his phone just before the alarm rang, silencing it before it woke her up. He slowly slid out from under Samantha, kissing the top of her head and tucking her back into the bed. She moved slightly, pulling herself closer into the pillow.

He smiled from the doorway as he put his shirt back on. Locking the door behind him as he left, he made sure to text her so she'd know he'd be back after work.

On his way in, he got a call from Greg — usually a bad sign as Greg never called him during the day. Come to think of it, Greg hardly ever called him at all.

"Hey, what's up?" he answered.

"Billy left me a voicemail late last night," Greg said. "We did great last night."

"We already know that, man. Get to the point, it's early."

"Saturday night we're playing downstairs."

The downstairs venue of the Middle East was nearly three times the size of the one they'd played just last night.

"Whoa, that was quick. How'd that happen?"

"I guess one of the bands slated to play can't make it, we're on at 10:30 until 11:45. I thought you'd want to know."

"Dude, that's awesome!"

The last few minutes of his drive to work were full of glee. He couldn't wait to get back to Samantha's to tell her the great news. The mundane activities of his day-to-day life at Starbucks seemed almost joyful today. After last night's show and his night in

Samantha's bed, he was on cloud nine. Making a thousand coffees couldn't deter him.

A new challenge occurred to him. They had a setlist that would suffice for 45 minutes and now had to come up with material for the extra half hour. They couldn't play the same setlist again on Saturday that they played on Wednesday. Sal began brainstorming on what songs they could use to fill the remaining half an hour.

Since last night's show, the flood of "You have a new follower" emails had been coming in pretty steadily from Twitter. Sal estimated that he saw at least a hundred of them throughout the day, and his phone kept lighting up with "So and So Likes So Say The King" Facebook notifications.

On his 15 minute break, he went outside to get some fresh air and opened his Twitter and Facebook clients on his iPhone: "Saturday night, 10:30, Middle East Downstairs. Be there. -SM" He'd just let their hundreds of Twitter followers and nearly a thousand Facebook fans know of the new show. He marveled at how easy they had it as a band these days. Thirty years ago it would have never been that easy to let your fans know about a show. Sal was amazed at how Woodstock happened; to get that many people to show up to an event when you couldn't just send an email about it, or send a Tweet? That amazed him to no end.

He sent quick text to both Paul and Derek to make sure they knew what was going on.

Greg called me earlier, it's too early. Replied Paul.

Me too, Greg woke me up an hour ago. Derek added.

In the afternoon, close to the end of his shift, a customer gave Sal a double take.

"I saw you at the Middle East last night, didn't I?" he said. "You guys were awesome. Seriously awesome."

"Wow," Sal was dumbfounded. "Thanks, man. We're playing downstairs Saturday night. You should come by. Bring your friends."

"I just saw it on Twitter," he said. "I'll be there for sure."

"On me," Sal said as his fan tried to pay for his drink. "Thanks for coming." He resisted the urge to add a high five or a squeal.

At two o'clock Sal left work and went straight back to Samantha's, knowing he didn't have much time before rehearsal.

He unlocked the door and she greeted him with a kiss.

"How was your day?" she asked.

"Fantastic. Like, wow! Fantastic."

"Wow, you're grinning ear to ear," she said. "What happened?"

"We're playing again Saturday night. Downstairs. Over five hundred people."

"Sal, that's so great! I'm so proud of you!" She wrapped her arms around him. "But wow, do you smell like coffee."

"I know, I came right here. I couldn't wait to see you," he said, stepping back. "Is it okay if you use your shower? I have my non-work clothes to put on."

"Of course. Help yourself. The towels are in the little closet in the hallway. The water's a little touchy, so test it before you get in."

"Thanks, babe."

He got halfway down the hallway before mouthing "babe" to himself in a questioning way.

He quickly learned that she wasn't kidding about the water being touchy. It seemed to go from freezing cold to scalding hot with a tiny amount of movement on the dial. He didn't care; he wasn't going to let a sporadic shower ruin his day.

After the shower, he found Samantha laying on the couch, watching TV. He grabbed some water and made his way over to her, sliding in behind her, just up high enough to see over her head.

"No work today?" he asked.

"I wrote a few pieces this morning, but there are no deadlines until next week," she said.

"So you're mine for the afternoon?"

"I'm yours for every afternoon," she said squeezing his arm as it wrapped around her waist. "Every afternoon."

Shortly into the afternoon's first episode of *Friends*, Sal's phone rang. It was Greg again.

"Hey," Sal answered. "What's up?"

"Jess needs our car tonight. Can you swing by to pick me up on your way into the complex?"

"Yea, no problem. I'm at Sam's anyway," he said. "I'll get you around five."

Samantha smiled to herself. It was the first time she'd heard him refer to her as Sam, a preference she hadn't yet mentioned to him.

Before Sal knew it, it was time for him to head out to band rehearsal.

"I've gotta go," he said. "I'll text you later when I get home. Deal?"

"I have a better idea. Come back when you're done. It's better when you're here."

"I think I can arrange that," he said, kissing her goodbye. "I shouldn't be back later than midnight."

"Take my keys with you, in case I fall asleep waiting for you. They're by the door."

He jumped over the back of the couch, so she wouldn't have to move, and made his way to the door to find her keys. He pulled the apartment key off the keyring, and dropped it into his pocket.

"I'll see you tonight," he said as he left.

"Ok, I'll be here. By the way," she said. "My mom loved you."

He smiled at the news and closed the door behind himself, making sure to check that the door was locked before making his way down the stairs and to his car. He couldn't help but think how lucky he was. In the short time since he'd met her, his band had become more successful, someone had recognized him at work, and he'd been genuinely happier overall. If things were this great already, he couldn't imagine how much better they'd get as time went on.

Chapter Twenty

SAL HONKED HIS HORN outside of Jess and Greg's apartment. Greg came out quickly, running down the driveway with his guitar and made his way towards the trunk. It was already open and waiting so Greg placed his guitar in and jumped in the passenger seat.

He fist bumped Sal and buckled his seatbelt before they drove away.

"Can you believe it, man?" Greg asked. "This is real. We got another gig already. Billy really came through."

"I knew it was going to happen, we've been working hard," Sal replied.

"We need to work out the setlist tonight, that should be our biggest goal for tonight. Maybe let's grab a pizza or two on the way in, so we don't have to stop for dinner?"

"That's a good idea. Arturo's is right around the corner. We can walk over after we park."

They hit traffic on their way, thanks to rush hour and a broken down MBTA bus on the side of a narrow road, causing all the other cars to have to go around it.

By the time they got the pizzas and made their way upstairs, it was after six and Paul had texted Greg to make sure they were coming.

"Dinner," Sal said, "is served."

He tossed the pizza down on the small table in the corner by the door and the guys dug in. Derek took a slice back to his drum stool, spinning around and clearing the whiteboard with his free hand. He wrote SETLIST in large letters across the top.

"We comfortably got through 45 minutes the other night," Paul said. "Another few songs and we should be golden."

"What if we added in some covers? It's been a while since we played any, but I think we could easily knock out some covers spur of the moment," Derek volunteered.

"I like that idea," Grey responded. "What were you thinking?"

"We have to play 'Foreplay.'" Paul interjected.

"Like *Boston's* 'Foreplay'. 'It's been such a long time', 'Foreplay?'" Sal asked, referencing the first line to *Boston's* "Foreplay/Long Time", one of his favorite songs from that album.

"That's the one. That place will go apeshit if we play a *Boston* song!" Derek said.

Before Sal could object and point out what a technically difficult song that was not only to sing but for all of them as well, Derek had already added it to the setlist.

They tossed around some other original songs, Derek jotting them down as they went along. Before they knew it, they had well over two hours of songs and had to start cutting things from the list.

"I don't think I can finish 'Night Before Dawn' before then," Sal spoke up. "We can take that one off."

"You sure? I know you've been working hard on it," Greg said. "You've got a few days to finish."

"I'm sure. If we were desperate for material, I'd say let's do it. But I think we have more than enough to get us through that show."

The thought of playing the song without it being perfect instantly caused knots in his stomach. He imagined rushing to get through the rest of the lyrics and having to perform it all within a short timeframe. He knew that'd be disastrous and he'd end up forgetting the lyrics. He couldn't let that happen again.

Derek got up, grabbing another slice of pizza before crossing "Night Before Dawn" off the list.

"I think there's still a few more that need to get cut so we don't go over," Derek said.

Paul proposed that they cut off their rendition of Taylor Swift's "We Are Never Ever Getting Back Together", but Greg vetoed the idea.

"People will immediately recognize that song and our version is super fun for everyone, including us. Can we leave that one?" Greg said.

"I agree," Sal said. "It's a lot of fun to play and I imagine people will want to sing along to stuff they know. What if we cut 'Polaroid' tonight? We played that Wednesday."

"I think that makes sense," Greg responded.

Derek ran through the list, jotting down approximate run times for all the original songs and referring to his trusty iPod to get the runtimes of the cover songs. He tallied everything up and came much closer to the hour and fifteen minutes they needed to fill.

"A little under the time we've got, but you figure with song introductions and Sal talking in between, that should fill the gaps," Derek said.

And so what if we run short a few minutes or even go over a few minutes?"

"I think we'll be fine. This is awesome," Greg said. "I'm stoked."

It was just two hours into practice, but they'd mostly accomplished everything that they needed to get done.

"Should we run through some of the covers that we haven't played in a while?" Sal asked. "I'm sure I could use a brushing up on the lyrics to a few of them."

"Good idea," Paul said. "The bass parts are mostly easy, except for 'Foreplay'. That thing's a bitch."

Before starting, Sal grabbed a bottle of water and the guys grabbed their instruments. They launched into the epic eight-minute-plus track. It took a handful of tries to make it through the intro, which was especially difficult for Derek, having not played it for a few years. Once they got past that, the rest of the song was smooth sailing.

Sal often referenced the late Brad Delp as one of the reasons he wanted to be a singer. His dad was a big *Boston* fan when he was a kid, and Sal often commented on how amazing Brad's voice was, hoping to someday be as successful as he was with *Boston* and some of his other bands later in life. "A life cut too short" he'd introduce the song on Saturday. Derek was right, people would respond to this song.

He knew the lyrics by heart, probably because he heard this song hundreds of times throughout his childhood into adulthood. It was one of two songs that he thought defined music, along with *Queen's* "Somebody To Love", which didn't make the cut for Saturday, but Sal was sure would make the cut for next time.

They ran through it five times, just enough to get the hang of it, but not so many times that they'd never want to play it again. As they finished the last run through and began shutting down their gear, someone knocked on the door.

Greg opened the door since he was the closest. Outside were two guys not immediately recognizable.

"Hey, sorry to bother you guys," the taller one said. "We have a space down the hall and heard you guys jamming that *Boston* tune."

"Oh, yea, sorry if we were too loud or played it too many times," Greg said. "We're going to play it Saturday."

"Where you playing?" the shorter guy asked.

"Middle East. Downstairs," Paul said, with pride in his voice.

"No shit," the taller guy said. "Wait, I know you guys. You're So Say The King aren't you? I follow you guys on Twitter. I dug the name when I heard of you."

They were starting to get recognized in places more than Starbucks, Sal thought to himself. That was twice in the past 24 hours that someone'd recognized him not just as Sal, but as a member of *So Say The King*.

"Thanks for stopping by," Greg said. "Hope to see you Saturday night."

"Gotta support each other, this is a tough industry," the shorter one said as they left.

It was still early by the time Sal got back to Samantha's apartment, barely 9:30. She was awake and startled by him coming in.

"I forgot you took my keys," she said, "and you're back so much earlier than I thought you'd be."

"We only played for a bit. We spent most of the night working on the setlist for Saturday."

"Any surprises?"

"A few. You'll have to come and see." He sat down next to her, his hand immediately taking hers.

"Did you eat?" she asked.

"Yeah, we got some pizza. I didn't eat too much. I think my brain's already nervous for Saturday."

"You'll be great, don't worry."

Fear of failure was something Sal would always deal with. No matter how great the last show was, that inevitably wore off before the next show would start. It was something that he told himself he'd have to work on as they started booking more and more shows.

Sal sat on Samantha's couch for a while, in silence, thinking about the upcoming show. Fearful that the first show was a fluke and the second would be a repeat of what happened years ago. He could still hear the boos as he dropped his guitar and ran off stage. He could still see the faces of people staring up at him while he fumbled for the lyrics to one of his own songs. It was something he'd never forget and always played back in his mind when preparing himself for a show.

Chapter Twenty-One

WITH YEARS OF WATCHING Greg and Jess as a reference, Sal expected an objection, maybe even annoyance, when he told Sam he and the guys would be rehearsing instead of attending Jess' weekly dinner. He wondered if she'd pout, and perversely found himself looking forward to it.

He bet she was pretty cute when she pouted.

To his surprise, Samantha didn't need coaxing or apologies. Instead, she just told him to go and practice. She sent him off with a smile and a kiss on the nose.

It wasn't a pout, but it was cute. And he liked that it was becoming a habit.

Derek and Paul met them at the room, already working on the tough beginning to "Foreplay", which Derek was starting to nail. Sal smiled to himself while he was making his way down the hall and could hear the song coming from their room. It almost sounded too good, like they were loudly playing the actual recording of the song loudly.

They spent the next six hours running through their entire setlist four times, only stopping for half an hour to run down to Arturo's to get another couple of pizzas and some drinks. Paul offered to go grab the food while the other guys kept working on the arrangement for their cover of Taylor Swift's "We Are Never Ever Getting

Back Together," which, as much as Sal tried not to, made him smile the entire time.

When Paul got back with the pizza, they each grabbed a slice and sat down.

"Tomorrow is both nerve-wracking and amazing. I can't wait," Derek said.

"I dunno," Paul said. "I was nervous on Wednesday, but I'm not really nervous for tomorrow."

"You realize there's going to be, like, five or six hundred people there, right?" Sal asked.

"Yeah, but so what? We have this material down. The only way that it's going to go bad is if one of us implodes on stage."

Sal didn't have to be called out by name. Paul immediately looked guilty, like he'd just been caught stealing.

There it was, someone had finally said it. Paul had brought up the gig that they'd played nearly two years ago, the one where Sal forgot the words to three of the five songs they played that night. Sal would never forget what it felt like to be booed off the stage.

Sal didn't leave his apartment for a whole week after that show. Everyone was convinced he was going to quit the band. It took almost an intervention to talk him down off the proverbial ledge.

He stood and took a moment to compose himself.

"That was then," Sal said. "This is now. This is different. You're right, we've got this."

He talked a big game, but he was more worried bout the show than he imagined any of the other guys could be. He'd never admit it to them, but the thought of screwing up as badly as he had kept him awake at night. The closer they got to the show, the longer he lay awake at night, thinking about the sound of those boos.

He finished his pizza and made his way back to his iPad that was sitting on a music stand. While rehearsing, he used an app that he'd bought for the iPad to display the lyrics to songs. He liked it because it would listen to his voice and auto-scroll at the right points. It wasn't perfect but it was good enough for practice.

The night wrapped up and everyone went home for one last night of rest before the show. They took the extra half hour at the end of the night to break down all their gear and get everything packed up for the next night so it'd take less time to prepare tomorrow.

As they left the rehearsal space, Sal could tell Paul was uncomfortable from the comment he made. While it had bothered him a bit, Sal wasn't one to hold grudges.

Sal called Samantha on his way home.

"Hey," he said, "I'm heading home now."

"I hope by home you mean here," she responded.

"I do still have your keys. How have you been locking your door?"

"I didn't have to, I haven't left since yesterday. Jess came over here."

"I thought she said you guys might go to the spa and use Greg's Amex?"

"We ordered pizza and an on-demand movie instead. It was nice to hang out with just her. Don't get me wrong, I love your band, but it's nice to have girl time."

"That's cool. So I guess I'll see you in twenty then?"

"I'll be here," she said. "Can you swing in downstairs and grab me a bag of salt and vinegar chips? I'm craving them."

"You got it. See you in a bit."

By the time he got Samantha's chips and made his way upstairs, it was just about 10:30. Unlocking the door and leaving his shoes inside, he made his way across to the couch where she was sitting watching TV.

"Hey," he said while leaning over her from behind. "Here are your chips, my dear."

Offering a kiss while thanking him, he took a seat next to her, immediately recognizing the episode of *Full House* that she was watching.

"I'll have to run home in the morning for some clothes. I feel like I've been in these ones forever."

"For. Ev. Er." Samantha said mimicking Squints from *The Sandlot*. Sal chuckled. She was almost as big of a movie buff as he was.

Hand in hand, arm in arm they sat for another hour.

"I'm getting sleepy," she finally said, rubbing her eyes. "Do you want to go to bed?"

"As you wish," he said smiling. "Lead the way. Or do you need me to carry you?"

"I can walk. I'm not that sleepy."

Truth be told, she enjoyed falling asleep on the couch just so that he'd carry her to bed. Waking up to him leaning over her, kissing her forehead was one of her favorite things of recent history.

"Don't take this the wrong way," he said. "But I'm taking my pants off. I can't sleep another night in jeans."

She laughed, "I won't take it the wrong way, I promise."

She changed in front of him again, the same magic routine to get her bra off without exposing her bare breasts. He watched her from his side of the bed as he took his pants and shirt off and slid into bed, pulling back the comforter for her to join him.

Clicking off the light and making sure his phone was turned off, she climbed in.

"No need to wake up early tomorrow," she said. "We can sleep in."

"I like that plan," he said, knowing his body would still wake itself up by 7, "I like that plan a lot."

They kissed goodnight and she turned her back to him, reaching behind her for his arm. Wrapped around her like a backpack, they fell asleep together. He made sure to kiss her shoulder before he fell asleep, as this was his new nighttime ritual.

He only thought back to the rehearsal complex for a minute or two before falling asleep. He played the conversation over in his head just one time, knowing that he not only had to show his bandmates that he was past what had happened years ago, but he had to tell himself, as well.

Chapter Twenty-Two

Sal promptly woke up at seven o'clock the next morning. Still wrapped around Samantha, he smiled and tried to pull himself away to get up and stretch.

"That's not sleeping in," she said with her eyes still closed. "Don't go yet."

"You're not supposed to be awake yet," he said.

"Neither are you," she pulled his arm back around her. "Stay."

He could feel her interlocking their fingers. Her hands were the softest he remembered ever holding. The morning sun was starting to peek through the houses that surrounded her apartment. Powerful rays found their way through the space between the shade and the window pane, shining over him and onto Samantha's shoulder. As she moved slightly to pull him closer, her shirt slipped off her shoulder to reveal a small tattoo of a flower.

"I didn't know you had a tattoo," he said. "Is it a daisy?"

"Oh, yea, I guess I never mentioned that. It's a daisy. My mom and I got matching ones when I turned 18. Sort of a symbol of being a grown up for both of us."

Sal leaned in and kissed her tattoo. She released his hand from hers and reached behind her to cradle his head. She managed to pull him around in front of her to kiss him.

"I'm sorry for my morning breath," she joked. "But you're worth kissing any moment I can."

Sal smiled and kissed her again.

"Breakfast?"

"Not just yet. Let's just lay and enjoy the morning."

He lay back down and she placed her head on his chest. With every breath his chest pushed her head up and down. He stroked her hair, running his fingers through its entire length down her back. On the way back up, he ran his fingers along her spine, slowly and sensually.

"How did we get here?" she asked.

"In bed?" he joked.

"No, here. As in us. It seems too good to be true, doesn't it?"

"No. It seems like it's supposed to. You and I are destined for great things, Sam."

Sam wondered if she should be cautious about things. Had she let her guard down too quickly? So many times she'd heard that if things seemed too good to be true, they usually were.

They lay still in the bed for another half an hour or so before Sal got up to make breakfast. This time before he could make two of everything, Samantha joined him in the kitchen while still in her pajamas.

"Can I have two eggs over easy?" she asked.

"Of course."

"Big night tonight. Are you nervous?" she asked while getting juice from the fridge.

"A little bit, but we've been through the setlist enough times that I think we'll do okay."

"Any big surprises?"

"We're playing a Taylor Swift song," he said, and immediately grinned ear to ear. "I don't think anyone will see that coming."

"Wait, *the* Taylor Swift?"

"Yep. 'We Are Never Ever Getting Back Together'. Our own rendition."

"Wow, I can't wait for that!" she said.

After breakfast, Sal got ready to head to his apartment to change before the show. "Do you want me to come back and get you for the show, or do you want to just come with me?"

"I need to jump in the shower first. My hair is gross," she said.

"I can wait, if you want," he said noting that her hair was nearly perfect right now, shiny and straight. "Go ahead."

Following her to the end of the hallway, he went back into her bedroom, turning his phone back on and laid back down in bed. From the doorway, he could hear her opening the closet in the hallway to get towels. A moment later she appeared in the doorway, tossing a towel at him.

"That's for you," she said before pulling her shirt over her head. "Join me."

Before he knew it she was already in the shower, but had left the door to the bathroom open.

Sal waited for just a second, making sure that he was ready for something of this caliber. Would he be able to restrain himself from having sex with her when standing in front of one another, naked?

He got up after another moment to join her. He made his way from the bed to the bathroom quickly, but not too quickly as to appear desperate.

Sal pulled back the curtain and marveled at her naked body. Standing there, smiling with the shower water dripping off her perfectly round breasts. He dropped his boxers and stepped in, pulling her in close to him and kissing her.

They spun together slowly, taking turns under the hot water. Their bodies pressed together, kissing. Her hands ran over his chest and down to his abs, exploring him. He followed suit, running his hands down her already familiar back, making his way down to her ass, grabbing it, pulling her into him. She turned her back to him, and pressed up against him, arousing him, and reached back putting her hands on his hips.

"I'm sorry the water pressure here is so terrible," she said. "But I'm glad you came in."

"Me too. You are gorgeous, you know."

She smiled and reached for her shampoo.

Chapter Twenty-Three

"YOU LOOK LIKE A groupie waiting for a band to come out after a show," Sal joked while carrying his amp by Samantha on his way into the venue.

They were the third band scheduled to play that night, the first two going on at eight and nine, giving them half an hour after the 9pm band to set up on stage. They stored their gear off to the side of the stage, setting up as much of it as they could before having to move it out onto the stage around 10 that night.

Once they wrapped up dinner, they made their way back down Mass Ave to the club, getting let in the side entrance reserved for performers and their people. They found a spot near the back of the venue and watched as the two earlier bands played their sets. Samantha danced a bit to some of the songs from the second band out of Connecticut called Marksman. Samantha seemed to enjoy them.

Once Marksman was done on stage, the guys quickly got their gear in place, making sure everything was set up, and going through a quick soundcheck with the sound guy. Downstairs was much larger, so they had to make sure their amps and drums were all miked up correctly, which took most of the half hour buffer between them and Marksman.

As the sound guy confirmed that their levels were good, and each member of the band individually signed off on their own gear, Greg nodded to Billy who jumped up on stage to introduce them.

"Some of you may have been blown away by these guys on Wednesday night upstairs. They were so kickass that we asked them to come play down here tonight. Give a warm hometown welcome to So Say The King!"

Billy left stage left, high-fiving everyone that was in his path on the way off stage.

Without a word, Derek counted them in with four stick clicks, launching right into "Mark My Words", a song more or less about their band and their struggle to make it. It was fairly well received; the crowd cheered and clapped as the song wound down.

"This next song is a hometown favorite. Feel free to sing along if you know the words," Sal said. "Brad Delp was taken from us way too early."

A good portion of the crowd recognized the name and began chanting "Boston! Boston!" repeatedly.

Derek counted them in with another four stick clicks, and away they went on "Foreplay." It was one of the hardest songs they'd play tonight, but they made it seem easy. Everyone hit all of their marks, Greg nailing all three guitar solos and Sal hitting every note that he'd been singing most of this life. Having sung it countless times throughout his life, it was one of the least stressful songs that he'd sing tonight. There were no nerves anywhere in Sal's body when he sang the first words.

During the second guitar solo, he had a moment to look out in the crowd for Jess and Sam, who were still in the back where he'd left them about 45 minutes ago. Sam was smiling and clapping, looking happier than he'd seen her before. She looked him with proud eyes in a way he'd only ever seen in his Mom when looking at his Dad.

"Foreplay" finished to such a thunderous ovation that Greg high-fived Sal.

"They loved it! We have to do more Boston songs when we play shows around here," Greg yelled in Sal's ear.

The applause was loud enough that Sal could barely make out what Greg was saying but he nodded in excitement and couldn't wait to get started on the next track. He looked over his should to queue Derek to count them in.

From "Foreplay," they went into "Inside."

"From 'Foreplay' to 'Inside'," Sal thought to himself "The innuendo is unintentional, I hope."

But Sal ultimately didn't care, he had fun with it, and sang his heart out.

A few more original songs and it was time for them to cover the Taylor Swift song.

"This next song," he started, "is something we like to play for fun. A little something unexpected for you. This is a cover of a song that's guaranteed to make you smile," he counted them in.

The first few notes were unmistakable. Sal could see people in the crowd looking at each other, puzzled, positive that they recognized the opening music, but baffled.

By the time the chorus hit, though, everyone was dancing, jumping, clapping, and singing along. Remarkable for a crowd of people who should not have even known the words, Sal thought to himself, they threw their arms in the air for each part of the chorus. Sal loved it. He took a look around at his bandmates whenever he could, knowing full well that they were enjoying this as much as he was. This was, after all, what they'd practiced so hard at all week.

The night had gone well and the crowd seemed really receptive to everything they played. Each song got a more thunderous response than the one before. To their surprise, the crowd even seemed to enjoy some of the more ballad-like songs, which Greg insisted they play.

"It's defines who we are and it lets people get to know you as a songwriter," he'd told Sal.

When their set was over, they quickly vacated the stage and made their way back to where Samantha and Jess were waiting.

Samantha greeted him with a giant hug when the guys got to the back of the venue.

"That was amazing! Did you see them go nuts for 'Foreplay'?"

"Everyone loves 'Foreplay'," Derek joked. "Right?"

Samantha pulled Sal in so she could get his ear.

"That was phenomenal," she said. "I may have to throw myself at you later tonight."

"I may just have to let you."

Once the headline act was done, the crowd thinned out pretty quickly. The occasional new fan stopped to say "Hey" to the band as they packed up their gear, asking for Twitter handles and if they were on Facebook. Greg handed out some of the contact cards they'd made, thanking everyone for coming out.

Sal noticed the tall guy from the other night leaving and gave him a nod.

"I just want to get home and to bed. It's past my bedtime," Jess said through a yawn.

"We're almost done," Greg replied.

"I'm so alive right now, I'm not going to be able to sleep," Paul said.

Once the gear was all packed into the van, they began their trek back to Allston to unload everything back into their room.

"Let's leave everything and set up Monday night before we start," Greg suggested.

"Sounds like a good plan, I want to go out and party!" Derek said.

Derek took Paul home in the van. Being the only one with a driveway meant Derek got to keep the band van at his place. Greg and Jess went home and Sal headed back to Samantha's apartment with her.

"I couldn't help but smile," Samantha almost yelled.

"Me too," he said. "It was amazing."

"I've dated guys in bands before. They've always said how great they were and were absolutely terrible. When you told me you were in a band a few weeks ago, I was skeptical. But, wow! You guys really are special."

"You've dated shitty musicians before?" he laughed.

"Some really shitty ones," she said. "You're not shitty."

They went inside Samantha's apartment, left their shoes behind and immediately grabbed each other. Sal noticed a look in Samantha's eyes that he hadn't seen before, one of passion and fire.

They awkwardly walked, still entwined with one another, from the entryway towards the couch, where they toppled over one another, laughing. They stayed there until around one o'clock that morning enjoying each other's company while mostly ignoring the TV, when she got up from on top of him and pulled him towards the bedroom. Shutting each light off as they made their way, she led him down the hallway, pushing the door to her bedroom open.

Before he knew it, she pushed him down on the bed and climbed on top of him.

"I'm not ready for sex yet," she said. "I'm sorry if I've revved you up and now am telling you to turn it off."

"It's okay. I don't want to do anything you don't," he said.

"We can still play," she said winking and reaching for the light to turn it off. "Right?"

She reached up over her head to take off her shirt and pressed his face into her perfect cleavage. He followed suit and removed his shirt, pressing his chest against hers. He held her close with his arms wrapped around her back. They stayed like this for no more than a few minutes before he unhooked her bra and tossed it to the floor.

He quickly stood up, easily lifting her tiny body and spun her around, putting her down on the bed and lying on top of her. He made his way down her neck, and spent ample time on each breast, kissing and licking her nipples which were erect almost immediately. He marveled, again, at how tone her body was as she ran her fingers through his hair.

Unbuckling his belt and taking his pants off, he felt her squirm below him while doing the same. In a moment's time, they were naked together, lying next to one another, exploring each other's bodies. Her fingers ran down his chest, finding his penis and squeezing it with just the right amount of firmness. He was immediately erect and wanting more.

Making sure not to leave him in a state that was uncomfortable, she made sure to wind the evening down slowly. Going from intense levels of foreplay to hand holding, to a simple kiss goodnight. Sal kissed her bare shoulder, right above her daisy tattoo.

"Goodnight Sam," he whispered and they were both asleep within minutes.

Chapter Twenty-Four

SAL AWOKE GENTLY THE next morning to the sound of the shower. Unsure if joining her was acceptable or if the other day was a one-time offer, he knocked on the door before stepping into the bathroom.

"Come on in," she called from inside. "The water's just getting hot."

Ensuring he had a towel, he climbed in and pulled her close to kiss her good morning.

"I forget," she said. "Do we have to leave here by 10:30 to make it to the party?"

"Yea, that should give us enough time. Are you nervous?"

"To meet your entire extended family all in one shot? No, not at all," she said as she splashed water at him.

Today they were celebrating the Maggione's 35th anniversary, a milestone that Sal was beyond proud of for his parents. He was almost more excited for Samantha to meet them and Cassie for the first time, than the party itself.

They were both ready to go with plenty of time to spare.

As she joined him in the living room, Sal lost his breath for a moment. He hair was perfectly straight and so shiny that he could see the sun reflecting off of it through the window. She'd picked an elegant dress to wear that fit her snugly and flowed down to her knees, exposing her perfectly tanned legs.

She looked beautiful with what appeared to be very little effort.

Noticing him looking at her, she smiled at him.

They headed downstairs to the car. After opening Sam's door for her, he noticed a ticket on the windshield. "No resident permit" it read, twenty dollars.

"It had to happen eventually," he said, "and it's only twenty bucks."

They buckled up and headed out to the party in the North End, a Sunday lunch with the entire family. Cassie had taken care of arranging the whole thing; she had a knack for being a party planner. Last he spoke to her, she'd told him that there were 125 confirmed guests. They had a typically large Italian family who liked to come out of the woodwork, especially when there was food involved.

Samantha fiddled with the radio for most of the drive. She'd find a song that she liked, sing along for a few seconds and then the song would end.

"I seem to keep finding the last ten seconds of songs I like," she said and smiled at him. "Just my luck. That seems to always happen."

"What do you mean?" he asked.

"I change the radio station and it's the last bit of a song playing. Like I'm cursed to only get the end of something I want to hear."

"That does sound like some sort of curse," he joked.

He knew that Samantha must have been nervous, but knew that everything would go swimmingly. They'd been dating for almost three months at this point, spending most of their free time together and this was her first introduction to his family. Meeting a new partner's parents for the first time could be nerve-wracking enough — meeting their entire extended family all at once was something that would give most people an anxiety attack. Sal wasn't worried. He knew that his family would love her, and she'd love them.

The old buildings that were inhabited by so many Italian and Jewish immigrants over the years stood tall this Sunday morning, beaming of their history. The various paths they took between side streets were cobbled and their age showed. The Old North Church bell rang. Centuries ago it warned Paul Revere that the British were coming; today it warned Sal and Samantha that it was 11 o'clock.

The doors were still locked since the place was technically closed for lunch today, as the family was renting the entire restaurant. Sal knocked loudly and a waiter opened the door a hair.

"May I help you?" the man asked.

"We're here for the Maggione party. My sister should be inside getting setup," Sal responded.

"Sal?" the waiter responded.

"That's me."

"Come on in, I'm Marcus, I'm one of the few here to take care of you guys today," he said opening the door and extending his hand. "Nice to meet you."

Marcus was shorter than Sal and much thinner. His bottle-blond coiffed hair was gelled into place. He clearly had weekly manicures and visited the tanning bed often.

Marcus led them to the dining room where Cassie was bounding around hanging streamers and a banner, smiling and looking like her usual chipper self.

"Cassie May," he called out from across the dining room. "We're here."

"Sal!" she yelled running towards him and throwing her arms around him.

"Hey, kiddo, how's everything going?"

"Good, I'm just about done," she said, turning to Samantha. "You must be Samantha. He hasn't shut up about you in months!"

"Cassie May!" he said, turning away so Sam wouldn't see he'd turned red in the face.

"It's so nice to meet you, Cassie. Sal's told me how fantastic you are to have as a sister. Congratulations on your graduation, by the way."

"Aww, thank you," Cassie said heading back towards the banner. "Samantha, could you give me a hand. Sal, you can get the gift table set up by the front there."

Sam and Cassie made their way back toward the back wall, chatting and hanging the banner together. He knew they'd immediately hit it off.

Just before noon, the three stood in the doorway together double-checking that everything was perfect.

"What time will Mom and Dad be here?" Sal asked.

"Everyone else is showing up by twelve-thirty and Mom and Dad will be here at one."

"You're sure they have no idea?"

"None, whatsoever. They think it's just you and I meeting them here. They're going to be hugely surprised!"

"This is so sweet of you guys," Samantha said. "When's their actual anniversary?"

"Next week, Friday," Cassie said.

"Then this really will be a surprise. They'll have no idea."

Guests starting pouring in at noon. Marcus and the rest of his team showed them into the dining room, offering everyone wine and other beverages. Soon the dining room was completely full except for the head table, a sweetheart table, like they had at their wedding all those years ago.

Sal and Cassie greeted each guest, hugging and kissing everyone on the cheek as they came in. Some of the closer family members were introduced to Samantha, most of whom said "Maria's told me all about you!" as they met her. A handful of times she'd turned red, but Sal could tell she was flattered that his whole family was so warm and welcoming to her.

As the clock on the wall approached one o'clock, Sal and Cassie headed towards the entrance to the restaurant to wait for their parents, taking a seat by the *Please wait to be seated* sign, pretending like they'd just arrived and were waiting for them.

Typical of his dad, they arrived exactly on time. Cassie often joked that he'd wait outside of a place until the exact moment they said they'd arrive, just to be on time. As they entered, Sal and Cassie rose and nodded to each other.

"Salvatore, Cassandra," their Dad, Vincenzo, said. "How are you?"

Their parents were always very formal with their names. Sal felt like his dad had given him them traditional Italian names just so he could have something substantial to yell when one of the kids had done something wrong.

"I'm good, Daddy," Cassie said. "Hi, Momma."

Maria and Vincenzo Maggione could have easily just stepped off the boat from Italy. They wore basic clothes with no brand names on them and did not carry any electronics of any kind. Vincenzo always made sure to leave his cell phone in the car when they entered any building.

"It's good to have, but I lived most of my life without it," he'd tell everyone later. "In case of an emergency, it's in the glove box."

Maria was dressed in her best dress — ankle length and dark green, it complimented her well. She was a short woman — barely five feet tall — and it showed that she had enjoyed Italian cooking her whole life.

Marcus played along with the surprise. "Right this way," he said and lead them into the dining room.

Had it not been for the banner, Sal was pretty sure his parents wouldn't have even noticed that there was a surprise party happening for them.

As Marcus led them to the head table, Sal and Cassie took their seats at their own table, where Greg, Jess and Samantha were waiting and enjoying some fresh bread and olive oil. Sal's mom teared up a bit.

"I had no idea," she kept saying, "did you guys do this?"

"It was all Cassie May, Mom. I swear. Happy Anniversary!" Sal responded.

Members of the family were taking turns coming up to Vincenzo and Maria to greet them and give their congratulations.

Vincenzo broke free for a moment and clinked his water glass. This was his way of telling the family to stop yammering so he could say something,

"This is such a pleasant surprise. Thank you all for coming out today to celebrate with us. It was 35 years ago that I married the love of my life and the greatest woman on earth. She gave me our two beautiful children and gave up her life and career to stay at home and help them grow into the amazing kids that they are today. *Possa la vostra vita che conduce in direzione di amore.*"

Samantha leaned over and whispered, "What does that mean?"

Sal took a second to process it, "I'm a bit rusty, but I think it means 'May your life lead you in the direction of love'."

She smiled and kissed his cheek.

Family-style platters of food — preselected with input from Sal and Cassie — began coming out almost immediately, starting with the appetizer course of fried mozzarella triangles, pasta salad, and traditional house salads, along with some Italian Wedding Soup.

"Wow," Cassie said. "This is delicious."

"You know how to pick 'em," Jess said. "This place is gorgeous. Honey, take me here some night for a date."

"Whatever you'd like, love," Greg said.

Once they'd had a chance to get some food into themselves, Sal's parents got up and started making their rounds to say hello to the extended family, many of whom they hadn't seen in many months. His Mom started at Sal's table, pulling his father behind her.

"Gregory, Jessica, thank you for coming," she said, kissing both cheeks on each of them. "And you must be the beautiful Samantha that Salvatore has been telling us about."

"Congratulations. Thirty-five years is amazing," she said. "And it's so nice to finally meet you."

Vincenzo spoke up from behind.

"Salvatore, you said she was pretty, you didn't say she was so beautiful. What are you doing with my son?" he ribbed Sal. "You're too beautiful to be with my boy!" he laughed, and the table joined in. Truth be told, his dad thought the world of him. He didn't necessarily understand Sal's desire to be a musician, but he supported him.

"It's so nice to meet you, Mr. Maggione," Samantha said.

"Please, Vincenzo. And my wife is Maria. None of the mister and missus nonsense. Manga. Enjoy!"

As quickly as they'd arrived, they were gone, kissing and greeting everyone else.

When they'd made it all the way around the room, back towards the front, Vincenzo noticed the long banquet table full of gifts.

"I'm almost 65, I don't need your presents. Who told you to bring presents?" he announced to the room.

"Oh, shush," Maria interrupted. "Thank you all. I'm sure we'll love each and every one of them."

As Sal's parents sat down at their head table, Marcus and his team brought out the platters of entrees. Pastas, parmiagnas, caccitorres, lasagnas, and meatballs as far as the eye could see. Steaming piles of delectible foods made their way across the restaurant, making their way from table to table.

The food was worth every penny. Sal made mention to anyone who'd listen throughout the day, even before he got the bill. Thankfully he'd been saving for this party for the last six months, which was about how long it'd take to pay it off. He brought his Amex, just in case he didn't have enough on his debit card to pay for everything. He knew Cassie would insist on helping pay, but she'd been out of school for almost five weeks now and still hadn't found a job yet.

"I'd like to make a toast, if I may," Sal said, standing and waiting for the family members to quiet down. "Thank you.

"My parents are the greatest two people I've ever known. My whole life I've aspired to be as amazing as I've seen them be. It's no secret that we didn't have a lot of money when Cassie and I were kids, but we never wanted for anything. Our parents taught us the value of a dollar and that when you want something, you have to work for it. I've aspired my whole life to be as great to a woman as my Dad is to my Mom. After 35 years, there's still a twinkle in his eye when she enters a room. He still smiles when she's not looking and they're still as in love as they were the day they met. I hope that in 35 years I'm as in love as they've been my entire life. May the rest of our lives be blessed with as much love as my parents have been fortunate enough to have in theirs." He raised his glass of sparkling cider. "Please join me in toasting the greatest couple I've ever been lucky enough to know. I love you both dearly."

Everyone in the dining room raised their glasses and began clanking them together. Maria had a few tears dripping from her eyes and Vincenzo offered her his napkin.

Dinner was followed by a dessert of endless piles of seven layer chocolate cake and tiramisu. Sal and Samantha shared a piece of cake, one of Sal's weaknesses that he was glad to share with her. While his parents shared their tiramisu, Sal made his way over to their table and gave them each a big hug.

"Congratulations. Here's to another 35 years, right?"

"Salvatore, if only we will be that lucky," his dad said. "I'd marry your mother again every day."

Though Sal doubted that his Dad had ever written poetry or a song for his Mom, he knew where he'd gotten his gift of words. His Dad was a romantic at heart and never let Maria go a day without being told how much she meant to him.

As dessert wound down, guests started making their way to their coats. Some of his uncles came up to Sal and tried to give him money to help pay for the bill, which he rightfully rejected.

"It's on me," he said more than a half dozen times, appreciating that his family was willing to contribute, but wanting to pay for the meal himself.

Marcus motioned from across the room with the small black folio that often contained a bill.

"Excuse me a moment," Sal said heading towards the back of the restaurant. Though paying a bill was not often a private matter, Sal knew that if his Dad had seen the check, he'd insist on paying it. That was something Sal wouldn't let happen.

With the tip included, the bill was more than Sal had anticipated, so he opted to put it on his Amex, knowing that he could pay it down in installments to make the burden a bit less overwhelming. He added in a small extra tip for Marcus' team.

A few beads of sweat dripped from his forehead as he signed the receipt.

Soon most of the dining room was cleared out and just Sal, Cassie, Samantha, Greg, Jess and Sal's parents were left.

"Would you guys mind helping load the gifts into my dad's car?" Sal asked.

"Not a problem. Mr. M, where'd you park?"

"It's down the block a bit. Do you want to pull it up?" he asked, tossing Greg the keys.

It took each of them two trips to load everything into the car. Their family had really gone overboard. Sal knew that many of the presents would contain coral, the traditional gift for thirty-five years.

"You guys outdid yourself," Maria said. "This was such as a surprise."

"We love you guys," Cassie squealed. "You're the best, you deserve it."

"I'm glad you guys had a great day," Sal Said. "I love you both."

"Samantha, take care of my boy," Vincenzo said.

"I intend to," she said pulling Sal in close to her side. "I promise."

"It was so great to meet you. You need to come up for dinner some night so we can get to you know you better. We didn't get a chance to really talk," Maria said.

"I would love that. Thank you for the invitation."

Sal and Cassie each took turns hugging their parents and walked them out to their car.

"Dad, if you need a hand unloading any of the gifts when you get home, call me. Don't hurt yourself," Sal said.

"I'll hurt you," Vincenzo said, faux-punching Sal in the stomach. "Thanks again, *miei figli*, you're the best."

With that, his parents were gone.

Chapter Twenty-Five

SAL WAS THE FIRST one to the rehearsal space Monday night.

On the ride to the rehearsal space, the radio station he was listening to played a lot of the songs that they'd played covers of on Saturday night. He accepted it as a sign and smiled to himself.

It was just after five o'clock, so he made his way up the stairs to vending machines at the top to grab a bottle of water while he waited for the others. Paul and Derek arrived as he was jamming a dollar bill into the machine.

"The show was kick-ass, wasn't it?" Derek asked.

"I can't wait to play again," Sal said as they walked back towards their room.

"How'd the anniversary go yesterday?" Derek asked.

"Great, it was a good time. My parents were surprised," Sal unlocked the band's room.

When five-thirty had rolled around and there was still no sign of Greg, Sal decided to call. It went to voicemail, but he immediately got a text message back.

be up in a min, on a call.

They waited around another few minutes before they heard Greg's footsteps coming down the hall.

"Sorry I'm late." Greg burst through the door. "I was on a call."

"Sal said," Paul replied. "No big deal."

"I was talking to this guy named Jack who called me. He was at the show Saturday night and is a manager. He wanted to know if we were interested in having representation."

"Wow, after one show?" Derek said from behind the drums.

Sal sat quietly on his amp, hoping to be able to get some more information out of Greg. He was optimistic that this could be the start of something big.

"How do we know this guy's not some shady scumbag looking to take all our money?" Paul asked.

"What money?" Sal asked.

"I told him we'd think about it, mainly so we could have time to research him," Greg said, "I didn't agree to anything. He wants to sit down with us tomorrow night to discuss. Plus it's not like we have any money for him to take, like Sal said."

"What's his last name?" Sal asked.

"DeBane."

Sal took out his iPad and proceeded to Google "Jack DeBane" and immediately found a very impressive Wikipedia page.

The photo showed a man gray before his time. His page said he was forty-one and had been active in the industry for twenty-three years, working his first job as a manager at the age of eighteen. His long graying hair was pulled back into a ponytail. It was clear from the photo that Jack was a large man. Standing at 6'4" and just over two hundred pounds, he was no slouch. He had drinker's nose, and his teeth were all veneers, too shiny and new to be his real teeth.

Sal was shocked as he read and reread some of the information on his screen.

"This seems too good to be true," Sal said. "Like, way too good to be true."

"What do you mean?" Greg asked.

"Well, according to Wikipedia, he's managed tons of bands from this area that went on to be huge. Godsmack, Mighty Mighty Bosstones, The Pixies. He was the original manager for Aerosmith before they moved onto someone else. He worked with the Dropkick Murphys, was close friends with Brad Delp, Bang Camaro before they broke up, and countless others. This guy seems like the real deal."

"And he's interested in us?" Paul asked.

"Yea," Greg said. "He said he likes to find new talent very early in their careers and mold them into a marketable band. He said we'd be perfect for a new agency that he just started, a flagship, he called us, whatever that means."

"It means he wants someone to become famous to give his new management agency a good reputation," Sal said, immediately feeling a pressure to be perfect. His stomach instantly in knots.

"Is that something he's been able to do before?" Greg asked.

"According to Wikipedia, yeah. It looks like he builds these agencies from the ground up and then sells them to bigger companies, pocketing a ton of cash."

"Shit. I say let's meet with him," Derek said. "What harm can it do? We won't sign anything without a lawyer looking it over. I can ask my dad to do it."

"I knew having you in the band would eventually pay off," Paul joked. "Lawyer dad to the rescue!"

Sal kept reading the page over and over again. He kept thinking that there was no way this could be happening. It seemed too fast, too perfect and too scary. He wondered if he was the only one who felt that this could have been made up information to fool them.

"People can make fake Wikipedia pages very easily," Sal said, "it's not hard to make yourself sound better than you are."

"I think Bryn has a new band that rehearses down the hall. We could go knock on their door and ask." Paul said, referring to Bryn Bennett, one of the founding members of Bang Camaro. He'd been friendly towards the guys when they ran into him in the hallway.

Sal, Greg, and Derek stayed in the room while Paul trekked down the hall to talk to Bryn. Sal managed to find an interview with Jack on The Huffington Post from a few years back where he talked about the agency that he'd just sold and what his next plans are. He had read most of it aloud by the time Paul got back from Bryn's room.

"He's on the up and up according to Bryn," he said. "He said the guy was awesome and helped them a ton."

"Be that as it may," Greg said, "we should still make sure to have Derek's dad read anything before we sign it."

"I already text him and asked if he would," Derek said. "No problem."

Chapter Twenty-Six

GREG HANDLED SETTING UP the meeting between the band and Jack for the next night. Sal lost his argument against meeting him at Legal Seafoods.

"If anything, he'll buy us some lobsters," Greg said. "And you can't beat a free lobster!"

"Unless you don't eat seafood," Sal responded with a scowl.

Jack was waiting for them when they arrived just after six o'clock. He'd arranged a quiet table in the back corner. They joined him, taking menus from the waitress and introducing themselves one by one.

"I know this is unusual for you," Jack said, "but I'm not a scam artist. I'm not a con-man. I'm a legit manager and my track record proves I'm not a hoax."

"We Googled you," Sal said. "The internet agrees with what you're saying."

"That's good. I'd be worried if you didn't look me up."

The waitress came back and Jack ordered a few different appetizers without even looking at the menu. The other guys ordered beers and the waitress rushed off to get them. Sal, as usual, was the designated driver, which was fine with him.

"Here's the deal," Jack said. "I was at the show two years ago. I know what happened. I was interested in you back then. I wanted to sign you to the agency I had back then."

Sal felt himself turning red. The butterflies that were in his stomach all day suddenly intensified. He'd been thankful to put that whole event behind him, but it was suddenly front and center, staring him in the face. He swallowed, hard, and tried to regain his composure and not go on the defensive.

"I was also at the show on Wednesday and obviously, on Saturday night," he continued. "The change is like night and day. You're the same band, but there's this new passion that clearly comes out in your performances."

"Thank you," Greg said. "But what does that mean? What exactly are you proposing?"

"Well, it's simple really. What I want to do is manage you. You don't have a manager right now, so let me fill you in on what that person would do. First, I'll get you gigs. No more calling Billy trying to get into some shitty venue that holds 50 people to play for 20 minutes. I'd take care of getting you on real stages in front of real crowds. Secondly, a record. You need one. There's no reason that you don't have at least an EP out right now. So you'd have to go into the studio sometime soon. I have connections at a few local record companies and could easily get you into a studio on their dime just from my word. Not to toot my own horn, but as they say, I'm kind of a big deal."

"And just like that some record company is going to just let us in and let us start recording on their dime?" Paul asked.

"There's a little more to it than that," Jack said. "But yeah. That's the gist of it."

"What's in it for you?" Sal asked.

"I obviously don't work for free. I take a fifteen percent cut of any money you make from shows, merch, or record sales. I take a larger percentage than most for two reasons. One, I'm fucking great at what I do. And two, I don't take any money up front. Some other managers do and those are the ones that are going to bend you over. By only making money when you make money, I'm motivated to work harder, faster and better than the other guys."

"And I suppose you want some sort of contract that you basically own our souls forever?" Sal said snidely.

"Look I'm not a bad guy. I get your reasons to be reserved. No one wants to jump in bed with someone you just met, right? I want to help you and I know I can. I'm not a bad guy, I swear."

"What kind of guarantees do we get?" Greg asked.

"You get the same as any other band trying to make it. Absolutely fucking none. Look at it this way -- eighty-five percent of millions is better than one hundred percent of nothing, isn't it?" Jack asked.

He had a point. If he could even do one tenth of what he said he could and what his history indicated he could, then they couldn't go wrong.

"How many other artists do you manage?" Derek asked. He'd clearly had some coaching from his father.

"Right now? Zero. Not a single one. I just closed the deal on my new office space and my lawyer's finalizing the paperwork on the new agency next week. You'd be my first and only band for the foreseeable future. And I'd be willing to put it in writing that I wouldn't take on another band for at least, let's say, a year. That way I can focus all my energy on getting you guys shows, getting a record recorded, and getting you in with a record label."

"What happens if we're not happy with what you do for us?" Paul asked.

"Then you fire me and we go our separate ways. I'm not a record company, so you're not stuck with me forever. If things don't work out, we're done. It's that simple."

"So tell us a bit about your process." Sal said.

"Well, to be honest, it's a lot like being popular in high school," Jack said. "The more people you know, the easier it is to do this job. Since I know so many people, I just call someone up and say 'Hey, it's Jack DeBane, I've got this kick-ass band that I want to book with you for an hour. When should I send them there?' and then we shoot the shit for a bit. Whoever I'm talking to tells me that I've never let them down and we book the gig. That's it. I do that three or four times a week and you guys go and play the shows. I collect the money, I negotiate the rates, I pay you guys and keep my cut. That's it."

"That sounds pretty easy. Why can't we just do that ourselves?" Greg asked.

"You can, don't get me wrong. But the reality is two-fold. One, I know way more people than you do, I've been doing this since you were all in diapers. Two, you should be focusing on your craft, not on the business side of this."

"That makes sense," Derek said. "But how do we ensure that the business gets handled?"

"That's what contracts are for. Contracts make sure I do my job and make sure I'm honest. Bottom line is that I like you guys. You blew me away with that Boston cover the other night, to the point where I honest-to-fucking-God thought Brad Delp had come back from the dead and was singing. You got some pipes on you, boy!"

"Thank you," Sal said, trying to remain humble. It was the first time that evening that he'd started to feel relaxed.

"I want you to be successful," Jack continued. "I want to hear your songs on the radio. And I know. I fucking know, that I can help you do it. You just have to put your trust in me."

Their meals came and as the waitress took away their appetizer plates. Another waitress came by with another round of drinks, saying, "They're on me, Jack" and winking at him.

"See, doors open when you're with me," Jack joked.

At first, Sal had thought that Jack came across as someone you'd expect to see in a movie playing a record executive. He said all of the right things at all of the right times. But, for some reason, it seemed to work for him. Every time Jack answered a question, Sal felt more relaxed and comfortable. Slowly but surely through the dinner, Jack was winning Sal over.

"Let's say we want to hire you. What happens next?" Derek asked.

"My lawyer draws up a contract. Your lawyer reviews it. We all sign it. I start working. There's not much more to it. Don't over-think it."

"And if we don't like the contract?"

"Then you either don't sign it or you propose changes to it to make it more agreeable. It happens every day."

As the meal wound down, the conversation trailed off.

The more Sal thought about it, he thought it couldn't hurt to try Jack out. He got the sense that Paul and Derek were in the same camp as he was. They both seemed pretty enamored with him. Sal could tell Greg, on the other hand, wasn't so sure. His body language and questions throughout the evening were defensive and accusatory, for the most part. Sal knew Greg would need some convincing.

"Listen, dinner's on me. Give it some thought. Greg, you've got my number. Give me a call in a few days when you've thought about it. No pressure at all. I just want what's best for you guys."

Jack paid the bill and shook each of their hands before he left. "It was great to sit down and pitch myself to you guys."

"Thanks for dinner," Paul replied.

"Yea, thanks for the food, that was good of you," Derek added.

"If you decide not to hire me, I want you to know that I legitimately think you guys rock. You're one of the most talented bands I've heard in a while. It'd be my honor to be your manager, but, I'll still buy your CD when it comes out one way or the other."

He left them there at the table. Everyone, as if on cue, looked to Greg, knowing he'd be the holdout.

"Well?" Paul asked.

"How do you know that I'm the only one who doesn't want to do this?"

"We know how you are with making decisions," Derek said. "Why would this be any different?"

"Sal, what do you think?" Greg asked.

"I really liked him. And what he said made sense. If he fucks up or is no good, then we fire him. It's not like he can do anything that's irreversible, right?" Sal said.

"Right, and my dad's an awesome lawyer. He wouldn't let us shoot ourselves in the foot," Derek added.

They gathered around Greg's car in the parking lot to mull it over some more.

"Why don't we each give it some thought and talk about it on Wednesday? That'll give us a couple days to think about it," Greg said.

Everyone agreed and went their separate ways. Sal couldn't wait to get back to Samantha's apartment to tell her, so he called to tell her the news.

Chapter Twenty-Seven

The lights were off when Sal arrived at Sam's. She was reading in bed, waiting up for him.

"How was rehearsal?" she asked.

"Pretty great. We all convinced Greg to give Jack a chance."

"So you've got a manager now?"

"We do. Jack was pretty excited when we called him a little bit after he left us at the restaurant. He used the phrase 'That's fucking awesome' when we agreed to hire him."

"That's great!"

"Yeah, it feels pretty great. I feel like this may be the start of something big for us. Like we're somehow official now. Like we're a real band."

"What's next?"

"His lawyer draws up a contract."

"And then what? Then you're famous?"

"If only it were that easy, babe. No, next we'll have Derek's dad review it and make sure we're not signing our lives away."

"And then you're famous!" She jabbed at his ribs, causing him to squirm away.

"Yep, then we're famous. And then you'll have to fight off droves of screaming women."

"Those bitches better know you're mine." She kissed him. "I'll cut one of them to prove a point."

"I feel like I haven't seen you at all this week. I've know I've been here with you, but I feel like there's so much else going on that I haven't spent any real time with you," he confessed.

"I know, honey. It's okay. You've got a lot happening right now and I'm supportive."

"You are supportive. It's kind of surprising. I don't know many women that'd stand by while their boyfriend pursued his dreams of being a rockstar."

"That's the first time you've said that," she said. "Boyfriend."

"Well, yea. I mean. I just kind of assumed. I figured we didn't really need to have that talk."

"I didn't want to jinx anything," she said. "These last few months have been so amazing I didn't want to point it out in case it was some elaborate ruse."

"I know what you mean. So far this has been amazing. And your lips, my God, I could kiss you forever," he said.

"And you should."

The light clicked off and Sal pulled her on top of him. She stayed there for the next hour before Sal fell asleep.

She quietly and slowly slid back onto her side of the bed and lay down next to him. He was so still while he slept.

It was nice to spend some time alone with him. Now that things seemed to be moving so quickly, she was feeling more alone than she had in the first few months of her relationship with Sal.

She lay awake for the next hour, wondering what it would be like to be the girlfriend of someone famous. She kept replaying his voice in her mind, hearing him call her his girlfriend for the first time. It made her giddy and she found herself dozing off with a large smile across her face.

Chapter Twenty-Eight

It didn't take long for Derek's dad to review the contract. He did some digging and fifteen percent was a bit high, so they proposed ten. Jack was surprised by the counter offer but said that he was proud of them for having balls and agreed to the ten percent.

"Ten percent of millions is still millions," he said.

Not even a day after the ink had dried on the contract, Greg got a call from Jack saying that he had a record company that was interested in hearing their demo.

"We don't have a demo," Greg said. "Is that bad?"

"It is for now, but we're heading into the studio later today. Get the guys to drop whatever they're doing. I'll meet you at the complex to help you break down the gear and get packed up in an hour."

"An hour? I'm not sure the guys can just drop everything they're doing. I have today off, but they're all probably at work."

"I realize that," Jack said, "but this is more important. Without a demo, you can't get a deal."

"Okay, I'll do what I can. No promises, but I'll try."

Greg called Sal first.

"Hey, you busy?" Greg asked when Sal answered.

"No, what's up? I'm just waking up and having breakfast with Sam."

"Jack got us into a studio, but we have to meet him in an hour. Can you bail on work?"

"What do you mean? Like not show up?" Sal asked, concerned.

Samantha looked at him across the tiny table. He could tell she was trying to figure out what the conversation he was having was about.

"We're meeting at the complex to get our gear in an hour. Can you be there or not? This trumps going to make coffee, Sal."

"An hour," he said, looking to Samantha. She nodded to give him permission to go. "Yeah, I can be there in an hour."

Sal put off calling his boss for as long as possible. The thought of missing out on a day's pay scared him. He was running numbers in his head, trying to make sure that he could afford this month's rent without the extra day's pay.

Samantha caught him staring at the wall.

"Are you okay?"

"I'm fine, just trying to figure out how to tell work I'm not coming today."

"This is more important, isn't it?"

"It is. Don't get me wrong. I just…" his voice trailed off.

"You what?"

"Nothing. I'm okay, I promise. I have to get ready."

"You know you can talk to me," Sam said.

"I know I can. Maybe later."

He got up from the table and called Paul on his way back to Sam's bedroom to get dressed. He was surprised at how easy it was to persuade Paul to leave work. Derek's response was also surprising.

"I work at Guitar Center, dude, I'm not curing cancer here. Guys leave all the time for shows. No one will care," he said.

Derek was wrong. He got fired on his way out of the store.

The guys all met up just over an hour later, working quickly to break down their equipment. Jack had been the first one there and Greg let him in when he arrived. By the time the rest of them showed up, Greg and Jack had broken down much of the gear, sure not to touch Derek's drums.

"Leave the drums for Derek," Greg said to Jack, "he's a bit finicky when it comes to who touches his babies."

All the gear was broken down and loaded into the van in record time, having the extra pair of hands there helped move things along.

"I totally just got fucking fired." Derek said when he arrived.

"For what?" Sal asked.

"They didn't want me to leave today. Said something about short staffed or whatever."

Knowing that his bandmate had gotten fired worried Sal even more. He had two hours before his shift was supposed to start at Starbucks and he still hadn't called to tell them he wasn't coming.

Greg, Paul and Sal rode with Jack while Derek drove the van closely behind. Sal finally decided to call into work and let them know he wasn't coming in today.

They arrived at the studio, an unsuspecting building that could have passed as someone's house. Sal looked up at the house, craning his neck to look all the way to the third story. On a quiet side street on the Medford–Arlington line, it was an unexpected location for a recording studio. The door was located next to the driveway where they'd all parked, containing no markings to indicate what was inside.

Jack rang the bell and a stocky man with long black hair answered, shaking Jack's hand and patting him on the back.

"Guys, this is Cee. He's the best producer and engineer in this state. This is the band. Singer Sal," Jack said.

"Nice to meet you," Sal responded.

"Greg, lead guitar."

"Hey Cee, nice to meet you," Greg called from the far side of the car.

"Bass player, Paul," Jack said as Paul walked around to shake Cee's hand.

"And that's the drummer Derek getting out of the van."

"Nice to meet all of you." Cee was short and stalky, five foot three inches tall. Sal guessed he weighed in at close to 250 pounds, which made him more round than tall. His long jet black hair was pulled back and tied so tight that he appeared bald in the right light.

"I inherited this place when my grandmother passed away years ago. Since I'm an engineer I figured it made sense to do a whole renovation and convert it into a studio as well as my house. I live on the third floor and the first and second are the studio. C'mon in, I'll give you a tour," Cee said.

Sal was in awe as soon as he walked into the room. Gear as far as the eye could see — guitars, amps, microphones, bass guitars, everything a band could want or need. The house had been gutted and rebuilt on the first two floors, allowing wires to be run through walls, Plexiglas windows to be installed, and a closed-circuit television and communication system installed.

"No matter where you are in the studio, you can see and talk to each other. The whole place is rigged with audio and video systems. Each sound booth has a little video screen in it," Cee said as he showed them one of the sound booths. "Every room is completely soundproof, not an easy feat, but worth the money. It makes isolating each instrument easier, which makes the recording sound better."

"Wow, that's pretty cool," Greg said. "I bet that wasn't cheap."

"Not even a little. But it's what I do."

Their tour continued upstairs where the old master bedroom had been converted to the control room. A mixing board extended the entire length of the wall, adorned with various sets of speakers, computer monitors, and video screens highlighting each of the rooms downstairs. The rest of the control room was rather unimpressive, a small fridge in the corner, a few desk lamps to light the place, and the windows were all blacked out.

"It's nothing to write home about," Cee said, "but it gets the job done and it's home."

"Cee's the best in the business. This demo is going to help get you guys a record deal," Jack said. "And the ball will roll from there."

After the tour of the studio, the guys headed downstairs and started bringing in their gear.

"I've got a lot of that stuff already," Cee said. "You don't have to bring it all in unless you want to use your own gear."

"Greg's kind of a snob," Derek said. "He likes his own stuff."

"I think the rest of us want to use our own gear, too. We brought it over, so we might as well," Sal said. "It makes sense."

It was almost noon by the time they'd gotten all their gear set up and levels tested. Cee spent very little time miking up the instruments — a sign that he was either really good at what he did or had no idea what he was doing. Greg looked worried.

Cee called down via the video system to have each member of the band adjust the volumes on their amp. He also had Derek go through a round of hitting each drum and each cymbal one by one to check its volume. "Okay, I think we're good to go," Cee's voice came through the speakers. "Can you all hear each other okay?"

Sal strummed a few chords on the guitar. Greg added in his guitar and was followed by Paul and finally Derek.

"I can barely hear Greg once the drums kick in," Sal said. "Can I get a little more of him in my headphones?"

He could see Paul nodding on the screen.

"Me too," Paul said.

Soon all of their adjusting had been completed and the guys played through a couple of riffs to make sure that they could all hear each other. Once satisfied with the levels, Cee called down.

"Come upstairs, let me walk you through the process," he said.

The stairway was narrow and steep, typical of old houses in this area. They made their ascent and found Jack and Cee waiting in the control room.

"The talkback system will automatically mute themselves when I'm recording, so there's no feedback," Cee explained. "How much material do you have that you want to actually record?"

"How much time do we have?" Greg responded.

"If you want to just do a whole album now," Jack interjected. "Let's do it. Cee owes me a favor, so his time is taken care of."

"A whole album? We haven't prepared for that" Sal said.

"Don't be a puss," said Paul. "We have more than enough for a full album."

"Right, but how much time do we have?" Greg asked.

"As long as you need. I cleared my schedule at Jack's request," Cee responded.

"And while you're working on recording, I'll clear your schedules as well. I need the names and phone numbers of all your bosses. I'll take care of work for you," Jack said.

Each member of the band took out their phone - except now jobless Derek - and started relaying the information to Jack, who put it into his phone before slipping it back in his jacket pocket.

"How does it all work? I understand the concept of a recording studio. But what's the actual process like?" Sal asked, knowing the rest of the guys needed to know as well.

"Don't worry about it," Cee said. "You do your thing, I'll do mine."

"And that's it?" Sal asked.

"You just go down there and play the songs. I'll tell you what's needed when it's needed," Cee said.

"And I'm here to be your shepherd." Jack said.

"Before we start anything, there's a deli at the corner of the block. Let's grab some lunch to sit and figure out what songs you want to record," Cee said.

They walked down the narrow stairs and out the door, many of them shielding their eyes from the sun.

The walk back to the studio was quick and before they knew it they were upstairs sitting around the small table in the back corner of the control room — safely away from the gear, eating. They kicked around a number of ideas for songs, Sal referencing his iPad for their last two shows' playlists, pointing out what original songs had done well and what songs hadn't.

"Can we record one of the covers we did?" Paul asked.

"Depends, did you license it?" Cee asked.

"Which song?" Jack interjected.

"I think it'd be amazing if we recorded the Taylor song. People enjoyed the hell out of that," said Paul.

"Which one? 'Never Getting Back Together'?" Jack asked.

"Yea, that's the one," Sal said.

"I know Max, I'll call him."

"Max who?" Derek asked.

"Max Martin. He produced the song and can give me a verbal agreement to let us record it while we work out the paperwork. They'll have to get a percentage of sales though. Is that okay?"

They all agreed that giving this Max guy and Ms. Swift some of their money seemed like the responsible thing to do. They agreed and Jack set out to call Max Martin to ask permission for them to record the song.

The guys tossed ideas back and forth until they'd come up with the setlist that they wanted to use for their first record. They decided that the Taylor Swift song would be simply titled as an acronym, which they hoped would entice people to want to listen to it first.

Lunch wrapped up and Cee gave them final instructions on what to do when they got back downstairs. "Give me a signal when you're done playing the song, so I know to stop the recording," said Cee.

Once he settled into his individual booth, Sal felt his nerves come over him. Though this is what he'd wanted for most of his life, he felt a sudden pressure to be better than he'd ever been before. Knowing that this record was actually happening meant more to him than he could rationalize in his own mind. Had they picked the right songs? Did they know the material well enough? Did they make a mistake hiring Jack? Everything flashed before him all at once and then he thought of Samantha. He took out his phone quickly to turn it off and made sure to look at the photo of the two of them from Greg's wedding. He'd set it as her default contact picture so it showed when she called. It gave him serenity and eased his doubt.

"Let's do this," he said. "Count us in Derek."

They started with "Mark The Day," an older song that they hadn't tried live, but one that Sal thought people would relate to.

"Everyone loses someone they love," he said. "Everyone dies. Everyone can relate."

Their first track was rough. They had to restart a handful of times due to either an adjustment with an amp or not being able to hear someone else clearly enough through the headphones. They finally got through their rough take on the sixth try. Sal signaled to Cee that the song was over by pointing to the camera mounted in the corner.

"Good first take," Jack's voice came through the talkback system. "Max says we're a go for the Swift song. Paperwork's been started already."

Sal felt good after the first rough take had been done. He could see Greg on the video screen smiling as well. Derek twirled his sticks in excitement and Paul bopped his head along as they were playing, offering his happiness in visual form.

From "Mark The Day" they went into "Welcome Home", a song Sal had written some 15 years ago when he was just a teenager. It symbolized how much life had changed for him once his baby sister had come home from the hospital. Not just that he was a big brother now, but also that he was no longer an only child. It was another song that he felt many people could relate to and he pressed to have it on the album. It wasn't his best work, but it was important to him to record it for Cassie.

"Welcome Home" went significantly better than "Mark The Day," They nailed the rough track in just two takes.

"The more we do this, the easier it'll get," Derek said from his drum booth at the back of the studio. "Seems easier already."

The recording took them through six o'clock. Greg joked that the microphones in the drum room were so sensitive that he could hear Derek's stomach grumbling.

The guys powered down all the gear and headed upstairs.

"Great first day, guys!" Jack said while giving them each a fist bump as they made it to the top of the stairs.

"It felt pretty awesome, I'm not gonna lie," Paul said, emphatically.

"I rarely get to tell bands that come through here that I like their sound and their arrangements. Normally I have to lie to them and then gently break the news that I have to basically recompose their songs for them. I'm glad to not have to lie to you guys," Cee said, "The music sounds great and I can't wait until it all comes together."

"Let's meet back here tomorrow morning around nine. I'll text you all the address," Jack said while typing away on his iPhone. "That work?"

"We just leave our gear here, all setup?" Greg asked.

"Unless you want to take your guitar home to work some more," Cee said. "I have state-of-the-art surveillance and security. Don't worry about it being stolen."

They each did a walk-through of their sound booths, making sure that their amplifiers were turned off and grabbing any personal belongings that they'd need for the night. As Sal grabbed his iPad, he took a photo of the empty booth he'd spent the day in, his guitar leaning against the corner.

Hard at work. -SM he tweeted as a caption to the photo.

A second fist bump from Jack and a handshake from Cee and they were out the door on the way home. Just enough light was left in the night sky to get them out of the city and onto the highway heading home.

Before he knew it, Sal was back at Samantha's. He took a few minutes to tell her how great his day was, yawning the entire time and before he knew it was sound asleep on the couch. She let him sleep, his head in her lap while gently stroking his hair. Just shy of 11:30, she woke him up and had him move to the bed, where she joined him. He was asleep again before she turned out the light.

Chapter Twenty-Nine

SAL AWOKE AFTER A restful night to the smell of bacon. He shook his head, still groggy and tried to remember how he got into bed last night. Surely she hadn't carried him. He must have just been exhausted and didn't remember moving from the couch to the bedroom.

"Good morning, beautiful," he said before kissing her neck from behind.

"Sit. It's almost ready. You were so exhausted last night that I figured you'd need a good breakfast to get you started right today. I talked to Jess last night and she said that Jack took care of getting you guys out of work for a while?"

"Yea, he worked some sort of magic to accomplish that."

"Magic or not, I made sure to turn your alarm off after we went to bed."

"You're the best," he said as he sat down. "I'm sorry I passed out. I must have been beat."

"You were. You were adorable. You barely got here, kissed me, and were asleep in an instant. We barely even talked about how it went."

"Invigorating. That's the best I can say."

"I know I've said it before, but I'm so proud of you. Everyone else, too, but mostly you."

She kissed him on the nose and joined him at the small table where he was sitting.

"Are you excited to get back into the studio today?"

"I am," he replied. "It's crazy how quickly this has all happened."

The guys were sitting around the various chairs in the control room when Sal arrived later that morning. Paul and Greg liked the idea of doing one song at a time, so they could focus on that, while Sal and Derek wanted to run through all of their parts all at once.

They decided to let Jack make the call.

"Let's do one song at a time," he said. "Then Sal will do all the vocals at once at the end. Then we'll master each song one at a time and see what final pieces everything needs."

The thought of having everyone sitting in the booth listening while he recorded the vocals made Sal uneasy.

Derek and Paul were up first. The backbone of any band is its rhythm section and it made sense to lay down those tracks first. They played along to the rough takes from yesterday, which were now referred to as scratch tracks since they'd be thrown away once every individual part was done again.

Derek had rehearsed his parts more than anyone else. He got through most of the drum parts in a single take, except for "Something's Wrong", which had some overly complex parts that he'd written and took two takes. He was done before noon and made his way up to the control room, where Jack was waiting to fist bump him at the top of the stairs.

"Paul, you're up," Cee said.

The bass lines were solid, the sound was smooth, and Paul nailed everything. A single take for every track and he was done. It was almost two o'clock when they finished his tracks so they decided to break for lunch before diving into the guitars.

They ate quickly before Greg and Sal flipped a coin to see who'd go next.

"Rhythm is probably easier to do first," Cee said, "might as well get Sal's guitar tracks done. That way he can rest while Greg does his tracks before having to do the vocal tracks."

"Fair enough, you're the engineer," Sal said before heading towards the stairs.

At the end of some takes, Sal asked if he could punch in another track at a certain mark in the song, harmonizing guitar parts with himself and making them sound fuller even before Greg's parts were added.

It took almost three hours to complete all of the extra tracks and punch-ins Sal wanted to do and it was just after five o'clock by the time Greg took his place in his little recording booth.

"Let's just power through until I'm done," he said before heading downstairs, "I'd rather do it now and not wait."

"You're the boss," Sal said. "Whatever you want."

Greg blasted riff after riff of lead guitar beauty into the songs, hitting note after note of his solos, trying new sounds he'd never played before.

"Something sounds off," Sal said.

"What do you mean?" Cee asked.

"His guitar. The sound. Something's not right."

Greg hadn't changed the sound of his guitar rig in as far back as Sal could remember.

Once Greg finished his first take, Sal called down "Did you change something? It sounds different up here."

"Yeah," Greg said. "I tweaked a few settings. I think I found a sweeter sound than I'd been using."

By the time Greg finished with his guitar parts, it was almost ten that night. They'd managed to finish all of the music for all thirteen songs they planned on putting on their first record.

"I don't think I've ever worked with a band that did a whole album of tracks in less than a week. That's kind of unheard of," Cee said.

"Tomorrow we'll tackle the vocals, post-production and do some listening to produce this bad boy into a store-ready album," Jack said.

"I'm pretty stoked to hear the whole thing," Paul said. "It's going to be a weird feeling to hear ourselves."

"Weird, but awesome," Derek added.

"Nine again tomorrow," Jack said as Cee nodded.

For the second night in a row, they made sure to power down their gear and collect their phones and other personal items from their respective rooms before leaving for the night.

As they walked out together, just the four of them, Greg was smiling ear to ear.

"What's with the shit eatin' grin?" Sal asked.

"This is just surreal, right?" Greg said.

"Who knew we'd be here so quickly? I thought we'd have more time to prepare," Sal said.

"Jack's right, though," Paul said, "we need a demo. And it makes sense to just do the whole CD as a demo, since it's on someone else's dime."

Sal had gotten more and more weary of performing his vocal parts throughout the day. As each member of the band got through their parts, Sal wished that something would go wrong so he'd have more time to prepare. If he'd had just one more day, he could rehearse more, or rework a chorus here or there.

He knew that he was ready and that once he was in the vocal booth, it'd just happen. But the time leading up to it was causing

Sal to feel unsure of himself or the songs he'd soon be sharing with the world.

Derek gave Paul a ride home in the van and Greg bummed a ride from Sal on his way back to Samantha's. Another long and exhausting day had ended and all Sal wanted to do was see her, kiss her, and fall asleep in her lap again.

Chapter Thirty

"You're home," Sam said as Sal opened the door to her apartment. "Are you exhausted?"

"Not as bad as last night," he said, kissing her.

"Are you hungry?"

"Starving, did you order something?"

"No, but I made pasta. There's some in the fridge for you."

Sal sat at the small table near the kitchen and took his shoes off, placing them next to Sam's.

"Today went great," he said. "We got so much done. I still can't believe this is all real."

"What's left to do?" Sam asked.

"Vocals, some final touches, mastering, and I'm sure some other things."

"Are you excited?"

"I am. I'm glad to be here with you, don't get me wrong. My mind just won't stop processing what happened today. And I'm sorry. I feel like I haven't been around at all."

"Don't be sorry. I understand."

Sam put a bowl of leftover pasta in the microwave to heat for him and pulled out the other chair and sat down next to him.

"Was it awesome? Tell me all about it." she said.

"I kind of feel numb," Sal said. "Kind of like I don't know what I'm doing and I'm just spinning my wheels."

She saw a look of concern suddenly appear. In that instant, things seemed to have become serious. The color left his face and he didn't seem interested in eating, despite saying he was starving.

"What do you mean? What's wrong?" Sam asked, reaching out for his hand.

"I don't know," he put his fork down and rubbed his temples. "I just feel like I'm starting to question all of this. I know this is what I want to do, but is this all too fast? Are we going about this wrong?"

"Okay, let's calm down. Why don't you eat and then we'll sit and talk about this."

"Sure," he said, picking up his fork. "That's fine."

He suddenly wasn't hungry, but knew that Sam wouldn't let him get up without at least eating something. He forced down a few bites and tossed his napkin on the plate.

They walked from the kitchen over to the living room and sat next to one another on the couch, turned slightly inwards, facing each other.

"I just feel like everything's too good to be true," he said. "This Jack guy shows up and suddenly doors are opening, people are doing favors. It feels strange, doesn't it?"

"I think he just wants to help you. He recognizes how astounding you guys are."

"I know. I get that part. I do. I just, I don't know. I'm questioning what I'm doing. I feel lost, even though I know exactly where I'm going."

"Okay, let's step back a second. What is it that you're worried about?"

"I don't know. That's the problem. I should be happy. I should be doing backflips. Shouldn't I?"

"Are you not feeling that way?"

"I'm not. I feel conflicted." He stood and began pacing around the coffee table. "I feel like this shouldn't happen this way. You don't get this far after playing one good show. Was no one there all those years ago when I forgot all the lyrics? What if that happens again? What if I can't do this?"

"Sal, try to relax. You're going to give yourself a panic attack," she said, pulling him back to the couch.

"What if I'm not made out for this?"

"There is no what if, Sal. You were born to do this. You have such a gift and you don't even realize it."

He turned to her and buried his head into her neck, closing his eyes.

"Sometimes you have to just suck it up and do it. 'Because if you take a risk, you just might find what you're looking for.' That's a quote from one of my favorite authors," she said.

"I can't."

"Yes, you can."

"I'm scared, Sam. I'm scared that I'll fail."

"You won't fail, Sal. You're too good at this to fail."

"I can't."

"Sal, you have to just man up. You were the one who wanted this, weren't you?"

"I was. I am. Yes."

"Then just do it. Go in there tomorrow and blow them away. You know you have it in you, so stop questioning yourself."

She was right. He had to just buckle down and do it. There was no more time for self doubt.

Chapter Thirty-One

Samantha woke him up the following morning with a gentle kiss.

"Let's jump in the shower before you have to leave," she said. "I miss you."

"I know, I'm sorry I've been gone so much," he said. "I'll make it up to you, I promise."

He wanted to make sure to spend as much time with her as he could before heading back to the studio for another day of recording.

"Thank you for last night," he said. "I really needed someone to kick me in the ass."

"You're welcome. I'm glad to kick you in the ass any time you need it.

After his shower, he grabbed a drink for the road, kissed her goodbye and was on his way down the creaky stairs when Greg called.

"Pick me up on your way?" Greg asked.

"Sure thing, I was just about to head out. Be there in ten minutes," replied Sal.

When they arrived at the studio, Jack was already upstairs with Cee, Paul, and Derek.

"Ready to hit it?" Jack asked.

"Ready as I'm going to be," Sal said, tapping his trusty iPad, "I've got my lyrics right here. Just in case."

"If you've got them digitally, I can put them on the screen in the vocal booth if that's easier," Cee said.

Sal had always had his iPad with him, holding the lyrics to every song he would be singing. It was his crutch and one that he'd always had ever since he was booed off stage.

"Thanks, I'm good with the iPad though," Sal replied.

Sal made his way back downstairs to the vocal booth, a completely separate room from the guitar booth he'd been in the last two days. It was a smaller room, still with its Plexiglas windows and door, but instead of a guitar amplifier, he just had a microphone. The room had square pieces of foam glued to the walls to reduce on the echoing, and the areas void of foam were stark white. In front of him was a music stand where he placed his iPad and adjusted the height. An expensive looking microphone was mounted to a stand that Sal moved up to a comfortable height.

His iPad carefully positioned at eye level, he was ready to begin recording the vocals for what would either be the best experience of his life or the biggest mistake he'd made.

He took a moment to pump himself up, literally shaking out the nerves.

One last look at the photo of he and Sam and he was ready to go.

"Let's start with 'Polaroid'," he said. "That one's the easiest for me. Give me a few to warm up."

"You got it. Just let me know when you're ready," Cee's voice came over the talkback system.

This performance was different from any other he'd done before, but he still prepared the same way. He ran his scales — up and down and back again — over and over until he felt his voice was ready to go. Having no formal training, he had no idea if what he was doing actually worked, but he felt better having done it.

"I'm ready," he yelled up at the camera. "Hit it."

Almost immediately the music started playing through his headphones. It was the soothing sounds of one of their ballads. Remembering the lyrics to this particular song was a benefit for him. Not having to look at the iPad helped him focus on singing the song the way it was meant to be sung. There were a few hiccups between verses, nothing that couldn't be fixed with their recording technology.

Once he'd finished with 'Polaroid', Sal smiled. He realized that he wasn't nervous anymore halfway through the first line of the song. It was as if all of his worries disappeared as soon as he started singing.

Song after song, lyric after lyric, Sal pushed through the recording, only once asking for a break to rest his voice. Before they knew it, all of the primary vocal tracks were done and just the backing vocal tracks needed to be done. By lunchtime, they'd finished everything. Just over two and a half days in the studio and they'd recoded their entire first album.

Sal fidgeted during lunch, getting up and pacing around the room while eating his sandwich, "We made pretty good time getting everything done, is that worrying anyone else?"

"What do you mean?" Jack asked.

"I just feel like things usually take months in the studio, don't they?"

"Not always. It depends on the band, their level of preparedness. Usually it only takes months if you're writing the material in the studio, too. Recording the actual tracks can be pretty quick," Cee said. "Once we're done eating, we'll start listening, tweaking levels, changing arrangements, and whatnot."

"How did everything sound coming together with the vocals?" Sal asked.

"Wait and hear. I really enjoyed it," Cee said, "Jack wasn't lying. You can sing, that's for sure."

Sal fidgeted during lunch, sometimes getting up and pacing around the room while eating his sandwich.

They started dragging chairs closer to the computer screens in the control room as they finished eating.

Cee started playing back the tracks one at a time. "Mark The Day" started off the session.

"Holy shit!" Derek yelled. "That's us! We're a recorded band! Sal, that's you!"

At the first sound of his own voice, Sal immediately felt satisfied. His nerves had left while he was singing and now that he heard himself, he had very few doubts left in his mind.

"For a pre-production recording, that sounds amazing. You're a genius, Cee!" Sal said.

They played back the song a second time and each compared notes on what they thought needed to change about the track. It seemed complete for the most part, but Greg asked if he could have a little more reverb on the guitar during the solo. Cee punched a few buttons, looped the solo on playback, and kept tweaking the settings on the mixing board until Greg smiled. Some songs needed more than a guitar solo tweak. Sal specifically wanted to add an orchestra-feel to one track in particular, "You".

"I love the idea of an orchestra," Greg said. "Can we arrange something for 'Night Before Dawn' too?"

The mere mention of the track bought back knots to Sal's stomach. He'd finished the lyrics last week but still wasn't feeling perfect about it.

"I'm not sold on that one just yet. I know the music's perfect, but the lyrics don't speak to me yet," he said.

"What's wrong with it?" Jack asked.

"I don't know. I'm just not satisfied with how it turned out as a whole. Let's listen to it and I'll see how it feels to hear it played back."

Sal closed his eyes as Cee queued up the track, letting it all sink in.

"Cee, can you boost the vocals a bit so I can focus on them?" asked Sal.

They played it back four times, each time at a slightly louder volume until Sal sighed.

"It's just not right yet. I'm sorry, guys."

Greg grabbed Sal's arm and pulled him aside "Sal, come on man. It's as perfect as it's going to be."

Jack and Cee looked across the room, trying to figure out what they were talking about.

"It's not perfect yet. This was supposed to be the song that people heard and fell in love with us.

"What if we revisit that one at the end?" Greg asked.

"Postponing it for a few hours isn't going to help," Sal said, "I'd need tonight to think about it."

"Can we hold that one until tomorrow morning?" Greg asked.

"Yeah, we'll come back to that one. If it's not right, it's not right," Cee responded.

They chugged through the rest of the songs, punctuating various verses and choruses with some level tweaks and effects added here and there. Cee punched a few buttons to bring up an orchestra add-on. In a matter of minutes they had a pre-arranged orchestra playing in key, at the same tempo, and for the duration of the chorus for "You".

"That's it? It sounds like an eighty piece orchestra," Sal said.

"That's it. Technology is powerful and impressive," Cee said.

"And expensive," Derek joked from behind Cee.

By the time the night ended, they had twelve of the thirteen completely produced and mastered. Cee had done nothing short of a miracle.

The only song left was "Night Before Dawn." Sal agreed to spend some time working on it that night and would record the final vocals in the morning.

As they left the studio for the third day, Sal hugged each of the other guys in the band and gave Jack his trademark fist bump.

"This is a dream come true," Sal said. "I couldn't do this without you guys. Thanks for hanging in there while I'm being stubborn about the last track."

"If it's not good enough for you, it's not good enough for me," Paul said.

"Same here," Derek said. "You'll get it, don't worry."

He dropped Greg off at home, waving to Jess through the window and made his way back to Samantha's apartment. Feeling defeated and frustrated, he climbed the creaky stairs and unlocked the door. It wasn't until this moment that he'd realized that he had never given her the keys back.

"Hey," he said. "I'm back."

"Hey you," she said, coming across the living room to hug him.

"I know I'm back, but I have some work to do tonight, if that's okay."

"What's up? You look stressed."

"It's 'Night Before Dawn'," he said. "We listened to it complete today and it just didn't feel right."

"Okay, well let's eat something and then we'll clear your mind and let you focus."

"You're so wonderful." he said, "You really are."

He kissed her on the forehead, and made his way to the kitchen to look for some dinner.

Once they'd eaten, she cleared off the small table in her living room where she kept her laptop, turned on the small desk lamp and turned off the rest of the lights in the room.

"I'm going to take a bath," she said, "you'll have some peace to work. It's not an invitation, not yet at least. If you finish and I'm still in there, you can join me."

"I can't. It's just not there," he said.

"What's not there?"

"The song. It's not in me. I don't know why I've put such pressure on myself for this one song, but I have."

All he wanted to do now was sit and sob.

"Sal, you can't put this kind of pressure on yourself. This isn't helping."

"I know that," he said back, a bit louder than he'd wanted to. "I know."

"It'll come to you. Just do whatever you usually do and it'll come."

She reached out and pulled him into her, holding him tightly.

Before he realized it, he'd dozed off.

When he woke up, he realized he'd been crying. The collar of Sam's shirt was wet and his eyes were sore.

"I guess I fell asleep," he said, "I'm sorry."

"That's okay. You needed it. I won't tell anyone you cried."

"I cried?" he asked. "What time is it?"

"Almost ten, I'm going to fill the tub and let you get to work."

A bit embarrassed that he'd been crying while asleep, Sal stood up and shook himself off.

"Thanks for letting me be stupid," he said, yawning. "I don't usually like to talk about this stuff. I'm glad I can with you."

"You're welcome," she said, kissing him. "That's what I'm here for."

She kissed him, rubbed his shoulders and was gone.

Taking the seat at her desk, he took out the pad of paper that he'd been carrying around with him for the last few weeks. He read and re-read the lyrics for the song, but couldn't pinpoint where the problem was. Frustrated, he got up and paced around the living room. Before he left the studio, he had Cee put the mixed music to the song on his iPad so he could listen to it while working on the lyrics. He did laps around the table while listening to the music on repeat.

An hour later, Samantha returned to the living room to check on him. She looked at the pile of crumpled up paper in the corner of the room and sighed.

"It'll come to you," she said. "Just stop trying so hard."

"I'll clean that up," he said looking at the pile of rejected attempts in the corner and said.

"I'm not so worried about the trash," she said. "I want you to feel accomplished. What you've done this week is amazing, honey. Don't let this one song get you down."

She hugged him around his neck from behind, squeezing him.

"I'm going to read in bed. Come in when you're done," she said.

Around four am the next morning, Sal had an eureka moment. He shouted "Yes!" at the top of his lungs, quickly putting his hand over his mouth in hopes he wouldn't wake Sam. He followed her advice and just stopped trying. Right before it came to him, he shut off his iPad, closed his eyes and sat in silence for a few minutes.

As soon as he stopped focusing on the song, an image of Sam flashed into his mind and inspired him. As soon as he pictured her face, the new lyrics came to him.

Once he finished writing, he paced around the living room, as quietly as he could, earbuds in place, listening to the recorded track and reading the lyrics again and again. There was no way he'd go back to the studio in the morning not knowing the new lyrics to the song that had eluded him for months.

Once he was convinced that he had the new lyrics memorized, he spent a few minutes transcribing them from his hand written version into the iPad.

The few short hours that Sal slept that morning were restless. He was excited and once again invigorated to get back into the studio. When the alarm went off at seven-thirty, he almost jumped out of bed, heading straight to the shower without waking Samantha up.

"Thank you for being my inspiration," he whispered before leaving that morning, "I owe you."

He got to the studio a bit early, glad to find that Cee was already awake and there to let him in.

"I know the guys aren't here yet, but I was too excited. I got it," he said.

"Yea?" asked Cee.

"Yea."

"Okay, come on in, let's do this."

They fist bumped and Sal followed Cee back to the vocal booth before Cee headed upstairs.

"You change any of the arrangement?" Cee asked through the talkback system.

"Nope, just the lyrics," Sal said in between warmups. "Music stays the same, same for the arrangement. Just lyrics."

Moments later Sal nodded to the camera. The music immediately began playing through his headphones and he knew, in that moment, that he'd gotten it right this time. The story he was about to tell would be one that no one would forget. His moment to shine was now and he was ready for it.

"Can we run through the chorus one more time?" Sal asked into the talkback system.

Cee punched them back to the beginning of the chorus, and gave him a three second buffer before starting to record.

He'd nailed it that time. As he was making his way through the third vocal part for the chorus, he saw the door outside the booth close and watched the guys silently make their way up the narrow stairs.

When he finished, Sal placed the headphones down on the stool, grabbed his iPad, and went upstairs. Jack was waiting at the top of the stairs ready for his fist bump.

"I was listening in the whole time, I got here before you did," Jack said. "It's perfect, Sal. I'm glad you took the extra time."

"Thanks. It hit me really early this morning. Sometimes you've gotta just listen to your girlfriend and stop overthinking. Once I did that, it hit me. I could barely sleep! I wanted to just come right here and get it all out."

"Shit, let's hear it!" Derek said.

They all grabbed their seats as Cee queued up the track with the new vocals, "It needs some post-production, but it's pretty great," he said. "Here we go."

Sal closed his eyes, ready to hear his masterpiece for the first time. After almost a full day of listening to himself yesterday, he still couldn't get over how different he sounded. When the song finished for the first time, he opened his eyes, waiting to hear the feedback from the rest of his bandmates.

All that came was one word from Greg.

"Perfect."

Chapter Thirty-Two

On his way up the creaky stairs to Samantha's apartment that night, Sal stopped and decided to head back down to the convenience store to grab some flowers. As soon as the door shut behind him, he got a text message from her. *Was that you? I heard the door.*

Yep, be right up. Forgot something.

Mr. Juang greeted him with a smile. Sal made his way to the back of the store where there were often a few varieties of fresh flowers.

Sal took his time finding a colorful arrangement that he thought Samantha would like, picking through the various bouquets that Mr. Juang had available. An arrangement of daisies in the back of the pile caught his eye. After pulling it from the display and letting the water drip off, he headed up to the counter, paid, and was out the door before he knew it.

Bounding up the creaky stairs and unlocking the door, Sal was greeted with a hug and a smile.

"Daisies! My favorite! Thank you."

"You're welcome. I felt badly that I haven't been around lately and I wanted to start to make up for it."

"You don't have to make anything up to me. Really."

"I know, but I want to. You've been trapped in your apartment since I keep taking your keys and I feel badly about it. I was thinking we could do dinner in the city, and take a walk through the Public Garden?"

"That sounds lovely! How much time do I have to get ready?"

"As much as you need. I'm going to run back to my place and grab some new clothes. Meet you back here in an hour or so?"

"Okay," she said and kissed him. "See you then."

Sal took his time getting down the stairs and back to his car. Having to just do the one vocal track this morning meant they were done by noon. He had all night to spend with Samantha and was on cloud nine after how great this morning had gone.

He kept telling himself that he didn't really care if he ever went back to work and that Starbucks was behind him now.

He'd saved the last couple of paychecks he'd gotten and would be sure to bring his credit card with him tonight, in case dinner was more expensive than he anticipated.

He got back to his apartment to find his mailbox stuffed to the brim. Try as he might, he couldn't remember the last time he'd been back here — it had to have been at least two weeks. He grabbed the mail and made his way inside. It was definitely a while since he'd been here. The apartment had started to have that no one's been here musty smell to it and the floors creaked as he made his way from room to room. He opened the window in the living room to let some fresh air in and headed back to his bedroom to grab some clothes.

A quick shower reminded him how much he missed his tankless water heater. Once shaved, he was dressed and on his way back to Samantha's apartment to pick her up. On the way he made a few calls to a variety of places in the city. He managed to get a last minute reservation at Top of the Hub. She'd be so surprised, he knew it.

It was just after four o'clock by the time he got back to her apartment. He made the reservation for seven, which gave them plenty of time to get into the city and walk through the Public Gardens and down Newbury Street on their way to the Prudential building.

She was ready when he arrived. Sal had opted for a button-down shirt, something he didn't often wear. Samantha had put on a sun dress. She looked adorable and spun to show off the flowery pattern.

"Well hello there, beautiful," Sal said in his best old-timer voice. "You look amazing."

"Thank you, Sal."

"May I surprise you with dinner? I got us a reservation somewhere nice and I don't want to spoil it."

"A surprise? I love surprises!"

Sal opted to park under the Common so they could walk together. With almost two and a half hours to spare, they'd have plenty of time to walk and enjoy. As they came out of the stairwell, Sal took her hand and they headed to the Public Garden.

"You've never been here before?" he asked.

"Nope, never. The closet I've come was when we came to the Common before. I've heard how beautiful it is inside, though."

"We're here at a good time," he said. "The flowers should all be in bloom by now."

It was mid-May and the weather was warm enough that neither of them needed a jacket. The sky was bright and the air smelled clean. They walked together hand in hand over the patches of grass towards the Public Garden.

While waiting for the walk signal to change to cross Charles Street, she leaned in and kissed him on the cheek.

"What was that for?" he asked.

"I like going on dates with you. I know you're my boyfriend or whatever, but I still like going on dates. I don't want that romance to ever die."

"I'm glad. This one should be a good one."

They ran across to the gates to the Public Garden and made their way inside. Immediately surrounded by roses as far as the eye could see, adorning the walkways in all directions, she gasped.

"It's beautiful," she said.

"It gets better," he said and took her hand again, walking toward the center of the Garden.

Every few steps Samantha would stop and bend over to smell the flowers, snapping photos here and there with her phone.

"The Garden has been here since 1837," Sal read from a bronze plaque. "The swan boats have been here over a hundred years. You'll see those when we get to the pond. It's just right up the path."

"Wow, so much history," she said. "This is really beautiful. Thank you for bringing me here."

Another few steps and she stopped to smell some more flowers. She wanted to take everything in all at once. There were so many flowers to see and so many people there seeing them as well. The Garden was, as she'd find out, a tourist hotspot.

"This is my new favorite place," she said. "I want to live here. I can just set up a tent over there, right?"

"Of course. I'm sure the city would love if we moved in right over there, by the pond!"

"And we can have a little patio right by the water?"

"I wouldn't expect anything less, would you?"

Halfway through the Gardens they came to the bridge that crosses over the swan boat pond. Man-made and filled at the beginning of spring, the pond was the center piece of the Public Garden. Pedal-powered boats shaped like swans, dubbed the Swan Boats, were filled with tourists floating around the pond, careful not to hit any of the real birds. The swans shared the area with the thousands of humans that visited here daily.

They paused at the start of the bridge. Sal stopped one of the passers by and asked if he'd mind taking a photo of them with Sal's phone. He gave the man a quick tutorial, as if he'd never seen an iPhone before, and quickly walked to Sam's side.

He pulled her in close to him and she pressed her head against his neck, putting her arm around his waste. He smiled bigger than he'd ever smiled before.

Sal thanked the man and took back his camera. "Do you want to go on a Swan Boat?" he asked.

"Maybe after dinner? When the sun has set it'll be prettier."

"I like the way you think," he said. "Let's keep going, there's more to see."

Samantha spent an extra moment or two standing halfway over the bridge, marveling at the city buildings around her. She watched as a few of the swans ran up on shore towards the woman who was tossing bread at them and laughed as the woman had to run away.

Sal stood behind her with his arms on either side, resting on the railing in front of her. His head gently lay on her shoulder, looking out at the water below. He noticed a few small ducks following along behind their mother and pointed them out to Samantha.

"How cute!"

"Ducklings are adorable, aren't they? They're all fuzzy and warm."

"Just like you," she said grabbing his hands. "Just like you."

They proceeded along the center path towards the statue of George Washington on his horse near the far side of the Garden. After stopping just for a moment to take a photo, they quickly moved to the crosswalk that would get them across Arlington Street and onto Newbury.

"So today went well," she asked as they crossed.

"Today went swimmingly. I knew as soon as I started singing the new lyrics in that vocal booth that it was perfect. That it was exactly what I hadn't been able to get through before. And I loved that feeling. I couldn't have done it if it weren't for you."

"Sal, that's so sweet."

"It's true. You've been so great with this whole thing. I'm glad this dream didn't freak you out and scare you away."

"You could never scare me away! So, what's next for the album?"

"I guess next Cee finishes up whatever production work he needs to do, and then Jack takes it and makes copies. I don't really know how that works, but that's what we're paying Jack for."

"I can't wait to hear it," she said, "I'm so proud of you guys."

"Well there's nothing really to be proud of yet. We haven't really done anything with it."

"Yes you have," she scolded. "You took the first step. And the second step can't come without the first."

The walk signal turned and they made their way across Arlington Street, walking one block to the left towards Newbury.

"If you can't find something you love on Newbury, you're either shopping wrong or you just can't afford it. Like us." he said.

"Is it really expensive?" she asked.

"Yes, very very expensive. But it's still fun to window shop, isn't it?"

In and out of stores they went for the next hour as they made their way down Newbury towards the Prudential building. Many of the shops were one of a kind, not part of larger chains, which made the window shopping interesting. There were certainly a fair share of big name brand stores, but Sal noticed her skipping over those for the more mom-and-pop-type places.

"Are we heading in the right direction for dinner?"

"We are. It's not far."

Before they knew it, they'd made their way over the few blocks they needed to go, to the base of the Prudential building. Samantha looked up and asked if they could go inside. The promise of dozens of shops intrigued her and he played along as if he wasn't planning on going in anyway.

They walked around the Prudential for a while before Sal's phone chirped to let him know it was almost time for dinner.

"Is that the dinner bell?" Samantha asked.

"It is, let's head up."

"Up where?"

"Up there," he said, and pointed.

The elevator to the top of the Prudential was one of the fastest in the city. It took just shy of fifteen seconds to go up fifty-two floors with the sound of wind whipping through the elevator shaft at immense speeds. When the doors opened at the top, Samantha stepped out and headed towards the hostess stand.

They were greeted promptly and escorted to their table. The waiter came over immediately, offering bread and a sample of wine. Sal asked for a water, and Samantha ordered a Diet Coke.

"We're going to look at the view. We'll be back." Sal said.

He took Samantha's hand and lead her to the far side of the restaurant. Occupying the entire top floor, the restaurant had views in all directions. The panoramic view of the city was beautiful. The sun was starting to set over the horizon, casting shadows of all of the buildings.

"You can see Fenway park from here!"

"You can see everything from here," he said. "It's beautiful, right?"

As they reached the last wall of windows, Samantha kissed him long and hard.

"This is breathtaking. Thank you. Really, thank you," she said.

"You're welcome. It's the least I can do to begin paying you back for all you've done for me. Let's hope the food is as good as the view," he said.

"Oh, it is," a man sitting at a table nearby said, overhearing their conversation. "It's fantastic."

"It's too expensive," she said in a hushed voice, "can we afford this?"

"Don't worry about it, it's my treat," he said.

"Are you sure?"

"I'm sure. I saved my last few paychecks and have my credit card, just in case. Let's not worry about the money, okay? Just enjoy yourself."

Sal wasn't sure though. He didn't know when he'd get any form of a paycheck again, and despite telling her not to worry about the money, he was very worried himself.

They talked through dinner and ordered a plate of fresh baked cookies for dessert.

As the waiter brought their cookies, Samantha said "Can I ask something?"

"Of course. What's on your mind?"

"Well, it's kind of stupid, but —"

"It's not stupid, tell me. What's up?" He caressed the back of her hand.

"Okay. I know this is new to us, and we've only been dating for a few months, but where are we heading? Is marriage in your future? Do you even want to get married someday? Not like tomorrow or anything, but someday."

"That's not stupid at all, honey. Of course I want to get married. And I honestly can't picture myself marrying anyone but you. You're right, this is new, but it's also amazing and perfect. I've known since the moment I met you that there was something special about you. Something different."

"Really?"

"Really. There was just this immediate and instant connection between us. I know you felt it too."

"I did. You're right. The moment you smiled at me, I thought 'I'm going to have his babies'," she said turning a bit red. "You're perfect."

The thought of spending the rest of his life with her made Sal smile.

"What about kids? I obviously want kids," she said. "Do you?"

"I'm Italian. Of course I want kids. I'd like a couple, maybe a few. But it doesn't matter what they are."

"I know! I hate that. I hate when people say 'I want one of each'. Blah. Be happy with what you get, some people can't or never have kids. I'll love any child the same no matter what."

"Me too. It's an honor to be able to have children and some people take that for granted."

They playfully fought over the last cookie before deciding to split it. Sal grabbed for it first and was met with puppy dog eyes from across the table. As much as he wanted to eat it, he wanted Sam to be happy more. They eventually agreed to split it.

The waiter had dropped the check on the table without Sal even noticing. Thankfully it wasn't as bad as he thought and he dropped his debit card into the slot, standing the black binder up so the waiter could see his card. As Sal took his last bite of his half of the cookie, the waiter whisked away the binder to run the card.

When the waiter returned with the signature slip, Sal and Samantha were staring into each other's eyes.

"You guys are adorable, I'm sorry, I don't mean to be rude, but you are," the waiter said.

Smiling, Sal made sure to tip the waiter well. He realized that the waiter likely waited until the end of the meal to give them this compliment as it'd add to his tip, but he didn't care. They were adorable and he enjoyed hearing an outsider say it.

They walked down Comm Ave on their way back to the car and were back at the Public Garden before long, passing the George Washington statue and crossing the bridge over the Swan Pond. It was nearly nine o'clock now, and the Swan Boats had all been docked for the night. From their vantage point they could see the shiny padlocks reflecting the stars that now filled the night sky.

"Tonight was amazing. Thank you for dinner and the walk through this breathtaking garden," said Samantha.

"You're welcome. I'm glad you enjoyed it."

"I enjoy anything we do together," she said. "I'm happy just being with you."

"I am too. You know, since I met you, so many positive things have happened. My life has changed so much and doors have started opening for me that I never thought would open. I'm in my thirties now and I finally recorded some music, something I've never had the motivation to do before. And it's because of you. You've inspired me."

"Sal, that's so sweet."

She smiled. Leaning against the railing, he held her close and kissed her.

"There's something important I want to tell you," he said. "Something that means a lot and that I don't take lightly."

"What's that?"

"I love you."

"Sal," she said as her eyes filled with tears, "I love you, too."

Chapter Thirty-Three

Though Jack had gotten him out of work for Friday, Sal didn't have to go back to the studio. They were still waiting for Cee to finish up his post-production work and the mastering of the album, so he spent the day hanging out at Samantha's apartment while she worked.

Before they knew it, it was time to head over to Greg and Jess' for dinner. Both of them were still smiling from the night before and they were excited to go see the rest of the gang.

"Don't let me forget that book that Jess wanted to borrow when we leave. I'm going to change. I'll be quick, I promise," she said while heading towards the bedroom.

"It's right by my keys, I won't forget it."

She was gone just a few minutes. Sal could hear her in the bedroom opening and closing the closet door and she was back before he knew it, looking as beautiful as she always did.

"I'm so lucky," he said to himself. "So so lucky."

They were on their way over to Greg and Jess' when Sal's cell phone rang. It was Greg.

"We're not late," Sal answered. "We'll be there in ten minutes."

"Not that," Greg said. "Put on WAAF. Jack got 'Night Before Dawn' into the Hometown Throwdown."

"What? Is it on right now?"

"We're up next. The DJ just said it."

The Hometown Throwdown was a Friday night feature on WAAF, the local rock station. They pitted two bands from the Boston area against each other and let people vote on who should move onto next week. You could vote by calling, tweeting, or posting to Facebook. The winner was announced at the end of the show.

Sal couldn't process what Greg had just told him. Their song was about to be on the radio for the first time. He reached over and grabbed Samantha's hand and squeezed it. She squeezed back.

"We'll listen to it in the car and then come up," he said to Greg, "we're almost there. Don't let Jess lock us out!"

Sal hung up and parked in front of Greg's apartment, waiting for the song that was playing to end. And there it was. He recognized the first few notes immediately and couldn't help but smile. His eyes filled as the first verse started.

"What's wrong? Why are you tearing up? Isn't this what you wanted?" Samantha asked.

"This is just so huge for our careers," he said. "We've never been on the radio before. It's so humbling."

He grabbed his phone from his pocket and sent a text to Jack: *You fucking rock.*

Next he posted to Facebook and sent out a Tweet: *Vote for us on Hometown Throwdown! #WAAF #SoSayTheKing*

Sal kept smiling as the song finished. This week was going his way and he didn't see it stopping any time soon. Sal and Samantha got out of the car and headed inside. His phone didn't stop vibrating the entire way. He knew it was emails about Facebook comments or people responding on Twitter. They could wait until later; it was time to celebrate with his bandmates right now.

When they got inside, Greg was waiting with Paul and Derek. As soon as he opened the door, Greg threw his arms around Sal.

"We did it!" he yelled.

"Yea we did!" Sal responded.

Greg hugged Samantha and the three of them moved into the living room where Paul and Derek were seated. Sal hugged each of them as well.

Greg had turned the radio in the living room on so they could listen in to the rest of the show.

"I hope we win," Paul said. "That'd be awesome."

"Of course we're going to win. Did you hear that other song?" Derek said.

Sitting together, they listened as caller after caller voted for their song. Greg grabbed his iPad from the coffee table and opened the band's email.

"Who tweeted?" he asked.

"I did it from the car," Sal replied.

"We've got over a hundred retweets and best guess on Facebook comments is over 50," Greg said.

"Wow, what?!" Derek said.

"That's awesome," Paul added.

"And we're up over 500 Twitter followers," Greg commented. "That's fifty percent more than we had an hour ago."

"Five hundred?" Sal said, excited.

"Are we getting more Facebook fans, too?" Paul asked.

"Let me check," Greg said, tapping in a frenzy. "Yeah! Yeah, we're up a few hundred fans, too! We're getting a bunch of people writing on our wall about the song and asking when the album will be out. Paul you've gotta update the website when you get home."

"I'm on it," Paul said. "Let's hope we win and we have more awesome news to post!"

Jess called them all over to the dining room table, but said that they could leave the radio on and listen at a low volume.

As they ate, they continued to listen to vote after vote for their song, only occasionally hearing a vote for the other band. Paul felt slightly bad for them, but not bad enough to call and vote for their song.

"I can hear all of your phones buzzing at once," Samantha said. "More Twitter followers or Facebook fans, I'm guessing."

"I'm sorry," Sal said reaching into his pocket, "I'll turn mine off."

"Boys, please do the same," Jess said motioning to Paul and Derek. "Greg, you can keep the iPad on to monitor things. But please don't be glued to it while we're eating."

"You're the best," he said while checking the mailbox. "Thanks honey."

Dinner was over in the blink of an eye and the guys were back in the living room. Samantha offered to help Jess with the dishes so the guys could listen to the results of the competition in the living room.

"To say it was a blowout," the DJ said, "would be an understatement. With eighty-eight percent of the votes, our winners this week are So Say The King with 'Night Before Dawn', which I'm told will be available on iTunes as a single before the week is out. Their full length record was just finished by my buddy Cee and should be available in a couple of weeks."

"We won! Holy shit we won!" Derek exclaimed.

"This is amazing. This is amazing, I can't believe it!" Greg said.

Sal jumped up and hugged each of the other guys, "I can't believe this," he said. "I can't believe we were just on the radio."

Sitting around the living room drinking champagne, they all felt like rockstars. It was just a small victory, but to them it felt like they'd just won a Grammy. They were on their way.

Chapter Thirty-Four

STILL REELING FROM THEIR victory on Hometown Throwdown, Sal felt like he couldn't lose.

He'd been fumbling with the idea for the last week or so and finally decided to just blurt it out.

"We should move in together, shouldn't we?" he asked on the ride back to Samantha's.

"You mean like right now?" Samantha responded.

"Yea, I mean, why not? I basically live at your place anyway, right? Why pay rent on two places?"

"It makes sense. Do you think we're ready for that?"

"I know I am. I don't want to rush you, though. If you're not ready, say so."

"I'm ready. I love you and I know that this is right. That we're right."

They arrived back at Samantha's apartment and went up the stairs one after another.

"I'm not sure if I'll miss these creaky stairs," she said. "We'd move somewhere new, right?"

"I think that makes sense. Start fresh with a new place that's our's. We can afford something bigger with both of us chipping in, so why not pick somewhere new?"

"Speaking of affording things, what's going on with Starbucks?"

"Well, I saved my last few paychecks."

"Right, but work? What about going back?"

"I don't know. I don't want to go back, but I know I probably should."

"No you don't. You're above that job, honey. You always were and always will be above working there."

"I can't rely on you to pay the bills while the next big thing happens or when we play our next show. I'll have to get another job somewhere else."

"You're not going to have to rely on me," she said. "Pretty soon you're going to start making royalties off the album."

"But what if it doesn't sell? What if we're poor?"

"Then I'll love you just the same and we'll figure something out. You'll still be playing shows, even if the album doesn't sell. You'll make some money from that."

"Loving me is fine, but what if money gets tight?"

"Then you'll get a job. I want to be supportive, but we have to be realistic. If the record doesn't sell or something doesn't work out, you get a job."

"I'm fine with that. I'm fine with looking for a job right now, if that'd make you feel more comfortable."

"It would, but let's wait a bit and see how this pans out."

"You're sure?"

"I'm sure," she said.

They'd made their way to the couch, turning on just a handful of lights. Samantha grabbed her laptop on the way by her desk and opened it up.

"Where do we want to live?" she asked as she went to Rent.com.

"I don't care, as long as it's with you."

Clicking around looking at various properties and comparing what they thought they could afford to what they'd get for their money, they found a few complexes that they agreed looked nice.

"I think we should move to an apartment complex instead of renting from a landlord like we are now," Sal said.

"I agree. Being in a complex makes sense," she agreed.

Together they could afford a little more money, which would get them something nicer. They'd also decided on a two-bedroom, so that Sal could have his privacy to write when he wanted to.

"This one looks nice," Samantha said, "and it's in our budget, too."

"And it's not far from here. Bookmark that, we can go look at it tomorrow morning."

They clicked through a half dozen more that they liked before calling it a night.

It wasn't until he lay down in bed that Sal realized how exhausted he was, both mentally and physically. It had been a long week and he was glad it was coming to a close.

"I love you," he said, kissing her shoulder before falling asleep. "Thanks for always supporting me."

"I love you," she said.

Sal spooned her, making sure to hold her extra tight tonight. Things were changing so rapidly for them, but he knew that he was making all the right decisions.

She lay in bed that night, listening to him sleep, and thinking. She wondered what would happen if things didn't pan out with Sal following his dream. She didn't make enough money to support both of them forever. What if she had to tell him to go back to some job he hated? Would that put a strain on their relationship? How would he take it?

She thought through the worst scenarios for hours before finally falling asleep.

Sal and Samantha woke up and dressed quickly the next morning, making sure to get on the road before the first complex opened so they would be the first to request a tour for the day. Sal stopped at the Dunkin' Donuts drive-through and ordered breakfast, which they ate on the way.

The first complex was grand, almost intimidating to them, but beautiful. The leasing agent was friendly but a bit pushy and insisted that they fill out an application immediately "as the units are filling up fast", a strategy that convinced them not to apply at all.

When they arrived at the last place on their list, just down the street from where Samantha was living now, they knew immediately that they were home. Greeted with the smell of fresh baked cookies and a friendly leasing agent, it felt inviting.

The large leasing office had high ceilings and warm natural tones. At the far end was a self service coffee area and some bottled water.

After greeting them, the leasing agent showed them the two available two bedroom apartments they had. One on the fourth floor, the other on the fifth right above it.

"The fifth floor is our top floor, so you wouldn't have any noise above you," she said. "The only downside being that there's a longer walk to the mailbox."

"Can we have a moment?" Sal asked as they looked around.

"Of course," the agent said. "I'll be out in the hall."

"What do you think," he asked Samantha once the agent had left them. "Do you like it?"

"The kitchen is gorgeous," she said, running her fingers over the marble countertops. "And it's brand new."

"I like that, too. I know they clean apartments between tenants, but this one has never been lived in."

Sam worried that they wouldn't be able to afford the rent. While beautiful, this apartment was just as expensive as their two separate apartments. And now that Sal wasn't working, she panicked that she'd not be able to cover all of the rent and other bills once he ran out of money.

"We'll need to buy some things to fill it up. I think this place is bigger than both of our apartments combined," she said, worried that she'd have to pay for those things.

"I think we can arrange that," he said. "I guess we should tell her we want it, right?"

They met the agent back in the hallway and followed her outside to view the pool and hot tub. She showed them the on-site gym and movie theater that they could use for free as part of their lease and ended up back at her office.

"What do you think?" she asked.

"We love it. Let's do it," Sal said.

"Great!" the agent said. "Let's start with an application. We charge $100 for the application plus fifty for the background check. I can take a debit or credit card, I doubt you brought a checkbook."

"Actually I did," Samantha said. "I figured some places may need a check."

"Perfect, go ahead and fill these out and I'll be right back."

They ran through the paperwork, making note of emergency contacts, previous addresses, and employers. When it came to his employer, Sal didn't write Starbucks. He proudly wrote "Musician - Self Employed" in the space provided. After their talk last night, he decided he wasn't going to go back to Starbucks. As much as he'd miss some of the co-workers, Samantha was right; his life was beyond that job now.

"When were you thinking of moving in?" the agent asked as she came back.

"It's empty now, we could move in as soon as it's ready."

"Normally we have to wait a week for the background check to come back, but they've been turning that around quicker these days. It'll probably take a day or two. I'll just call your existing landlord to verify everything ahead of time, is that okay?"

"We don't live together now," Samantha said, "we're moving in together for the first time."

"That's fine, dear, that just means I have to make two calls instead of one."

The leasing agent excused herself with their applications to fax them for the background check.

Sam had a moment of sheer panic. She tried to take a step back and think about what they were doing. She knew that he loved her as much as she loved him, despite the brevity of their relationship, but she still wondered, in that moment, if what they were doing made sense.

"Are you okay?" he asked.

"Yes, I'm fine. Why?"

"You just had a look. Does this scare you?"

"Honestly, yes. A little. Are you scared?"

"I am. This is a big step for us. I know it's the right one, though."

"You do? How?"

"Because there's only one of you. And I just know that you're the right decision."

She smiled, feeling slightly comforted by his sweet sentiments.

"I don't really have a lease," Sal said. "I hope that's not a problem."

"My lease is month to month, so I can really move at any time," Samantha said. "I'm sure it won't be an issue."

"Good news," the agent said when she returned to her desk. "Both of your landlords love you and say you always pay on time. That's a great sign. In a day or two, we'll hear back from the background check."

"Great," Sal said. "What does that mean?"

"Well, assuming your background checks don't come back saying you're mass murderers," she smiled. "You can move in as soon as soon as the check comes back. If you were to pay your first month's pro-rated rent on that day, I'll give you the keys and you officially live here."

"That's it?" Samantha asked.

"Sure is."

Samantha blushed, turning to Sal, "We could move in next weekend."

"We could. I bet the guys would help no problem."

"Okay, let's do it," she said. "How much would the prorated first month be?"

The agent did some calculations and wrote down everything they'd need, assuming the background checks would come back clean.

"It's a standard lease, no punching holes in walls, take out your trash. That sort of usual stuff, no surprises. I'll give you a copy so you can read it ahead of time and I'll call you when I hear back."

"Great! Let's just do a quick walk through of the apartment to make sure that any issues are noted, so when you eventually move out, you don't get hit for any damages."

"Is there a security deposit?" Sal asked.

"Nope, we don't ask for one, we just bill you for any damages when you move out. We're flexible with that, too. We know we're going to have to replace the carpet, so we don't charge you for that."

"That's unusual, isn't it? Not taking a security deposit?" Samantha asked.

"It is, but that's our corporate policy. Why should we get to hold onto your money in the event that you break something? It seems unfair to me."

After the walkthrough was done, they thanked the agent for her time and headed out.

On the ride back to her apartment, they stopped at UHaul to see if they could get a truck for next weekend on such short notice and to buy some boxes. Being the middle of the month, the employee told them that they could more or less have any sized truck they needed and that he could give them a deal.

Yet again, everything seemed to be going Sal's way.

Chapter Thirty-Five

It didn't take long for everyone to help them unload all of the boxes and furniture into the living room of Sal and Samantha's new apartment. The giant piles of boxes looked tiny in the new place. Their lives had filled their previous apartments to the brim, yet had barely taken up one room in their new place.

"I measured," said Sal. "This is literally twice the size of both our old apartments combined. And it's less than what we were paying separately."

"Good job us," Sam said with a high-five. "There's so much to do, though."

"Let's start with the bedroom. It's already mid-afternoon and we need somewhere to sleep tonight."

"This pile over here is bedroom stuff," she said. "Let's get moving."

The bed was already in place in the spot where they wanted it. Jack and Derek being bigger guys, had helped manhandle it into place with just enough room on either side to fit their mismatched nightstands. They'd opted to keep Samantha's bed as it was bigger and newer. Sal's previous landlord had agreed to buy his bed from him since he didn't need it anymore. It wasn't a lot of money, but enough to make it worth leaving behind.

They carried box after box down the hall, past the bathroom and into the bedroom. Samantha unpacked clothes, hanging them in the respective closet.

Once all the boxes for the bedroom were unpacked and broken down, Sal laid down on the bed, looking out the window overlooking the wooded area outside.

"It's so quiet," he said. "Peaceful."

Samantha lay down next to him, "And ours. This is our place, together."

She kissed him and pulled away, looking into his eyes.

"What is it?" he asked.

"Nothing. I just like to look at you sometimes. Your eyes are the windows to your soul, as they say."

"And what do my eyes say?"

"They tell me that you're not as tough as you think you are. You're not mister big-rock-star that you come across as sometimes."

"I come across that way?"

"You do, sometimes. But I know better."

"Do you?"

"I see you for what you are."

"And what am I?"

"You're Sal. You're deep and thoughtful and have so many stories to tell the world."

After they lay in bed together for a while, Sal suggested they get back to work.

"The kitchen should be next. We need to eat," he said. "Well, I need to eat. I'm starving."

"Why don't we see what's around here for delivery. I'm sure most of the places we used to order will come here, too, don't you think?"

Sal took out his iPad and did a few quick searches before finding that there was a Papa Gino's not far. They agreed that pizza would be fine, and put in an order, making sure to put in the new address and not either of their old addresses.

"We have our own address," Samantha said, "we live here."

"This is our home. This is where we'll get junk mail with our names on it and get to take turns shredding it. This is where we get to be together."

"This is where I get to love you," she said, kissing him.

She looked around, smiling at their view off of the small deck they had just outside the large sliding glass doors. The wooded area outside was beautiful and helped cut off the noise from the nearby roadways.

They continued unpacking dishes, plates, glasses and silverware until the pizza arrived. Sitting on the floor cross legged, they ate dinner in their new apartment together for the first time.

The next morning, Sal woke up in his new apartment, next to the woman he was sure he'd love for the rest of his life.

Knowing that the pieces of the puzzle were falling into placed made him feel secure and worry-free. He'd hardly worried about what would happen in the next weeks and months. Any time that he felt uneasy or concerned about life, he thought of her. Having a constant vision of her in his mind helped ease any troubles that came his way.

His phone was ringing on the nightstand. He grabbed it before it woke Samantha up and made his way out to the living room before answering.

It was Greg, conferencing him in with Jack, Derek, and Paul.

"Okay, we're all here, go ahead," Greg said. "What's up, Jack?"

"Glad I got you guys. Sorry it's so early. I wanted to tell you that Cee finished mastering the record over the weekend and it's completely done."

"That's great!" Greg said. "When can we hear it?"

"Today. Actually, when the stores open, you can go to any Newbury Comics and buy a copy. As a surprise to you guys, I had my graphic designer buddy work up all the artwork while we were in the studio last week. It's basic, but it's just a first self-released album. Once a label picks you guys up, they'll likely release it again with a full package attached to it. Once we had the artwork finalized, I sent it over to my friends at Discmakers with a rush order of five thousand."

"Five thousand? We can't afford that." Greg said.

"I know you can't, but I can. And it's my gift to you guys. The first five thousand are on me, and are already scattered across every Newbury Comics in New England. Their distribution manager is not only a friend of mine, but he heard you on Throwdown Friday night and actually called me Saturday morning asking to get some copies of the disc."

"That's bitchin'." Derek said.

"What does that mean? How does it work?" Sal asked.

"Well, they pay wholesale. So they'll sell the disc for $9.99, so I sell it to them for half that. So five thousand records at five bucks each. Who wants to do the math?"

"That's twenty-five grand," Sal said, "we made twenty five grand?"

"Well, you made twenty-two five. I took my cut off the top, of course," Jack said.

Sal couldn't believe it. In the span of a week they'd gone from hiring a manager to recording a full album to having it in stores. This was like a dream come true and he couldn't wait to tell Samantha. He suddenly felt less guilty about moving into a new apartment and hoping Sam would foot the bills for a while.

"They open at eleven," Jack said. "I'm hitting the one in the city for my copy."

"Thanks, Jack. This is great and super nice of you to front the first five thousand copies," Sal said.

"You guys deserve it. It may seem like I'm just being nice, but the reality is that it's a strategic business move. No one's going to sign you without having sold some records. So let's get out there on Twitter and Facebook and tell all of your friends to get out there and buy the record, okay? I've already got Cee submitting the tracks to iTunes. It usually takes 24 hours for them to show up in the store for a new band."

"You got it!" Greg said.

When they all got off the conference call, Sal creeped back into bed, kissing Samantha awake.

"Good morning," she said. "What time is it?"

"It's just after 9. Feel like getting up and taking a ride?"

"To where?" she asked. "It's early."

"I have to stop at Starbucks and tell them I'm not coming back. In case they didn't figure it out on their own."

"Do you need me to go with you for that?" she asked, rubbing her eyes.

"No, but then we're going to Newbury Comics. I'd like you to be there when I buy the first copy of our CD."

"Wait, what?" She asked, rolling over.

"Jack just called. He had five thousand copies of the album printed and got them onto shelves at Newbury Comics. They open in two hours."

"Sal, that's amazing. Really amazing. Can I sleep for five more minutes though?"

"Of course you can. I'll wake you up in fifteen minutes, okay?"

She nodded back off he grabbed his iPad from the nightstand, opening the Twitter app. *Newbury Comics has our album available at open today. Tracks coming to iTunes later this week. RT*

He posted the same status to Facebook and immediately the Likes and comments started flooding in.

He made sure to follow up saying that there were only 5,000 copies available from the first run.

Sal and Samantha met Greg outside before the Burlington Newbury Comics opened, looking in through the window like children at a toy store at Christmas, trying to find their album on the shelves.

Right at eleven, a girl with pink hair and a neck tattoo of Hello Kitty came over and unlocked the door. The three rushed inside and found the album right up front, then under the S section of Rock, and then in the New & Notable section. There it was, in all its glory and validation of all their hard work — their album, in print, waiting to be bought, a shiny "Hometown Throwdown Winner" sticker right on the front.

The artwork, as Jack said, was basic, but it did the job. The back of the CD listed all of the tracks, their runtimes, and the band's contact information — Twitter, Facebook, and Email, as well as Jack's contact information for booking purposes.

"I've got to get one for my parents and for Cassie," Sal said. "They'd be mad if I didn't."

"I just need one copy," Greg said.

"I want one too," Samantha said.

With five copies in hand, they made their way up to the register. The pink haired girl was there, evidently the only employee working this morning.

"Oh, dope," she said, "I didn't know these guys released a CD."

"Today, actually," Greg said. "These are probably the first copies."

"How'd you know?" she said, popping her gum.

"It's our band," Sal said. "Our manager told us it was going on sale today, so we came right over. Is that weird?"

"Nah," she said, "it's cool. Congrats on the win on Hometown. I heard the song on Friday. You got my vote."

"Thanks!" Sal said.

She rang them up and Greg paid for all five copies.

"You don't have a job," he said when Sal tried to give him money, "I do."

"Oh, you heard?"

"Yeah, your girl tells my girl everything," he said, poking at Samantha. "They're almost the same person."

As they left the store, Greg and Sal hugged each other.

"This is the beginning, my friend," Greg said.

"I hope so," Sal said. "As you so astutely pointed out, I don't have a job anymore."

From the parking lot, Sal tweeted a photo of the album with the caption *Get it before it's gone! #SoSayTheKing*, making sure to send the same photo to Facebook.

"Can you text Cassie to let her know? Ask her to let my parents know too, please," Sal asked Sam on the ride home.

"Of course. Anyone else you want me to notify?"

"No, I think just Cassie. She'll probably tell everyone else on earth, knowing her."

When they arrived home, Samantha insisted on listening to the whole album. They still hadn't setup the TV or stereo yet, so they played it through Sal's iMac speakers. While it wasn't the greatest sound, he loved every second of it.

"It could have been recorded in a tin can," he said. "That's me. That's us. That's amazing!"

He smiled ear to ear the rest of the day, constantly checking Twitter and Facebook for updates, followers, Likes, and comments. The support was pouring in from all over. Just before dinner he got a text message from Jack, addressed to the entire band: *2100 copies* *sold today, my buddy reports. Others expected to sell by end of week. We should talk about ordering more. \m/*

Sal told Samantha the good news over dinner and they celebrated by laying on the couch all night, listening to the CD on repeat from the newly set up stereo. He knew they'd get sick of listening to it eventually, but for tonight he just wanted to bask in the glory of what he'd created. He was proud of himself, but more importantly, she was proud of him. And that meant more to him than anything else in his life.

"I still can't believe this is me. This is my band, on a recorded CD, playing through a stereo." Sal said.

"I can't even imagine how great that must feel."

"I'm usually good with words, but I'm just a blubbering idiot right now. I can't express how excellent this feels. I don't even care if nobody were to ever buy a copy."

"Speaking of, my mom wants a copy. She says she wants an autograph from my 'rockstar boyfriend'."

"Shut up," Sal laughed. "She did not call me that."

"She did too! I told her I'd try to not let it go to your head."

The track finished and the next one started.

"Is it somewhat egomaniacal to want to listen to this over and over again?"

"A little bit, but that's fine. I can't say I'd react any differently."

"Is it wrong that I'm listening for faults?"

"No. Are you focusing on yourself or on the others?"

"Myself. Let's face it, if anyone's likely to screw up, it'd be me. Wouldn't it?"

"Sal, come on. That happened one time, years ago."

"It could happen again, couldn't it?"

"It could, but it won't. You're rehearsing a lot. You're focusing on what you need to focus on. You're ready for whatever comes next."

"I know. I just have to keep telling myself that. I'm ready. I'm ready. I'm ready."

"I know. I just have to keep telling myself that. I'm ready. I'm ready. I'm ready."

Chapter Thirty-Six

IN THE TWO WEEKS following the CD release, Jack came through in some major ways. Not only had they gone through two more runs of discs, this time ten thousand each, but their album was selling worldwide on iTunes at an astonishing rate. Tickets went on sale for a series of shows in New England, and the venues were selling out over the course of a day or two. Twitter followers skyrocketed to over twenty thousand and Facebook Likes were just about to cross that mark. Jack insisted that it was time to play shows to more than a few hundred people. He'd managed to get them onto a number of tours as an opening act.

"Often times," he explained, "bigger bands will go out on their own and just find local opening acts, instead of paying some other big band to tour with them. I got you to open a dozen dates for various bands over the next month."

"A dozen?" Greg asked.

"How many seats?" Derek said.

"From five to twenty thousand," Jack said. "Big time."

"We're going to need more CDs and some merch made up," Sal said.

It was Friday morning and they had all met Jack at their rehearsal space to discuss some band business. Now that they were selling out of CDs with every run and iTunes was making them a lot of money, they wanted to get together and plan the next steps.

"We'll start tomorrow night in Manchester," Jack said.

"Who are we opening for?" Paul asked.

"The band is called Quantum. Heard of them?"

"Yeah, I heard them on the radio the other day," Derek said. "They're pretty good."

"How much will it pay?" Greg asked, ever the businessman.

"We get fifteen percent of ticket sales and all merch that we sell would be ours as well," Jack said.

"Fifteen percent doesn't sound like a lot to me," Greg said. "Is that average?"

"An opening act usually gets around ten. I got you fifteen because I know the promoter personally. It may seem low, but keep in mind that tickets are fifty bucks each. Times thousands."

"That's tens of thousands of dollars," Derek said.

"And there's no doubt that a lot of people will pick up the CD and a t-shirt on the way out," Jack said.

"Can we get t-shirts that fast?" Sal asked.

"They're in my truck already. You guys still doubt me? That's cute. We'll get past that," Jack winked.

After pausing for a short while to take it all in, Sal stood up and paced around the room.

"What's wrong?" Greg asked.

"Nothing, that's the thing. It all seems too good to be true. A month ago we played a show for a couple hundred people, and now we're blowing up and playing to thousands. It's just surreal."

"It's fucking great is what it is," Derek said.

"Don't let the success go to your head," Jack said. "There's still a long way to go."

"Yeah, Derek, don't let it go to your head. But seriously guys, is this bubble going to pop?" Sal asked.

"It could," Jack said. "That's the nature of this business. One day you're up, the next you're down. Why do you think there's such a thing as one hit wonders?"

"We won't be that," Sal said.

"You may be," Jack said. "Let's be real. It could happen."

Before leaving for dinner at Greg and Jess', the band broke down their gear and agreed to meet back there in the morning to load up the van and head to the venue in New Hampshire.

Saturday morning Sal arrived at the rehearsal complex and began moving the gear down to the lobby in front of the garage door. On his third trip, Greg met him downstairs and they walked back up together.

"I'm glad we signed Jack," Sal said. "We wouldn't be here if it weren't for him."

"I was talking about that last night with Jess after you guys left. It's like the guy's a miracle worker or something."

Derek and Paul showed up with the van and started loading the gear in from the lobby, while Greg and Sal continued making trips back and forth to their room, bringing more gear down.

They packed the bare minimum — amps, guitars, bass, drums and cymbals. Jack had told them that the venue provided the sound gear and all the microphones, so they opted to not bring any of their lower-end gear with them.

As a show of unity, they all rode from the city to Manchester together. It took a little over an hour and a half. They arrived at the venue just before ten that morning. They'd have plenty of time to get set up, do a soundcheck, and relax backstage to work out the nerves.

"This is our first huge show," Paul said. "Who else is nervous?"

"I think I can speak for us all when I say I'm shitting my pants over here," Sal said as he unloaded gear onto the loading dock.

The tour manager, Michael, came out to meet them. He looked more like a business man than a tour manager. His hair was short and dark, slicked back. He wore a button down shirt and dress pants. No tattoos were visible, but his Blackberry was attached to his hip. He squawked into his radio and had someone tell Jack the band was there.

"Jack's inside, he'll be right out," Michael said while holding the door open.

When Jack came out he gave his fist bumps to the guys. He was wearing one of the band's t-shirts, and an all-access pass draped around his neck. He immediately distributed the passes to each member of the band and continued in stride to help unload the van.

They went through the double doors on the loading dock, following Michael through hallways pulling dolly after dolly of their gear. They emerged through a curtain and onto the stage. Thousands of empty seats stared back at them and countless venue employees milled about preparing for the show. The smell of popcorn and hotdogs was heavy in the empty arena.

"Do you have a banner you need hung?" Michael asked.

"No," Jack replied. "We have amp covers instead."

He pointed to a box on the far side of the stage.

"I had those printed," he said. "Drape them over your amps once they're miked up."

Sal walked over and opened the box. There were large black sheets of cloth inside with the band's logo printed on them.

Their logo, which Paul had designed, from afar appeared to be a simple crown. Up close the letters of the band's name twisted and conformed into the shape of a crown.

Michael introduced Derek to Vinnie, the drum tech that Quantum had offered to give them a hand. As they were setting up the drums on the platform, the rest of the guys from Quantum came out to introduce themselves. Quantum had heard this was their first show at a big venue and wanted to come out and wish them well.

"The most important thing," one of them said, "is to pretend you're back at the Middle East. You guys killed it there when we saw you. This place isn't that big, there aren't that many people here. It's normal to be nervous, but don't be. You're going to have so much fun, and meet so many awesome people when you're done."

After Quantum left, they ran through a quick soundcheck. Derek listened closely as the sound guy told him which drum to hit, one after another. Once the drums were done, they moved onto Paul, then Sal, then Greg. Vocals were last, and Sal was blown away by how low and echoey his voice was in the empty arena, jumping back from the microphone the first time he sang into it.

"That's normal," the sound guy said through the monitor on the stage. "It's less loud when the place is full. Don't worry. And you'll sound a lot less reverb when the sound is bouncing off people and not empty seats."

"Thanks," Sal said, still reeling. "That's good to know."

"Levels are set. Go ahead and play a bit. Make sure you can all hear each other through the monitors and let me know if anything needs tweaking."

Sal looked back at Derek, then to Paul, and finally Greg.

"What should we play?" he asked.

"How 'bout a little 'Stairway'? We haven't played that in a while," Derek said.

"Isn't that a little cliché?" Greg asked.

"It is, but so what," Sal said, nodding to Derek.

Rather than play through the whole song, they started where it picks up in the middle. They played it full-out, rather than holding back for the soundcheck, and Sal loved every minute of it.

"Can I get some more of Greg's guitar in my monitors?" he asked.

"I need some more vocals," Derek added.

"All set. Give it another whirl," the sound guy said.

"'Welcome Home,'" Sal said.

"Good choice," Greg said, as he began the opening riff. "Good choice indeed."

They played through the song as if the house were packed. They gave it all they had and left nothing on the table. During the intro, Sal stepped back from the microphone to warm up his voice. Still playing his guitar, he sang to himself, running up and down his scales until he was ready to sing the first verse.

He stepped up to the microphone and belted it out, flowing into the second and right into the chorus. The house lights were still up throughout the arena which made it easy for him to see the various food workers, janitors, ticket takers, and other employees start lining up around the walkways above the first row of seats. Dozens, if not hundreds, of people were stopping what they were doing to listen to them soundcheck. He smiled, and pushed a little bit harder through the last few versus and choruses.

When they finished, before Sal could tell the sound guy that everything sounded fine, applause erupted from the employees that had stopped to listen.

"Thank you," Sal said into the microphone. "Thanks a lot."

Jack came out and collected them, walking them to behind a big curtain and pointing to where they could put down their guitars. Derek put his drumsticks down there too.

"What?" he said, "I don't want to feel left out."

Jack then led them back to the waiting area. Inside was a set of plush leather couches, a table of snacks, a cooler of assorted beverages, and a TV. Sal took out his iPad and opened his Twitter app and sent out a tweet to their twenty-four thousand followers: *Who's coming to Manchester tonight? We're opening for Quantum. #SoSayTheKing*

The responses and retweets started happening immediately. Fans saying how excited they were to see the show tonight, others sending the message to their friends saying they should come. The instant gratification of Twitter was something Sal loved.

About an hour after Jack had left them there, he called Greg and asked them to come out to the front of the venue. When they found the front doors, Jack was waiting by their merch table. Behind it were Jess and Samantha.

"Surprise," Jess said. "Jack called us and asked us to be merch wenches."

"Merch wenches?" Greg asked, giving Jack a look.

"I didn't make up the term. It's a real thing," Jack said, innocently.

Surrounding the tables were boxes of different t-shirts, hats, wristbands, and a few thousand CDs.

"I brought everything I had made," Jack said. "If we sell it all, we'll have more money for the next show."

"When is the next show?" Derek asked.

"Tuesday night in Bangor, Maine. A twenty-thousand-seat venue."

"How many is this one?" Jess asked.

"I forget the exact count, but they've sold around sixteen-thousand tickets. There's probably a few thousand left at the door. I think it's twenty here."

"Twenty thousand!" Samantha said. "Holy shit!"

It was five now, and the doors were scheduled to open at six and the show scheduled to start at seven. The guys made their way back to the waiting area and had some snacks.

"After you're done on stage, I want you to make sure to thank everyone for coming. Introduce Quantum, too. People eat that up," Jack said. "And then head back to the merch booth. Make sure you say that's where you're going to be while Quantum performs, got it?"

"And then what? We sell t-shirts and CDs with the girls?" Paul asked.

"No, Paul, you mingle with the fans. You sign t-shirts, you sign tits. You be the rockstar that you are," Jack said. Paul grinned.

Michael popped his head in the door back at the waiting area around 6:30.

"People are starting to file in and the venue's filling up," he said. "You guys have half an hour before you go on. You'll play for an hour, no more, no less."

Jack nodded.

"Can I go take some pictures of the crowd?" Sal asked.

"You have an all access pass, you can do whatever you want," Michael said.

Sal walked back down the hallway towards the stage and poked his head out from the right side. He pointed his iPhone out at the crowd, which he estimated was over five-thousand at this point, and took some photos. He immediately uploaded them to Twitter with the caption: *Are you out here? #SoSayTheKing #Manchester.* Responses started coming in quickly.

"I am, I can see myself in the front," one girl said.

"I'm still waiting outside to get in!" another fan replied.

By the time he made it back to the waiting area, the rest of the guys were doing warmups. Greg was still on his iPad, Derek was drumming on his practice pad with a special weighted pair of drumsticks, and Paul was doing pushups.

"Pushups won't help you, Paul," Sal joked.

Paul did a pushup high off the ground and gave him the finger before falling back into another pushup. Sal laughed.

"Five minutes," Jack said. "You ready?"

"Ready as we're going to be," Sal said. "Ready as we're going to be."

Stopping to think for a second, Sal realized he hadn't questioned himself at all today. Perhaps he was finally ready to do this, and his mind had accepted that this was what he was born to do and that he was good at it.

I texted Cassie. She just got here and is helping us in the Merch booth. Sam text him.

:-) Sal replied.

I can't wait!

Me too.

Promptly at seven, Michael came in to get the band.

"Wait on the side of the stage until the stage manager tells you to come out," he instructed.

It felt like they were waiting there for an hour but in reality it was only about five minutes. The lights went out in an instant and the stage manager ushered them onto stage with a small flashlight. They'd decided in the waiting room that they'd go right into a song to start, no introductions of any kind, just right into "Lost Without You." It was one of the better selling singles on iTunes.

Standing there in the dark, Sal waited for a light of some kind. Through the monitor he heard the sound guy say "ten seconds" and he knew that in ten seconds his life was about to change again in a major way.

"Three, two, one" the sound guy counted down, and the lights came on the exact moment that the band burst into song. The crowd went nuts, screaming and cheering. He could hear some fans closer to the stage singing along and could sometimes see the crowd through the bright lights shining in his eyes. People were clapping, smiling, signing along, and taking photos and video with their cell phones.

When the song ended, Sal introduced them.

"We're So Say The King," he said, "and we're so honored to be here. Thank you all for coming out so early to see us."

Song after song, note after note, lyric after lyric, it was evident that they were well rehearsed and polished. They'd played some of these songs hundreds of times over the years and it showed. The crowd was warm and receptive and Sal liked to think that they earned some new fans throughout the night.

"Last song" a voice came through the monitors. "Play the single."

"We've got time for one more," Sal said. "This song you may know if you listen to AAF. It's called 'Night Before Dawn'. Once again, we're So Say The King. Thanks for coming out. Quantum is up next," the crowd went nuts, and Sal could barely hear himself. "We'll be at the merch booth in the back for the rest of the night. Stop by and say hey."

"Night Before Dawn" had never sounded so good. Whether it was the arena or the sound system or the pure adrenaline that they were firing on while playing, the band couldn't figure it out, but the song was perfect.

The song ended and the guys took a bow at the front of the stage. It was something that they'd seen other bands do in the '70s and '80s on old VHS and DVDs of concerts and they liked the idea. They tossed some guitar picks and Derek threw his drumsticks out to a screaming girl in the front row.

A few members of the event crew were on stage before the band even left, ushering the band's gear off stage to make room for Quantum's gear. The guys made their way down the hallway and through the curtain to where Jack was waiting. A round of fist bumps were had.

"You guys were fucking brilliant. They loved you," said Jack.

After taking a few minutes to recuperate from the rush, they made their way around the halls of the arena to their merch booth. Jess, Samantha, and Cassie were waiting there, fighting off the hundreds of people who wanted to buy a t-shirt or a CD.

"We're out of CDs, I'm sorry," Sal heard Jess yell a number of times.

"Just small or medium in that one," Samantha yelled to a fan. "I'm sorry."

The guys made their way closer until the fans noticed that they were there. Squeezing in behind the tables, the guys spent the next few hours signing autographs, taking pictures, meeting some new fans, and reconnecting with some old fans.

It was a night they'd never forget and they knew they got to do it again in a few days.

Sal took a moment to lean over tables, taking it all in. Dozens of yelling fans trying to get closer to him, yelling his name, trying to get his autograph or buy a copy of the CD that he'd poured his heart and soul into. This was the life he wanted and this was just the beginning.

Chapter Thirty-Seven

"Hey," Sal said as Greg answered the phone. "What are you doing today?"

"Not much, why? What's up?"

"I was thinking we should go get some new toys. Think the guys would be up for it?"

"You want to go get a new guitar, don't you?" Greg chuckled.

"I'll pick you up in half an hour. Call the other guys and see if they want to go."

Sal had given himself ample time to relax and recuperate after he and Sam's recent move and the string of shows they band had been playing. Sam had been unpacking and putting things away, going as far as labeling all of the cabinets in the kitchen with sticky notes so they'd know where everything was.

"Hey Sam," he called to her from the bedroom.

"I'm in the living room," she yelled back.

He walked out to find her hunched over the coffee table, sliding the remote controls and coasters around amongst the magazines, trying to find the perfect spots for it all.

"I'm going to pick the guys up and go to Guitar Center."

"What are you getting?"

"I think I'm going to pick out a new guitar. Jack's been pretty quick about paying us when we sell through records and I have the money, so I figured I might as well treat myself."

He kissed her on the top of her head.

"I'll be back later tonight. Text me if you want me to bring dinner home."

"Okay, I'll see you later. Maybe I'll call Jess and see if she wants to come over."

"That sounds like a good plan. Bye."

He grabbed his wallet, keys and cell phone and made his way out the door and down to the car.

Greg was waiting in the driveway when he pulled up.

"Any idea what you're going to buy?" Greg asked.

"No idea, but I feel like we've earned something new, don't you?"

"Absolutely. Derek and Paul said they'll meet us there with the van, just in case."

When they arrived at Guitar Center, Derek and Paul were already waiting by the entrance, eager to get inside and see what things they could find for themselves.

They entered like rockstars, swinging the door open and walking in one uniform line, marching into the store like they were million-aires and would buy everything.

It didn't take long for them to each separate into three; Derek headed into the enclosed drum room, Paul made his way toward the bass section and Sal and Greg stood in front of the massive wall of guitars. Floor to ceiling, perhaps twenty-five feet tall, lined with hundreds of shiny brand new guitars.

They were both like kids at a candy store with no parents. One of them would pick up a guitar they liked, play it for a minute or two and then put it back, grabbing another. It didn't take long for one of the sales guys to come over and ask if they needed help.

After introducing themselves and shaking hands, Sal asked him to grab a ladder. There were a few guitars up higher that he wanted to play and he couldn't reach them.

"Sure thing, Sal. I'll go grab a ladder."

When he came back, Sal began pointing to guitars up near the ceiling that he wanted. From the ground, he couldn't see the price tags on those guitars, but he told himself he didn't care what they cost. He'd wanted a new guitar for years and was finally in a position to buy himself something nice. Something that'd rival Greg's gorgeous guitar that he'd been envious of for years.

As soon as he struck the first chord on the Paul Reed Smith that he'd picked, he knew that was the one. It was love at first note. Its transparent blue tiger finish reflected every overhead light in the building, shining its rays onto the array of guitars scattered around the wall in front of him. The fretboard felt like an extension of his fingers, his hand fitting perfectly around it like it was made just for him. The sound that came out of the test amp was glorious with very little adjusting.

"This is the one," he said to Greg. "This is it."

"PRS, man. That's gorgeous. How much is it?"

"I don't even care," Sal said. "It's mine."

He handed the guitar to the salesman without even asking how much it was. Sal told him to put it behind the counter so he could keep looking at other guitars.

By the time they'd finished, Sal had amassed a total of three guitars; the Paul Reed Smith, a Taylor acoustic electric, and a Fender Stratocaster.

Greg had found a new multi-effects pedal for himself and had followed Sal up to the register to pay.

Just as he finished checking out, Paul made his way back — a new bass in his arms. From the sounds of it, Derek was still in the drum room, wailing away on one of the demo drum sets.

"Paul, can you go retrieve Derek for me?" Sal asked.

"Sure thing. I'll drag him away from whatever sparkly thing he's beating on."

"Your total comes to $5,150 with tax," the salesman said. "I gave you a slight discount because you're buying three."

Sal looked to his left at Greg and sort of shrugged at him.

"Gotta do what you gotta do," he said, almost telling himself more so than Greg.

Between the four of them, they'd spend almost ten thousand dollars that afternoon, the bulk of it being Sal's spending. Derek had picked up a couple of cymbals in addition to the rest of the band's loot.

Shopping had been tiring and Sal couldn't wait to get home and just hang out on the couch with Sam. While tired, he felt accomplished today. He'd finally made enough money that he could splurge on himself, though he assured himself that this would be the only time for a while.

"Are you mad?" he asked as he entered the apartment, a guitar in each hand. "There's one more in the car."

"Oh Sal. How much did you spend?"

"More than I should have. They're just so amazing."

"How much?" She folded her arms trying to look angry.

"Over five grand."

"Sal!" she yelled. "That's a lot of money!"

"I know. I know! I feel terrible. I just couldn't help myself. It's the first time I've had that kind of money to spend."

He dropped the two guitars off on the floor by the TV and went back down to grab the third.

"Well, let me see," she said as he piled the third case on top of the other two.

"Later. Right now I just want to sit on the couch and spend time with you."

She curled up next to him after grabbing the remote and flipping on the TV. He put his arm around her and pulled her in closer than she was already sitting.

"I'm proud of you," she said. "You're on your way."

"Thank you. I still can't believe any of this is true."

Chapter Thirty-Eight

THE FIRST ELEVEN SHOWS happened in the blink of an eye. Over the course of four weeks the band had played show after show all over New England. From Maine to Connecticut, even sneaking into Rhode Island for two shows. Their Twitter feed had broken fifty-thousand, and Facebook just surpassed the sixty-thousand mark.

Self-funding their shows was tough, but Jack helped them manage the money. The money that they got from one show was paid forward to the next, funding their travel, hotels, food, and other expenses. By Greg's estimate, each member of the band had already pocketed close to fifty-thousand dollars, once they factored in all the expenses and Jack's cut. Not bad for a band with no record label, he said a handful of times.

Once a week, Jack would show up at a venue with more cases of CDs and t-shirts. They were selling out faster than they could have them delivered. He estimated that between concert sales and the copies sold at Newbury Comics, they'd sold close to two hundred thousand copies. Well on their way to a gold album.

"There's going to be twenty-thousand plus here tonight," Jack said. "They always sell around one or two percent more seats for standing room than actual seats in the venue."

It was early on a Saturday morning and the guys were setting up their gear for the final show of the twelve that Jack had booked them. They'd played in front of tens of thousands of people over the last month and ended up back in Boston at the TD Garden, opening for Waxing Electric, one of the hottest new bands out of London of recent history.

Once set up, the band members met backstage in the green room, where they enjoyed free drinks and warmed up for the show. As had been typical of their entire run, Jess and Samantha were with them. The bus that Jack had arranged for them to travel in had WiFi, so the girls could work while they were traveling on off days.

"I can't believe we're playing the Garden," Sal said, "I've dreamed of this since I was a kid."

"It was a different building back then," Derek said, "but me too."

They spent the afternoon working up a setlist that was different from what they'd been playing all month. The crowd pleasers would still stay, but they decided to add some new covers to the list at the last minute, trying to give the hometown crowd something to be excited about.

Though they were still the opening act, Waxing Electric had agreed to let them play for ninety minutes. Given that they preferred to play later and usually had two opening acts, they figured they'd go on around ten, giving So Say The King from eight to nine thirty to play, with half an hour in between.

Despite being the largest show that he'd play to date, Sal wasn't nervous. He felt rock solid in his performance, and that of the band, for weeks. Thinking back to the first show they played on their tour, Sal had a hard time even remembering being nervous.

He worked on his vocals, running through the new setlist to make sure he knew the words to the new covers that they'd added. Nothing would be more embarrassing than forgetting the words to a song in front of twenty-thousand plus people. He didn't want a repeat of what happened years ago, especially not in front of such a large crowd. Even though he wasn't nervous, he still worried that he may not remember all of the lyrics to all of the songs.

Before they knew it, the afternoon had ended and dinner time was approaching. They decided to walk over to the North End. Jack called ahead and got them a private seating area, so they wouldn't be disturbed by any fans. When they left the Garden, some fans were waiting outside by the bus asking for autographs. They made sure to sign each and every one before leaving.

Sal and Sam held hands as they walked together to the North End. It had been a few weeks since they'd had any alone time, but Sal knew that nothing had changed. Though their apartment was empty, the lights all turned off, and the heat turned down, he knew it was still home. He knew he'd eventually make it back there and resume his normal life of loving her.

"How are you feeling?" Sal asked.

"About what?"

"About all of this. About the concerts and the touring."

"It's a lot," she said. "It's very draining. I can't wait for it to all end and we can go back to bed."

"Is that all you want to do? Be in bed?" he pulled her to his side.

"With you, yes."

"That's sweet, honey. But what if this all lasts for years?"

"Eventually it'll stop. And then we'll be back in bed."

When they arrived at the restaurant, some fans were waiting outside. Somehow word of their visit had gotten out. After signing some more autographs, they made their way inside to be greeted by a friendly Italian man. He introduced himself as the owner and thanked them for coming in, quickly showing them through the dining room to the private area in the back.

"I can't say again how proud of you all I am," Samantha said. "This tour has done so much for you guys. I'd like to propose a toast." She raised her glass and everyone around the table followed suit, "To So Say The King, the nicest, most honest, most talented guys I've ever known. I love you all."

"Here, here," everyone said, clinking their glasses together.

When they exited the restaurant, applause erupted, surprising them all. They tried to make their way through the crowd of fans, saying that they'd be signing autographs and hanging out after the show. Some fans made it more difficult than others and Jack had to yell at everyone to get back.

"Looks like we're going to need security for next time," Greg said. "This is nuts."

They finally made it back to the Garden and waited in their green room for the word that they'd go on soon. The arena had mostly filled up by this point, so Jess and Samantha headed to the merch area to meet Cassie, where there was more than enough merchandise waiting to be sold. Jack had learned his lesson that it was better to have too much stuff available and had gone overboard with the last order of merch.

"Newbury Comics said they'd take whatever we didn't need after tonight," he said, "so we'll sell it all one way or another. But retail at a concert makes us more money than wholesale to Newbury, so try to sell some t-shirts."

"What if we tell them that this is the last show they can buy that t-shirt at and we retire it?" Derek asked.

"It's technically true," Greg said. "We don't have to tell them it'll be available at Newbury comics."

"Okay, I'll say that towards the end of the set," Sal said. "I'm sure that'll help."

At quarter to eight the tour manager came into the green room to get the guys, walking them to the curtained area on the side of the stage. As they left the green room Jack fist bumped them one more time, making sure to tell them all how proud of them he was. Over the last few months he'd grown to be a father figure for them.

While they waited, DJ Kim walked up next to them, introducing herself. She was the DJ that had originally played "Night Before Dawn" on the Throwdown a few months back.

"I'm glad I found that submission that night," she said. "Jack insisted that I played it and I'm glad I did. You guys deserve all of this."

"Thanks so much," Sal said, "it's awesome that you've supported us since that night. Everyone keeps telling us how you keep playing us on your show."

"As much as I can," she said. "When you're ready to do an in studio acoustic set, you call me first."

"Consider it done," Sal said. "We're there."

"Awesome. I got to run," she said, running out onto stage and grabbing the microphone.

"She's going to introduce you guys," the tour manager said. "Be ready."

"You all know me," DJ Kim said on stage, "and you know the band I'm about to introduce, too. I played them on Hometown Throwdown two months ago and you fuckers went apeshit over it. They're still the reigning champions and you'll hear them again next week because they won again last night! Give it up for my homeboys So Say The King!"

They charged out on stage. The applause was thunderous as they made it to the center.

"It's good to be home," Sal said as they started their first song. The crowd worked into a frenzy. Sal had learned that no matter where you were, if you said you were happy to be there, or mentioned the city's name, the crowd went bonkers. Having that place be your hometown was even more exciting and the locals knew it.

Sal decided to switch things up a bit in conjunction with the new setlist they'd worked out. They'd allotted a few minutes in between songs for Sal to talk a bit while the guys changed instruments or got water, whatever they needed to do.

"This next song has been one of my favorites since I was a kid. It seems like so many great songwriters and singers die before their time. Freddie Mercury was one of my biggest idols as a kid. I thank my parents for introducing me to Queen when I was still in the womb. This is for my parents."

The rendition of "Someone To Love" was one of the most beautiful cover songs they'd done to date. Jack had arranged accompaniment from some Berklee students. They performed the song completely a cappella with the exception of the orchestra accompaniment. It was something they had rehearsed a handful of times last year. Despite having no formal training, the guys could harmonize with one another really well.

It was well received and the crowd played into it holding their cell phones in the air, waving the light left and right. Jack, standing on the side of the stage, made sure to get some pictures for them to post online.

"Smile for the internet," Greg said into his microphone pointing to Jack, "you're being Tweeted."

The crowd ate that up and cheered louder than it seemed possible.

Each song seemed to get the crowd to cheer louder and louder, with not a moment of silence during their entire set. Their ninety minutes flew by faster than any other show they'd played on the tour.

"This is our last song," Sal said. "It's been a true honor to play here in front of you all. Thanks so much to Waxing Electric for letting us do this on our home turf. Thank you all for coming. We'll be in the back hanging out for the next few hours, so come say hi. We've got exclusive concert shirts for the last time on this tour back there, so be sure to get yours. We love you all."

"Night Before Dawn" was their closer. It was the song that everyone expected them to play. Sal felt every word and savored every moment that he was performing in front of this enormous crowd on his home turf.

The merch table had quieted down just long enough for Sam to walk over to where she could see the stage. Hundreds of feet away she could barely tell that it was Sal, but she felt every word he sang. He leaned into the microphone while singing the verses, pushing up against it, almost knocking it over. Many times, in between lines, he looked to his left and right at his bandmates, clearly smiling and enjoying himself. He loved what he was doing on stage, and Sam felt it.

"Good night. We love each and every one of you," Sal said as the other guys joined him for their bow. "We'll see you again soon."

After their bow, they left the stage and made way for the techs to come and move all their gear off. Jack was waiting in the wings and hugged them all.

Once cleaned up and changed, they made their way to the merch area where there were hundreds of people waiting. Sam and Jess were waving fistfuls of cash around, reaching over the people who hadn't made their decision yet to those who had, handing t-shirt after t-shirt out to the crowd of fans.

"There they are!" someone yelled, and the crowd turned.

Sal waved and the band quickly made their way behind the row of tables to protect themselves. They formed a signature line and passed CD after CD along, each signing their name. Sal lost track of how many times people asked to take a photo with him, but basked in it all. At one point he lost track of what he was signing and just kept saying "thank you" and passing things to his right. Over his left shoulder he could hear Jess and Samantha selling merchandise at a record pace. Jack had planned well and they didn't run out of anything, but came close to selling out of CDs.

As the night wound down and the venue emptied, the guys stayed at their tables. Until the last fan had left and the house lights came up, they continued to sign autographs and take pictures with their fans.

Before leaving with their gear, Sal took a picture of the empty venue from the stage. The venue was cluttered with trash and smelled of sweat. He tweeted the photo to all of their followers and posted to Facebook for all to see: *We love you all. Thank you, from the bottom of our hearts, thank you.*

Chapter Thirty-Nine

Everyone piled into the tour bus after the show. Teeming with excitement, Derek and Paul quickly decided they wanted to go out and get some drinks to celebrate the night and the tour.

It was just after eleven o'clock that night and there was no chance that anyone would be ready to go to sleep any time soon.

"We'll leave you kids alone," Greg said to Sam and Sal. "Jack, why don't you come have a late dinner with Jess and me."

"That sounds good," Jack said, following them out of the tour bus.

"Looks like we've finally got some alone time," Sam said, smiling.

"Finally. It feels like we haven't been alone in months."

Sal stood and began pacing around the long and narrow bus.

"I can't believe how much has happened," he said. "This just all seems surreal, doesn't it?"

"You deserve this, Sal."

"I couldn't have gotten here without you, you know that, don't you?"

"Don't be silly. You got here because you worked hard at it."

"No. I got here because you let me. You've supported me through-out this whole thing, even though it seemed like a pipe dream for so long."

"I didn't do anything any other girlfriend wouldn't do."

"Yes, you did. Don't downplay it. You're the reason I'm here right now."

"Sal…"

"No, Sam. You are. I wouldn't have made it here without you being by my side. Please know that."

He paced around the bus some more before finally sitting down next to her.

"Tell me something I don't know about you," he said, suddenly.

"What do you mean?"

"I don't know. Something you've never told me before. Something that might surprise me."

"Okay, let me think," she said. "Oh, I've got it!"

She stood and walked to the fridge to get herself a drink before proceeding with her story.

"I won the National Geography Bee when I was in fifth grade," she said, sitting back down.

"National? Like you beat the whole country?"

"Yes. I have a good memory and studied a lot when I was a kid. So I knew where all the countries were and what their capitols are."

"That's so dorky!" he said, poking her ribs.

"It's only a little dorky to be smart," she said.

"I never won anything as a kid."

"Really? I won my share of things you may call dorky."

"What else?"

"I think I won a spelling bee once, too."

"So you know where the countries are, and you can spell their names?"

"I never looked at it that way, but I guess you're right!"

It had passed midnight when Sal took her hand and pulled her up.

"Let's go for a walk. It's a clear night and we should take advantage of everyone leaving us alone for a while."

"I like that idea," Sam said. She smiled and took his hand, heading towards the bus' exit.

Sal helped her down the few steps and out of the bus' door. The couple walked hand in hand through the large parking lot through a few side streets and alleys and eventually came to a small playground.

"Swing with me?" Sam asked, making her way across the sandy playground to a swing set with two swings dangling gently in the night air. It was late August and the air was still warm at this hour. A single lamp post illuminated most of the small playground. The sky was clear and the surrounding buildings shielded the busy city lights from their playground, allowing them sight of the stars.

"It's beautiful," Sam said, "I love astronomy."

"You do?"

"It's always fascinated me. I memorized the major constellations when I was a teenager."

"What's that one?" he asked, pointing.

"That's Cassiopeia, that one's easy."

"What about that one?" he tried to stump her.

"That's Ara, it means Altar in Latin."

As they took their seats on the only two swings in the playground and began swinging, Sal stared at Sam smiling at the stars. Seeing such a large smile on her face brought one to his. He took a moment to think about how quickly they'd come together and how important she'd become to him. Over and over he'd tell himself how he couldn't have done any of this without her and how he'd still be working at Starbucks, practicing a couple of times a week, but not going anywhere.

While off deep in thought, Sam looked over and noticed him staring at her.

"What?" she asked.

"Huh?" He snapped to attention.

"You were staring."

"Was I? I'm sorry. I didn't mean to."

"It's okay. I find it flattering."

"You find it flattering that I'm a creeper and am staring at you?"

"No, Sal," she said. "It's not creepy when you're staring with affection."

He locked eyes with her for a moment before looking back up at the stars. The night was so clear tonight that he felt like he could see every star in every galaxy in the sky.

They swung in silence, in harmony, each taking turns looking over at the other.

The sounds of the night calmed Sal: the night air whooshed past each of them as they swung in unison, the chains clanking an almost melodic harmony with one another, the far off faint sounds of traffic from the nearby highway. His feet dragged each time he crossed the bottom of his arch while Sam's feet made no noise. The sound of sand kicking up each time he flew by the low point in his swing reminded him of childhood.

Her legs being shorter than his meant she was pumping harder than he, though unintentionally. He found himself slowing down a few times to let her catch up, so they could swing in harmony. He felt like, at any time, he could reach out and grab her hand and she'd be there for him.

Before long, Sal realized that they'd been swinging for over an hour without saying a word. He looked at his phone and suggested they get started heading back to the bus.

He smiled to himself as he took her hand to walk back. They'd sat together, swinging, in silence for over an hour. It didn't seem to bother either of them at all. They didn't need words to appreciate each other. They were just together, swinging, enjoying the peace, and watching the stars.

Chapter Forty

AFTER THE TOUR ENDED, the guys decided to take a few weeks to rest up before going back to the rehearsal complex to work on new material. In the weeks since the last show at the Garden, they'd been signed to Sony, and had gotten national distribution for their album.

Sony footed the bill to go through the process of re-doing all of their album artwork. They also took care of forming a business for the band to collect their royalties from, to make filing taxes easier on each individual member of the band.

The show had done wonders for them; opening for a band that was so hot on the last date of their mini-tour had been the right move. "Night Before Dawn" had made it onto the Billboard charts at number 6, and it had a snowball effect — get on the radio, sell more records, get more radio play because people own the record. The more they heard themselves on the radio, the better the record sales were.

Sal was at home with Samantha on a Tuesday afternoon when Greg called.

"Hey, what's up?" he answered.

"I've got everyone else on the line, Jack wanted to tell us something."

"Hey guys," Jack said, "I've got good news to report."

"What's up," Sal asked.

"Well," Jack said, "I just got off a call with some of the execs at Sony. Normally they don't count self produced sales in the total sales for an album because it's not tracked through Soundscan. However they're bridging the close to three-hundred-thousand copies we sold ourselves at shows before they signed us. That means that, as of the numbers yesterday, the album's gone gold. Gold!"

"Gold? How many is that?" Derek asked excitedly.

"Half a million," Jack said.

"Half a million?" Greg yelled so loudly Sal had to pull the phone away from his ear and Samantha perked up from the other end of the couch.

"Half a million," Jack repeated, "and you deserve every copy sold."

Sal reached over and pulled Samantha across the couch to him, so she could listen in.

"There'll be a ceremony, and they'll want you to play a show somewhere big to celebrate. I think we should have them book a headlining show at the Garden and make a party out of it."

"Don't we normally do a listening party when we release a CD not after we sell a bunch of copies?" Sal asked.

"Yea, normally," Jack replied. "But we could blow it up. Halloween is coming up, what if we did a costume ball at the Garden?"

"That's a great idea" Samantha whispered to Sal.

"Yea, let's do that. It'll be a lot of fun for the fans," Sal said.

Jack asked them to wait until Sony confirmed their plans before sending it out to their fans via social media.

"We wouldn't want hundreds of thousands of people to be disappointed if this didn't work out," Jack said, "that'd be bad for business."

Sony came through and arranged for a costume ball at the TD Garden on Halloween night. The official press release, which Paul put up on their website, informed fans that it was a costume party and anyone not in costume would not be allowed in, ticket or not. They'd also boasted that the costume party would have prizes for best costume, door prizes, and special guests. The costume contest registration was done through the official website, so Paul kept track of entries via a database, and would report to the rest of the band every few days. By the time Halloween rolled around, there were a few hundred entries.

Some of the reps from Sony said they'd take care of arranging everything at the venue, which took some of the stress off of Jack's shoulders. Jack told them on Halloween morning that the guests that were showing up would be some of Boston's local music heroes, and they'd be judging the costume contest. Aerosmith's Joe Perry, Boston's Tom Scholz, and Godsmack's Sully Erna would be their special guests that night.

Jack had also arranged for the three of them to join in and accompany the band for the encore of "Night Before Dawn" and "Something's Wrong." When asked if they should rehearse, Jack said it wasn't necessary.

"It'll be better if it's spur of the moment," he said. "Just be sure to introduce them as they come on stage. The place will go nuts."

"How can we perform something we've never done before?" Sal asked.

"You're professionals now, Sal," Jack said. "You'll be fine, don't worry. This happens every night at dozens of venues across the world. Improvising your way through it makes it feel more genuine. Fans eat that shit up."

But he did worry. Not being in control of the situation and having no rehearsal worried him a great deal.

Samantha and Jess showed up a few hours before the show and made their way to the green room where the guys were waiting.

"Hey," Sal said.

"We're here," Jess said. "At your disposal. Merch area all set up?"

"Yeah, but you guys don't need to work it tonight," Greg said. "Sony sent some people to do it. You guys can hang out at the side of the stage, as long as you're in costume."

"What are you guys dressing up as?" Samantha asked.

"After disagreeing with everything we suggested," Derek said, "we finally got Greg to agree to 1980s era Metallica."

"Seriously? That's awesome," Jess said. "The crowd may not get it right away, but that's still awesome."

As showtime approached, the special guests started arriving. Jack brought them back one at a time to meet the band, and then lead them to their own dressing rooms where they could get ready for the show. Sony had arranged for the costume contest to happen on the far side of the stage, to the band's right. Each person participating would be able to come up on stage from the left and walk to the right in front of the band, as sort of a parade in front of the crowd.

"It's such an honor to meet you, Mr. Scholz. I've been a fan since I was a little kid," Sal said, extending his hand.

"Thanks. It's great to meet you all. I have to admit, I love your record."

Sal was elated to hear that one of the founding members of one of his favorite bands had enjoyed his album. He smiled and replayed that over and over in his head until it was time to get out on stage.

"Got everything ready?" Greg asked Sal before they started changing into their costumes.

"Yep," he said while patting his pockets. "I'm ready."

As each member emerged from the bathroom, clad in Metallica gear from the '80s, the rest of the band applauded. Denim jeans, big hair wigs, and ripped t-shirts made their attire complete. Derek had also custom-ordered a bass drum head with So Say The King on it, in the same font as Metallica had used.

The arena was sold out and then some. Everyone that came was in costume, and it was evident that their constant Facebook messages and Tweets had worked. The party was a success.

When they took the stage, the crowd went nuts and a Metallica chant started.

"Look at all you beautiful costumed freaks," Sal said. "Happy Halloween!"

After the first song, Sal pointed over to the table at his right. "Looks like we're going to give away some prizes for some costumes. I know a bunch of you registered, so let's get a move on, shall we?"

The crowd screamed more.

"Who's ready to meet our special guest judges?"

The volume of screams increased.

"Let's first welcome the legendary guitar player from one of Boston's most successful bands in history. Ladies and gentlemen, Joe Perry."

Joe came out on stage, shaking hands with everyone in the band and waving to the crowd. He took his seat at the table and the spotlight came back to Sal.

"Up next, another Boston legend. From my all-time favorite band, give it up for Mr. Tom Scholz from Boston."

Tom came out, hugged Sal, and shook the other guys' hands. He took his seat next to Joe Perry at the table and leaned over to whisper something to him.

"Last, but certainly not least," Sal said, "we've got someone who started out just like we did. On local radio, winning battles against other local bands. Godsmack's Sully Erna!"

Sully came out and shook everyone's hand.

"It's fucking awesome to be here," he said into Sal's microphone. "Happy Halloween you guys!"

The band launched into song, while various workers started leading costumed fans up on stage, and telling them to walk across the stage, but not to touch or do anything to the band in any way. Each judge took notes as people walked by. Most were women wearing next to nothing — a feat not to be overlooked in October in Boston. Men were dressed as firemen, policemen, some comic book characters. It was, overall, a fun experience for everyone.

"If I could, I'd like to take a minute to acknowledge a few people. We wouldn't be here if it wasn't for them," Sal said. "Jack DeBane, our manager. Without him we'd still be wondering how many people fit in the Middle East. Jack, come out here."

Jack came out on stage in his Iron Man costume and took a bow, fist bumping each member of the band. He sat down on the drum platform and made himself at home.

"Jessica Wincomb, Greg's wife. She's been supportive of us for as long as I can remember and I'm proud to call her family. You may all recognize her from selling you a t-shirt months ago. Jess, come take a bow."

Jess came out, dressed as Annie, and took a bow. She kissed Greg, which got the crowd cheering again, and hugged the rest of the guys before taking her seat next to Jack.

"And last, but certainly not least by any means," he continued. "Samantha St. Allen. Samantha's been helping with so many things that I can't even begin to list them all. Samantha, as many of you from Twitter and Facebook know, is the love of my life. Come out here, honey."

Red in the face and dressed as the Little Mermaid, Samantha came out onto the stage. She hugged Greg on her way by and kissed Sal.

"Take a bow," Sal said. "A good bow."

As she turned to the crowd, Sal reached into his pocket and bent to one knee. When she turned back, she instantly started crying.

"What did you do?" she said, trying to rush off stage.

"Come here. It's okay," Sal said, pulling her back towards center stage.

He pulled her in towards the microphone stand, and turned to face her.

"Samantha, since you came into my life, you've made me a better person. You've allowed me to follow my dreams with these guys and you've supported me the entire way. I love you now, I loved you then, and I will love you for the rest of my time here on this earth. Nothing would make me happier than if you agreed to marry me in front of twenty thousand of our friends here. I love you. Will you marry me?"

After a collective "aww", the crowd started chanting "say yes" over and over again, but they didn't need to. Before he could even finish talking, she was nodding and saying yes repeatedly.

Sal slipped the ring on her finger, stood up, and put the microphone back on the stand. He wrapped his arms around her, kissed her, and squeezed her.

"I love you so much," she said. "I had no idea you were going to do this. You're full of surprises."

"I love you," he said.

He took her hand and turned them both to face the crowd, arms raised in the air, hands clasped firmly together as if they were going to take a bow.

The crowd erupted in thunderous applause.

When Sal and Sam got back to their apartment that night, they couldn't keep their hands off one another. The excitement of their engagement brought them to a state of bliss.

"I can't believe you proposed to me on stage," Sam said. "In front of all of those people!"

"I wanted everyone to know how much I love you," he responded while kissing her.

"You know I'm a sucker for a surprise."

"I know. I don't think I'll ever top that one, though."

They made their way, arms tangled, twirling around, from the front door to their bedroom. By the time they made it to their bedroom, they were both left in their underwear.

"I love you," she said, looking deep into his eyes.

"You are my world," Sal replied. "None of this would be possible without you."

As they each shed their last article of clothing, Sam reached over and turned the light out.

Sal's eyes took a moment to adjust, but he could soon see her body laying next to his. He studied it, moving his fingers over her, touching her skin, holding her hand.

They celebrated their engagement at home, in their own bed. They made love until dawn.

Tired and covered in sweat, Sal laid back onto his pillow, pulling Samantha close to him.

"Why did we wait so long to do that?"

Still trying to catch her breath, Sam replied. "That was perfect. Let's do that a lot."

Exhausted, they fell asleep with their fingers interlocked with one another. For the first time in months, Sal slept in.

Chapter Forty-One

AFTER SAL'S SURPRISE PROPOSAL at the Halloween show, Jess worked with Cassie and Sal's parents to plan an engagement party for them in the North End. She'd snuck Samantha's phone one Friday night and got her mom's phone number to call and invite her.

A hundred of their closest friends, all of the immediate family members and the happy couple arrived at around the same time on a Sunday afternoon in early November. It was brisk, but not quite cold yet. Jess greeted Sal and Samantha as they arrived, leading them into the dining room where the guests were waiting. It wasn't a surprise, per se, but Sal and Samantha didn't know of the details of the party. Jess wanted some of the elements to be a surprise.

"My mom's here!" Sam yelled.

"Hi baby," Vanessa said. "Congratulations you guys. I'm so excited! I wouldn't have missed this for the world!"

She hugged them both as they went by her table towards Sal's parents and sister.

"My son," Vincenzo said. "I'm so happy and proud of all you've done." He kissed Sal on each cheek before moving onto Samantha.

"My baby," Maria said. "You're not old enough to be getting married. I'm not old enough for a married child."

Once they were seated at their table, the waiters and waitresses began bringing the food out. Jess had opted for some of their favorite foods, served family style, like at Sal's parents' anniversary party. Marcus, the head waiter, was there again, and came by to give his congratulations to the couple. Sal remembered him and thanked him.

"I know it's tacky," Marcus said, "but I'd like an autograph before you guys leave. I'm a big fan."

"Consider it done," Sal said. "Remind me when we're leaving. I'll get the guys all together."

The clanking of a knife on a glass caught their attention and Greg rose from his seat.

"Could I have your attention," he asked. "I'd like to say a few words."

"Sal has been my best friend for most of my life. We've been through so much together, and we've accomplished so much this past year. But all of that pales in comparison to what's happened in the last few weeks for him. Finding someone to love and spend the rest of your life with is something that no amount of record sales can top."

Everyone chuckled.

"Please raise your glasses and join me in congratulating my best friend and the love of his life in eternal happiness," said Greg.

The crowd cheered and raised their glasses, clinking with the people at their table before drinking.

As Greg sat, Cassie stood.

"My turn. My brother, Sal, is the greatest person I've ever known and will ever know. I love him more than anyone else. Sorry, Mom and Dad. When he first told me about Samantha, I knew immediately that one day we'd be celebrating their marriage. I knew that they'd be in love forever and I knew that she'd make my big brother happy. Thank you Sam, for being the love of Sal's life."

Another clinking of glasses and the crowd drank together again.

When dinner had ended, Jess wheeled over the cart with the piles of gifts on it.

Sal's parents had gotten them a gift certificate to Kayak.com, so they could use it towards their honeymoon.

"Thank you Dad, Mom," Sal said. "That's very generous of you."

"There'll be another as a wedding gift," his father said. "Help you along the way."

Once the gifts were done, Marcus brought out the cake. A half-chocolate, half-vanilla cake. Jess quickly wheeled it over to their table and showed it to them.

For the rockstar and his future wife

"Jessica," Samantha said. "You're too sweet. Thank you for this."

When dessert finished, the night had turned dark and gotten colder. Sal and Samantha thanked guest after guest for coming.

"Mom, where are you staying?" Samantha asked.

"I'm at a hotel not far from here. I'll be fine, don't worry," she said.

"Sal, can you give Mom and Dad a ride home? They rode in with me, but I have to go pick up a friend of mine from the train station who's in town for the week for job interviews," Cassie asked.

"Yeah, I can do that. Sam, do you mind bringing the gifts home and I'll meet you there?"

"Sure," she said. "As long as you help load the car up."

Jess and Greg lent a hand loading Samantha's car. Sal had bought the car for her with some of his earnings after the tour ended. While they'd been fine sharing a car for months, she had asked to get her own, so she could have more mobility and freedom when Sal wasn't around.

"I'll meet you back at home," Sal said before getting in his car, "I love you."

"I love you, too."

A few minutes later she thanked Jess again, hugging both her and Greg before heading home with their car full of gifts.

Just after ten that night, Samantha got a text from Sal. *Got caught up at my parents. Heading home now, don't wait up. See you when I get there. Love you.*

Okay, tired, going to bed, love you.

She waded through the piles of presents that adorned their living room floor and made her way to the bathroom, preparing herself for bed.

Once ready, she climbed into bed and was asleep in a matter of seconds.

Her phone startled her awake at one-thirty in the morning. Stumbling around looking for it, she noticed Sal wasn't with her and the light was still on. Her eyes adjusted slowly to the bright light and she managed to find her phone on the nightstand.

"Hello?" she said, expecting to hear Sal's voice.

"Sam?" the voice on the other end asked. "Is that you?"

"Yes, who is this?"

"It's Maria."

She knew then that something had happened. She hoped she was wrong as tears filled her eyes and she steadied herself on the edge of the bed.

"What's wrong?" she asked, walking into the living room, expecting to find Sal on the couch, asleep. He was going to be on the couch. He had to be.

"It's Sal." Maria was clearly crying. "He… he was… oh, Sam."

"What happened Maria?" Her voice was getting louder and filled with concern when she found Sal wasn't on the couch. She looked on the counter where he normally left his wallet. It wasn't there.

"He left here hours ago. We thought he got home to you. They just called."

"Who called, Maria? What happened?" She was shaking her head in disbelief and opening closet doors, hoping she'd find him hiding somewhere, but Sal wasn't anywhere in the apartment.

"He was two blocks away from being home to you," Maria said, blubbering. "A drunk driver. He was hit."

"Where is he? Is he okay?" Samantha heard herself, as if from far away, yelling the words.

"He's… I… he's gone. I told them I wanted to call and tell you."

"Tell me what, Maria? Gone where? Where did they take him?" she said. "I'll go to him. I have to get to him."

"They didn't take him anywhere honey, he's gone."

"Gone?"

"They said he died instantly." Maria had trouble saying the words. Sam barely heard the words that she'd hoped weren't coming.

Samantha dropped the phone to the ground and fell to the floor. She felt sure the crack it made was the sound of her heart.

From the floor, she could hear Sal's mother sobbing into the phone, still hysterical. She reached down and picked it up.

"Where did they take him? I need to see him," she said. "This can't be real."

"He's at Lahey in Burlington. We're on our way there now."

Once she'd hung up the phone, she sat in silence on the couch, not knowing where to go or what to do. In an instant, her love was taken from her. She'd never see him again, she'd never hold him again, she'd never get to marry him. Her entire life was upended and changed in the blink of an eye.

"This can't be happening," she told herself. "This isn't real."

She was lost.

In a daze, she walked to the door and took her keys, heading outside. She got to the elevator before realizing she hadn't gotten dressed or put shoes on.

When she finally got outside, she started walking out of the parking lot, wandering in hysterics, not realizing where she was walking or what direction she should be going. She made it almost two blocks before she realized she should drive there.

She quickly walked back to her car and fumbled with the remote trying to get in. She let out a primal scream when she dropped the keys for the second time. She yelled loud and long, not caring who heard her or who she woke up.

When she finally got into the car, she grabbed the steering wheel so tight that the plastic strained and her knuckles turned white. She shook the wheel, hard, screaming as loud as she could. Not words, but pain.

The first few times that she tried to start the car, the key didn't fit. She couldn't focus on the keys in her hand and didn't realize she was trying to put the apartment key into the car.

Once she finally got the car started, she sat in it for close to half an hour, hoping that she'd be able to drive herself to find him. She had to see him. She had to find out that this wasn't real and if it was, she had to say goodbye.

Chapter Forty-Two

Samantha approached his body just after three that morning. It was Sal, there, laying before her. Cold and lifeless. A smile was still on his face, but his color had started to fade.

"Most of the injuries were internal. I'm sorry for your loss, I'll be right over there. Take as much time as you need."

"Was he in any pain?" Samantha asked.

"I don't believe so," the coroner replied. "Based on the photos they showed me of the scene, I believe he died on impact."

She let out a tear and quickly wiped it from her cheek. She kept wiping the tears as they came out, eventually giving up and realizing she wouldn't be able to keep up.

"There was this," the coroner said while reaching into an envelope. "He had it on the front seat with him."

It was two photos taped back to back. On one side was the photo of his grandparents and Dad; she'd recognized it as the inspiration for "Polaroid." Taped to the backside was a photo he'd printed of him and Samantha dancing at Greg and Jess' wedding.

The overhead lamp illuminating Sal began to spin around in a confusing flash of light and the room began to spin. Sam's knees were giving out beneath her and she realized that she was about to faint. She began to fall to the ground, when the coroner caught her before she hit her head on the corner of the table.

"I can't do this. How do people do this every day?"

"I wish I had that answer, dear," he said. "I really do."

Sam forced herself to fall to the floor, shaking the coroner off of her. The cold tile shocking her immediately back to the reality of where she was. Sal was gone.

His parents had taken care of the preparations for the funeral. The drunk driver who'd hit and killed him was charged with vehicular manslaughter and would likely go to jail for many years.

It was two days after the accident when they'd all gathered at the funeral home to say goodbye.

"Sal would have wanted it this way," she said to Cassie. "His fans, friends and family."

"I can't believe he's gone," Cassie said hugging Samantha. "It doesn't seem real. This is my fault."

"What do you mean, your fault?" Sam asked.

"I was supposed to drive my parents home that night. Sal should have gone home with you to celebrate," Cassie couldn't finish through her sobs.

"Cassie, you can't blame yourself. This isn't your fault. This is that man's —" Sam couldn't bring herself to say the driver's name. "That man's fault."

"I can't help but blame myself. If I had driven my parents home, this wouldn't have happened."

Vincenzo was right behind Maria, waiting to hug Samantha as Maria moved on to hug Cassie.

"May God bless his soul," he said. "My baby boy."

"I'm so sorry for you guys. I know I loved him, but I can't imagine what you're going through," Sam said.

"We're here for you. You weren't married, but you're family now, Samantha," he said. "We love you."

It was just about time for the wake to start and the close members of the family and Sal's bandmates had been there for an hour already. They milled about, mostly avoiding the casket.

"Hey, Sam," Greg said as he approached.

"Greg," she said, hugging him.

She didn't have the right words to say, and neither did he. They held each other for a minute before the funeral director came in to tell the family that they were opening the doors in a few minutes and warned them that there were hundreds of people waiting outside to come say their farewells.

"I'm not sure I can do this," Samantha said. "This is too hard. I'm not ready to say goodbye."

"I'm right here with you," Jess said. "I won't leave your side."

A line formed to the left of Sal's casket as people began funneling in. The first few people were family members — aunts and uncles, cousins — all saying their farewell and offering condolences to Sal's family and his fiancée. As the line progressed, the faces changed from familiar to unfamiliar.

"I'm so sorry," one woman said. "Sal touched me in so many ways, I can't begin to sympathize with you."

Sam heard the same apologies and appreciations countless times that day. She politely nodded to most visitors, allowing a handful of them to hug her, but she didn't speak. She didn't thank anyone for coming and didn't tell them that Sal would appreciate it. She quietly grieved to herself and went through the motions.

The faces all began to look the same after a while. Fan after fan made their way through the line, taking a moment to kneel by Sal and say their silent goodbyes. A few asked if they could place a small token in the casket to be buried with him. "Die-hard fans" they called themselves.

Maria asked that they didn't do so, but said they could leave their items on top, and she'd make sure they got buried next to him. "Not in the casket," she said. "Not with my baby."

Many fans had a hard time dealing with the wake and broke down into tears while saying goodbye. Sam felt bad for them and hoped that someone else would usher the hysterical people away from Sal.

The hours passed by and people kept coming. The line was never-ending and at one point Greg looked outside to see hundreds more still lined up.

DJ Kim stopped by to show her support and brought a number of other of the staff from the radio station where they'd gotten their start.

"Way too soon," she said. "He was in his prime."

Many fans left letters with Samantha, offering their support and showing their love for the band through their own words. She'd read them all eventually, but could barely keep her eyes open at the moment.

On the far side of the casket Greg, Paul, and Derek stood. They thanked their fans for coming out.

"Get this guy out of here!" Greg yelled.

"Dude, I'm sorry. I just wanted to get an autograph."

"Asshole, do you not see this isn't the fucking time?" Derek snapped back.

Two of the funeral home's employees came and grabbed him and he was gone in a matter of seconds.

The commotion had caused a stir and everyone seemed to be staring at the door the guy had been rushed out of.

The funeral director came up behind Samantha.

The people keep coming," he said. "Let's just keep going as long as you need to. We scheduled a break between the two sessions but we'll just leave the doors open for everyone to come and go."

"Thank you," she said, "it's amazing to see how many lives he'd touched and how many people truly loved him."

"The funeral," Samantha said loudly, "is tomorrow morning across the street. Thank you to all who can attend."

After the wake, Greg had insisted the Samantha join the guys and Jess at a bar to drink away their sorrows.

"It'll do you some good to not be alone," he said, "come with us."

She declined a number of times before Jess persuaded her to go.

They spent the better part of the night at the bar, ordering round after round.

"You're all drunk, and I insist that you all get in a cab and get home safely," she said.

"There's been enough loss for one lifetime," Greg said with slur. "We'll take a cab, Sam. I promise."

Samantha drove back to her apartment, alone. Her apartment, she told herself. She lived alone now. That she had no choice about.

The door seemed heavier than she remembered. She pushed it open and forced herself inside after standing in the hall for a short while.

"You can do this," she said, but she didn't believe herself.

She made her way to the bedroom before collapsing on the bed. Grasping onto his pillow, she breathed in deeply, smelling him. She knew that eventually his smell would be gone so she savored it while she could.

She tried to scream into the pillow, to somehow get the frustration trapped in her mind out, but nothing came out. She'd yelled and screamed and cried so much that her body was refusing to do anymore of it. At least for tonight.

Lying in bed, Samantha's mind raced. She thought about all of the ways that Sal had been cheated. Not just because she didn't get a chance to marry him, but because his career was just getting started.

He was on the verge of becoming great and that was ripped away from him.

Early the next morning, her mother knocked on the bedroom door. Vanessa had insisted she sleep on the couch and arrived shortly after Sam had got home the night before. She wouldn't let her only daughter spend the night by herself after such a stressful day yesterday.

"Thanks for flying in, Mom."

"I got the first flight I could. I'm sorry I didn't get here earlier."

"It's okay," Sam said.

"You shouldn't be driving today," her mother said. "I'll do the driving."

"Thanks, Mom. Being here was hard last night. Thanks for staying with me."

"I know, angel. I understand."

"How am I supposed to handle today?"

"No one knows that answer, sweetheart. You'll just have to do the best you can."

"The best I can do is staying here, smelling his pillow."

"You can get back here this afternoon. I'll make sure of it."

Vanessa helped her up and forced her to the shower. The sight of Sal's toothbrush on the sink brought Sam to tears. From shows on the TiVo that were his, to seeing his iPad, to someone posting a photo of him on Facebook. Everything made her cry.

After Sam was done in the shower, Vanessa helped Samantha get dressed. Her black dress and black shoes befitting of the event were pressed and waiting when she got home last night.

They hugged for a long time, but Samantha didn't feel any better.

"I'm a wreck Mom, I can't do this."

"You can, honey. Sal needs you to get up there and tell those people how you felt about him. He's watching you."

"I know, but it's so hard."

"He's always going to be watching you," she said. "That man loved you more than any man has ever loved any other woman."

Samantha smiled and led her mom down to the car. They got to the funeral home and looked across the street. There were thousands of people lined up trying to get in. Local police had to stop traffic on the road to prevent anyone from getting hurt.

The funeral director came out and again gave his condolences.

"I've never seen anything quite like this," he said. "Sal must have touched a lot of people."

"He did," Samantha said. "So many."

Maria, Cassie, and Vincenzo showed up and made their way inside. Maria had been crying already and made her way right to the casket to say a private goodbye.

Quiet with just the family in the building, the funeral home was peaceful. Just the five of them present, with the funeral director outside getting his men ready.

When Maria was done saying goodbye, Vincenzo went up to do the same. A strong Italian man, and one that Cassie said never cried, wept like a baby.

"My boy, my boy," His words echoed through the mostly empty room.

The smell of the flowers was strong and the silence heavy.

"Do you want to say goodbye?" Vanessa asked Samantha.

"No, I'll wait until we put him in the ground."

"I'm going to go up," Cassie said. "I have to do it now."

As she made her way to the casket, she passed her father and stopped to hug him.

"I love you, daddy," she said.

"I love you too, Cassandra," he responded, wiping the tears from his eyes.

"Big brother, it's me, Cassie May. I know you can hear me, because I believe in that sort of thing. I'm sorry you're gone, but I want you to know that you touched all of the people outside. Your words and your songs, you made the lives of so many better. People felt understood, people felt like they weren't alone because of you. You made everyone feel the love that you showed, and I love you for that." She started to cry. "You were the most important person in my life. You were the one I always looked up to and who I will always look up to. I'm not sure how I'm going to get through the rest of my life without you, but I'm going to be the best I can be. I'll take care of Samantha for you, don't worry. She's my sister now, and I'll make sure she gets through this. I love you."

Cassie gave the sign of the cross and stood, making her way to the back of the room.

The funeral director came in. "It's time," he said, and led the family outside.

His men entered and prepared Sal to travel across the street to the church. Sal wasn't overly religious, but his mother was. She insisted that he have a proper Catholic funeral where people could say goodbye and grieve properly.

While they waited outside, the funeral men inside packed up the flowers and closed the casket, moving it onto the wheels they'd used to get it across the street. Standing just outside on the porch, Sam could see Greg, Jess, Paul, and Derek in the doorway to the church ahead of the crowd of thousands.

"Where are all those people going to fit?" Samantha asked.

"Anywhere they can," Cassie said. "They just want to be near."

The funeral director nodded as if to give his permission to cross the street, and they did. Samantha lead the family members to the church, holding the hands of Cassie and Maria.

A local police officer, with the aid of a bullhorn, said that there wasn't enough room inside for everyone and asked them to line up on the lawn next to the church. Jack was there working with some sound folks to set up some speakers outside so that people who couldn't fit could still hear the service.

When they made it to the front of the church, the family sat down in the front row still holding hands. The rest of the band and Jess filed in behind them, offering hugs and placing their hands on various shoulders to show their support.

Samantha estimated that the church held close to 500 people and it was packed. Hundreds more stood outside, while the outer aisles inside were jam packed as well. There must have been close to a thousand people inside alone, all waiting to say a farewell to Sal.

This particular church had been one that Sal attended with his family as a child. Stained glass windows adorned the long aisle casting multi-colored light shows on the walls and floor. Their mother and father still came here twice a week and were friendly with the head priest who offered to do the services.

The center aisle of the church seemed to go on forever. The walk from the entrance at the back to the seats that Vincenzo and Maria usually sat in on Sundays seemed to be a marathon's distance away.

The pulpit seemed to have been made of solid marble. A seemingly giant structure that Father Jacobs had stood behind day after day, week after week, telling everyone in attendance about God's greatness. Today would be no different.

Father Jacobs took the pulpit and the hundreds of people sat, silencing themselves. He looked to the back of the church where the pall bearers began wheeling Sal's casket to the front, where it would rest for the remainder of the service.

"Gone far too soon," he began, "was this young man of God's creation. A man of many talents and loved by everyone he met,

Salvatore Maggione was someone that we'll truly never forget. I've known him since he was just a baby, and have watched him grow into the remarkable young man that he was, blossoming and using his God-given talents to share his voice with the world. He will be sorely missed and we will all love him through God's spirit."

Sobs were heard throughout the echoing church and Samantha held Cassie's hand tightly.

"Sal's best friend, Greg, would like to address everyone," Father Jacobs said, motioning for Greg to come up.

As Greg took the pulpit, reaching into his pocket, he took a moment to look around. The church was packed full, people standing as far back as the eye could see. He took a moment to look down at the casket where his best friend was. He let out a tear and quickly wiped it from his cheek.

"Sal was my best friend, but you all already knew that. He was there for me through almost my entire life. We grew up together, we grew into men. We set out a goal of making music for a living when we were ten. We didn't even know how to play an instrument then, but he insisted that we'd be rockstars some day. And look, he was right.

"It's hard to imagine not talking to my buddy every day, or not having him be there when I'm a dad, or not being able to continue down this amazing path that we've begun together.

"I can't begin to even tell you how much I'm going to miss him. To try to explain how much he meant to me would be lost here in this setting. Sal was the brother I never had. He was the Cory to my Shawn. The Jesse to my Danny. The Joey to my Chandler. I'm sorry if you don't get those references, but Sal would have.

"Sal would have appreciated all of you coming here today. Even if he didn't know you. His lifelong dream was to touch the lives of strangers and I think it's safe to say that he has. Those of you that never got to meet him have missed out. I'm sorry that you'll never get to hear him tell a terrible joke, that you'll never get to have him be your designated drive, and that you'll never get to see the moment in his eyes when he realizes he's written a song that's perfect. I'm sorry that he's gone.

"Sal, you're my brother, you're my best friend, and you're always going to be in my heart and mind," he said, looking towards the casket. "I'll miss you every day. Thank you for insisting we take this journey together all those years ago. We couldn't have done this without you."

Greg stepped down from the pulpit, crying, as Father Jacobs stood and took his place.

"Some of you may have had the honor of being there," Father Jacobs said, "when Sal proposed to Samantha not long ago. She's prepared a few words that she'd like to share with you all. Samantha, please come up."

"What can I say about Sal that we don't already know? How can I," she began, "even start to go on in my life without him? Most of you knew Sal as the musician, the singer of the band and the guy that you paid to spend a few hours of your life with. To hear him, to feel him, to connect with him. To me, Sal was a man that was made for me. He showed me light and life in ways that I never thought I'd see. He brought me flowers and he held my hand. He loved me in ways that I always wanted to be loved.

"When I first met Sal I was a shy and reserved introvert. I kept to myself and didn't trust most people. He helped me become who I am today. It was as if some by some miracle I was a different person around him from the moment I met him.

"He took me to heights I didn't want to reach and he helped me down when I didn't think I could come down. He took me to places

I wanted to visit, and he let me be myself when I didn't know how to be.

"Sal was the greatest person I've ever known and I'm lucky to have known him for the short time that we had together.

"I stand before you today, sad but not crying. I'm sad that he's gone, yes, but I'm glad at the same time. Glad to have gotten to know him. Glad to have loved him, and most importantly, glad to have been loved by him. Sal enriched my life, and made me happier than you could even begin to imagine.

"He leaves behind a group of talented friends, his mom and dad who loved him dearly, and his younger sister. All people who are lucky to have known him as long as they have.

"It's hard to say goodbye, but we all know we have to. Sal has gone on, not to a better place, as they say, but to a place where he's waiting for us to join him in our due time. When we meet again, we'll hear his voice, we'll hear him sing again, we'll see him move, and we'll get to hug him again.

"I love you, Sal. I will love you for as long as I live, and I will be with you again. Death won't keep us apart and I'll be there with you as soon as it's my time. You're my reason to keep trying, you're my soul mate, and I promise that I'll do the best I can without you. Your energy will give me strength and your music will give me hope. Any time that I miss you, I'll listen to your songs and you'll be there with me. If I just close my eyes, you'll always be there with me."

As she stepped down from the pulpit, she kissed the casket.

As she took her place between her mom and Sal's, she thought about the many nights that she and Sal had spent together. Their night stargazing on the swings was, she thought, her favorite. She replayed it in her mind, hoping it would make this day go by faster, and ease the pain in some minor way.

"We'll now move outside," Father Jacobs said at the conclusion of the services, "to bid our friend farewell. Please join us out back."

The cemetery was just behind the church and it was the one that Sal would have wanted to be buried in. The family followed the pallbearers out, still holding each other's hands, making sure not to break the chain.

Once outside and seated around the grave, Father Jacobs instructed everyone else to join them, including those still left inside the church.

It was a small cemetery, but still large enough to house the thousands that had joined them to bid farewell to Sal. The guests filled every nook and cranny of the space.

Row after row of headstones led the troupe of fans, family, and friends to the Southeast corner of the cemetery. An oak tree had been growing here for years and stood tall over the site where Sal would be laid to rest. His headstone would read *Touching the lives of all he knew*, a phrase that Samantha and Cassie had picked out together.

The sky was overcast and the threat of rain was real. The funeral home had set up a canopy over the grave and some of the seats.

The box of items that people had requested to be buried with Sal was off to the side, waiting to be lowered in on top of his casket. Samantha'd made sure to keep her word to those of his fans that needed this closure. She'd make sure that the funeral director put the box in before closing the tomb over his casket and piling the dirt down upon him.

"We say goodbye," Father Jacobs said, "to our brother. Our son. Or loved one. We say farewell to Salvatore in our own way, on our own terms. But we do say goodbye. We loved him and he us, and we will never have that taken away from us."

Mourners took their turns placing flowers onto the casket, some taking one or two for themselves. The floral arrangements were in no short supply, having been sent from all over the world. Sony had sent a dozen arrangements and Jack had a few delivered himself.

The crowd began thinning out after a few hours, and Samantha noticed the band standing off towards the entrance to the cemetery with Jack and two men she didn't recognize. The band declined autographs and photos, but were courtesy to grieving fans, offering hugs and thanking them for coming.

She made her way over and greeted everyone through tear-soaked eyes.

"Samantha, I'm so sorry," Jack said. "If there's anything I can do."

"Thank you," she replied. "I just need some time."

"This is Cee. He produced the album," Jack said as Cee extended his hand, "and this is William, a lawyer from Sony."

"Thank you both for coming," she said. "Sal would have appreciated it."

"Sal was an amazing man," Cee said. "We're all lucky to have known him and the music he made with these guys."

"Thank you," she said.

"I'm actually here somewhat on business," William said. "I'm sorry. I know this isn't the time."

"What business?" Samantha said, taking Jess' hand.

"Sal wasn't prepared for this, as you know. This was unexpected. He didn't have a will," William said.

"Okay."

"That means that he didn't specifically have any final wishes, and any of the money that he made or items that he owned separate from you would go to his next of kin."

"What does that mean?" she asked.

"It means that anything that wasn't in both of your names would go to his parents," William said.

"You picked a pretty terrible time to tell me all of this," she said crying, "why not now? What other bad news do you want to give me?"

"There's some better news, I'm sorry to do this now," he said. "I came to pay my respects. The record company told me to take care of this while we're here."

"What's the better news?" Greg asked.

"We just got finished talking to Maria and Vincenzo. They said that anything that Sal would leave to them by default should go to you. His dad says that there's nothing they need, and they want you to have everything. All of the money and all of the future royalties. Everything. It's yours."

"What? Just like that?" she said.

"Just like that. They already signed the papers," William said.

Samantha cried, not sure who to thank or what to do, or what it meant. She just knew that she was thankful and that Sal had found a way to take care of her even after he was gone.

"I'm going to go say goodbye. Thank you all for coming," she said, "Jess will you wait here for me?"

"Of course. Go ahead."

Samantha walked back through the small cemetery and looked back towards the row of cars, where Sal's family was waiting. Rain had started to fall now and most people had run back to find shelter. Jess and Greg were the last two standing by the gated entrance under an umbrella. Samantha looked back over her shoulder at them as she approached his grave.

Standing under the tent that the funeral home had provided, alone, she leaned into his casket to be sure that he could hear her.

"I know you're gone," she said, "but I know you hear me. I know you're watching over me. I'm better for having been loved by you. My life is better for having you in it. I can't even begin to think how I'm going to pick up the pieces from this. I can't begin to fathom how I'm going to bounce back and continue living my life without you. But I know that if I don't try, you'd know. You're watching over me, and I know that you'll watch out for me. I know that you'll keep an eye on me and make sure nothing bad happens to me. You'll be my guardian for the rest of my life.

"And when that life is over, I'll join you again. I'll be together with you in the gates of Heaven. I'll be with you in the place that we can be together forever.

"If that's not the case, and you're already somewhere else as a new person, as someone new, reincarnated as a new life — I'll find you. Death won't keep us apart. I will be with you again.

"I love you with all that I am, and I miss you deeply. I miss your smile, and your warm touch. I miss your hands and your kiss. I will never forget our first kiss and the way it sent lightning bolts through my soul.

"You're the greatest thing that ever happened to me. Or ever will. Farewell, my love."

She made her way back to the gateway where Jess was waiting and looked back one last time as he was lowered into the ground. She waited one last moment to make sure that the funeral director placed the box of farewell items in with him. She smiled a bit, knowing that the photograph of his grandparents and his dad were in that box. The photograph of her and he dancing from the wedding nestled tightly into the inside breast pocket of his suit.

"It'll help him remember me in the afterlife," she had told Jess, "so when we meet again, he'll recognize me."

Chapter Forty-Three

WINTER HAD ENDED AND spring soon began. The sun brought more warmth, the snow had all melted, the roads were cleared of the excess salt and sand, and So Say The King had to make a decision on how to proceed without Sal.

They sat around a conference table in Jack's offices. A large, round table, likely made of some expensive or rare wood sat centered in a large conference room. Dead center was a conference phone that execs from Sony would be calling into in just a short while.

"I'll be the first to say it," Greg said. "I don't think we can replace Sal."

The rest of the room nodded in agreement.

"There's no one else that can do what he did, at least not in my opinion," Jack said. "We could hold auditions and try to find someone, but I don't think anyone would fit in as well as Sal did. Journey and Queen have never been the same since their singers passed."

"I don't think I want anyone else," Paul added.

They hadn't been to their rehearsal space since Sal died and hadn't played any concerts.

The execs from Sony were starting to get a little agitated and had called a meeting to discuss the band's future.

"It's not really up to me," Jack said. "What do you guys want to do?"

"I think," Derek said, "if we go on… If we get a new singer and that's a big if, then we're a new band. We're not So Say The King anymore. We're a new band with a new singer."

"And we don't play any of the same songs," Paul added.

"I like that idea," Greg said. "But I doubt Sony's going to."

"So what, we'll deal with that," Jack said.

As if they knew they were being talked about, the conference phone rang, connecting the guys in Jack's conference room with a half dozen execs and lawyers on the Sony side.

"Hello? Jack here," he answered.

"Hey Jack, are the guys there with you?" the voice on the other end asked.

"Yep, everyone's here," he responded.

"Great, let's get started. This is William. We met back at Sal's services. How are you guys doing? I'm so sorry for your loss, again."

"We're doing the best we can," Greg spoke for the group.

"Glad to hear it. If there's anything we can do, please let us know," William responded.

"We will, thank you," Greg said.

"In the room with me here, I have a handful of lawyers and my colleagues, but I'll be doing most of the talking, if that's okay with you guys."

"That's fine," Jack said, "what did you have in mind to discuss?"

"Well, it's obvious that things have changed quite a bit on your end with the band. Things have been hard the last few months and rightfully so. We, as your record company, need to stand behind you and whatever decision you make. That said, you have fans and obligations to those fans. Do you have any idea what you'd like to do?"

"We were just discussing that here," Jack said, "and we came up with a solution that works for us. I don't have the contract paperwork in front of me, so I can't say if this'll work on your end. You tell me."

"Go on," William responded.

"Okay," Jack began, "the existing contract with So Say The King is done. That band no longer exists as of November, when Sal passed. The guys and I will begin a hunt for a new singer and will present you with a new band, a new album, and a new plan to make that band as popular as So Say The King was when Sal died."

"I'm listening," William said.

"Royalties for the So Say The King album continue to be paid. It continues to get printed and sold, you'll still promote it. But there'll be no new singer in the band. The guys won't do any press about the band. The legacy will live on with just the single album."

"I'm looking around the room at the lawyers. They're flipping through pages of the contract and trying to find out if that's something that we can allow. If it were up to me, I'd say let's do it. But hold tight," William said slowly.

"We're not going anywhere," Jack said.

"How do you feel about this, guys?" William asked.

"It was our idea," Greg replied. "We can't be the same band without Sal."

"I understand. The lawyers are telling me that there's nothing specifically in the contract about what happens if someone dies. We had contracted the band to put out three albums and do three stadium tours, but I think we can safely say that's null and void now that the band doesn't exist anymore."

"And there's no penalty or fees to the band or me?" Jack asked.

"Given all that's happened," William responded. "I don't think that would be very fair."

"Okay. Thank you," Jack said. "We'll begin our search for a new singer and be in touch when we've made some progress."

Chapter Forty-Four

She still woke up looking for him, even after all these months. The dreams she'd have of him were so vivid and lifelike that she could have sworn she was talking to him at night.

Many of his belongings were still in her apartment, scattered around in various locations. Some of his things she still used. She slept with his pillow every night, though it didn't smell like him anymore.

She'd taken over using his computer and kept his plastic bin of songs at the foot of his desk, just like he'd have had it.

After Sal's death, she'd taken some personal time from work to grieve. Her mom had come up to stay with her for a few days immediately after the funeral, but had long since gone back home to upstate New York.

Sam had been alone in her apartment night after night for months now and it hadn't gotten any easier. Some nights she'd fall asleep on the couch, partially expecting to wake up in bed, having been carried there by Sal. Those mornings when she woke up still on the couch were the worst.

The outgoing message on the answering machine was unchanged, still Sal's voice. "You've reached Sal and Sam. We're not here, please leave a message!" Every time the phone rang, Sam would let it go to voicemail, just to hear his voice for those few precious seconds.

The trial of the drunk driver that hit Sal had only taken a few days. Sam was present every day, as were his sister, his parents, and dozens of his fans. The jury only deliberated for ten minutes before coming back with a verdict of guilty. Sentencing took place a few weeks later and the judge handed down a sentence of 30 years. Fifteen years for operating under the influence, the maximum allowed in Massachusetts and fifteen years for vehicular manslaughter, also the maximum allowed. Though it didn't heal her wounds, Sam took some pleasure in knowing that the man who killed her soulmate would be behind bars for the next few decades.

She was closer than ever with Jess. The two of them, along with Cassie, got together every Saturday night and went out. They didn't go clubbing or dancing or to concerts. They did simple things together: bowling, dinners, fondue parties. Just being with those that knew and loved Sal helped Sam feel better.

Night after night she'd tell herself that this would get easier, that she'd eventually be able to look at a photo of him and not cry. Night after night she'd tell herself that he was looking down on her and that she needed to be strong. Night after night, she'd cry and miss him.